THE
DOG THAT
WHISPERED

ALSO BY JIM KRAUS

The Dog That Saved Stewart Coolidge

THE DOG THAT WHISPERED

a novel

JIM KRAUS

New York Boston Nashville

Copyright © 2016 by Jim Kraus
Reading Group Guide © 2016 by Jim Kraus and Hachette Book Group, Inc.
Cover design JuLee Brand
Cover image by Getty Images
Cover copyright © 2016 by Hachette Book Group, Inc.

FaithWords
Hachette Book Group
1290 Avenue of the Americas
New York, NY 10104
www.faithwords.com
twitter.com/faithwords

First Edition: June 2016

FaithWords is a division of Hachette Book Group, Inc.
The FaithWords name and logo are trademarks of Hachette Book Group, Inc.

The publisher is not responsible for websites (or their content) that are not owned by the publisher.

The Hachette Speakers Bureau provides a wide range of authors for speaking events. To find out more, go to www.hachettespeakersbureau.com or call (866) 376-6591.

Library of Congress Cataloging-in-Publication Data

Names: Kraus, Jim, 1950- author.
Title: The dog that whispered : a novel / Jim Kraus.
Description: First Edition. | New York ; Boston : FaithWords, 2016.
Identifiers: LCCN 2016001569| ISBN 9781455562565 (paperback) | ISBN
    9781455562558 (ebook)
Subjects: | BISAC: FICTION / Christian / General. | FICTION / Humorous. |
    FICTION / Family Life. | GSAFD: Christian fiction.
Classification: LCC PS3561.R2876 D65 2016 | DDC 813/.54—dc23 LC record
available at http://lccn.loc.gov/2016001569

ISBNs: 978-1-4555-6256-5 (trade paperback), 978-1-4555-6255-8 (ebook)

Printed in the United States of America

RRD-C

10 9 8 7 6 5 4 3 2 1

To all veterans and the dogs who love them.

THE
DOG THAT
WHISPERED

Chapter One

*G*RETNA STEELE shuffled past the television. She kept the set muted, but it stayed on for the entire day.

"Nobody in this 'retirement village' can hear worth beans. Why should I turn up the volume? I'm already being forced to listen to six other programs from every apartment on this floor."

What was being shown on the screen caught her eye. She shuffled to a stop and pulled the remote out of the pocket of her pastel housedress. She stabbed at the yellow button while turning the remote toward the TV, to help push the electronic beam into the set's electric eye.

She knew the extra push made the television respond faster.

The older analog TV, the size of a small refrigerator, barked into full voice.

Sad music was playing.

"No. Not sad. Plaintive. Manipulative."

Gretna often self-narrated the small events in her daily routine.

She leaned forward and narrowed her eyes. She had glasses somewhere, but seldom wore them.

"They make me look old. I may be eighty-five, but I don't have to dress the part," she often said.

The commercial continued. A series of dogs with sad faces appeared on the screen.

"Adopt one of these," the announcer said, with just the right amount of gravitas, "and you'll be making the world a better place for one lucky dog or cat. And yourself."

And then Gretna noticed something. The commercial was not the finely tuned, slick presentation of a national campaign. It was not a video done by some corporate animal rescue organization. This had to have been locally made and produced—perhaps by some volunteer at the shelter who happened to have a decent video camera.

In the foreground were two sad dogs, each apparently selected because they could emote maximum pathos. In the background stood another dog. This dog was black and active and bouncing and grinning and looking directly at Gretna, almost as if he was daring her to look away, to not be affected by the announcer's plea, smirking and wiggling and grinning cheek to jowl.

"That dog has guts," she said to herself. "He's not buying into their propaganda."

Then the black dog in the background stopped and simply stared, but his grin remained at half power. Gretna was sure the semi-happy beast was staring directly at her.

She thought for a moment.

"So where is this place, anyhow?"

And in a few seconds, the announcer gave the address. Twice. And asked for donations three times.

It took less than an hour for the taxi to arrive. Gretna climbed in, pulled out a small pocket-sized notepad, and made a most deliberate show of writing down the cabbie's name and cab number. She made sure the cabdriver saw what she was doing.

"Mizz Steele, you don't scare me. I drive you six times in a month," the driver said with a thick accent. Gretna thought it was perhaps Caribbean, perhaps Middle Eastern. Even African. He was from somewhere else and not here—of that Gretna was certain.

She leaned closer to the Plexiglas partition, narrowing her eyes, determined.

"Maybe."

"I did, Mizz Steele. Last time, we go to de Giant Eagle. Remember? You paid in quarters."

"Maybe."

The driver, one Sharif Moses Yusry, sighed and put the cab into gear.

"Where to, Mizz Steele?" he asked. "De Giant Eagle again?"

Gretna scowled at the rearview mirror.

"No. I don't eat that much. Or spend that much. Who do you think I am? A drunken sailor?"

The cabdriver sighed, signaling that he knew arguing, or even adding a comment, was futile, but stopped when he reached the end of the circular driveway.

"So . . . where to, Mizz Steele?"

Gretna flipped the page on her notepad.

"Sixty-six twenty Hamilton Avenue."

Sharif did not pull out.

"What's there?"

Gretna scowled again, then responded with a more agreeable tone.

"You're a cabdriver, for heaven's sake. If you don't know where it's at, then let me call for another cabdriver who does know."

Sharif slumped in the front seat.

"Mizz Steele, I know address. I know street. What will I look for? A house? A store? What?"

"And that's none of your business, actually. But if it helps you find the place without taking me on a wild-goose chase, then it's the Animal Rescue League of Western Pennsylvania."

Sharif remained still, even though his surprised expression was reflected in the rearview mirror.

"You adopt a kittycat?"

Gretna leaned back in the seat.

"Again, none of your business. But, no. I'm adopting Thurman."

Professor Wilson Steele set his cup of coffee down on the round kitchen table with precision—the very same table that had been in the kitchen since Wilson was a child: chrome legs and Formica top, the table surface mainly gray with a squiggling pattern of red and gray lines, which Wilson always thought looked like snakes, or some sort of 1950s virus, worn almost colorless in a couple of spots by several thousand meals eaten at those very places.

Wilson had rotated the table one-half turn fifteen years ago and now sat at a relatively unworn location, his chair still facing the same direction as it had when he was younger—the same direction he had always faced, since birth, the truth be told.

Or at least since being able to sit in a high chair.

His seat faced the kitchen window over the sink and had a prime view of the large oak tree in the side yard.

Or *used to* have a view of the oak tree.

The tree had succumbed to natural causes a decade earlier, and it cost Wilson an obscene amount of money to have it cut down, chain-sawed into smaller sections, and hauled away. He would have left that spot bare, but without the oak tree as a shield, he could see directly into the kitchen of Rod and Linda Heasley, an overbearingly friendly couple who were relative newcomers to the neighborhood, having arrived some twenty years earlier.

Linda Heasley had had the temerity to wave to him after the oak was dispatched. Yes, wave to him as he sat and enjoyed his cup of coffee in the morning.

He assumed that social protocol required him to wave back.

And on that same day, between the writing classes he taught at the University of Pittsburgh, he had ordered an obscenely expensive thirty-foot maple tree to replace the oak and harangued the nursery to deliver it the following day.

The maple wasn't as full or as large as the oak, but it was a serviceable screen between the two houses.

"Good fences—and big trees—make good neighbors," he said to himself, the same thing he had said to himself every time he sat at stared at the maple tree, which was now coming into green.

Wilson's house, originally his parents' house, sat, as the crow flies, only two miles from where his mother now lived.

It had a phone that had been placed in an alcove. This was the same alcove that had held that phone ever since he was young, during the time when the family owned only a single phone. Wilson believed that the architect of the house had designated this small niche to be the "phone alcove," on the premise that a family would have but one phone and one outlet only—as God intended it to be.

Now Wilson had a wireless phone system with four separate phones scattered throughout the house. But to Wilson, talking on this specific phone, located in the alcove, made it an official phone call. So it was the one he usually used. That phone began to ring and Wilson picked it up.

"Are you home?"

Wilson sighed.

"No, Mom, I'm hang gliding off of Mount Washington. Of course I'm home. You called the landline. I have to be at home to answer that, remember?"

"Do not get snippy with me, young man. I was merely making conversation."

Wilson took a deep breath and stared at himself in the hall mirror. He wondered how many reflections this mirror had seen over the decades it had hung there. He ran his hand over his short salt-and-pepper hair. It was only just a bit thinner than it had been when he was young, but it still gave him a very average, nearing-senior-citizen-status, grayed appearance. He had never considered himself handsome, nor notable in any physical way, just average—average height, average weight, average coloring, modestly blue eyes, average, all of it average, tending to invisibility.

Sweet invisibility.

"Well... you have to come and get my dog."

Wilson did not speak for a long moment. He did not have a dog growing up. As far as he knew, his mother never had a dog growing up. No one in their family had dogs. So this was probably not a flashback to some childhood memory.

"Your dog? You do not have a dog, Mother."

He typically used the word "Mother" rather than "Mom" as his exasperation rose.

He heard her sigh with an increased degree of that same exasperation.

"I do too. He's right here. Aren't you, Thurman?"

Wilson heard some sort of rusty noise in the background. A manner of vague growling.

It could be the TV. That was always on.

"Mom. A dog? Are you drinking enough water? Remember what Dr. Farkas said. You get dehydrated and you start hallucinating. That happens easily with his older patients."

He heard his mother snort in derision.

"I'm not an 'older patient,' that quack. And I am not seeing things. Thurman is here with me. And he can't be. With me, I mean. Because he is definitely here. So you have to come and get him."

Her grip on reality was clearly starting to become tenuous.

"Okay, Mom. Settle down. I have to go to class now. I'll stop over when it's done. This afternoon. Okay? And take care of your 'dog.' Okay?"

"You're a good son," Gretna replied. "Such a good boy."

And then she hung up and Wilson was not sure if she had addressed the last comment to him or to the dog, imaginary or otherwise.

Chapter Two

WILSON'S ONLY CLASS that day was a master's-level graduate class, "Writing the Short Story," that met on the fourth floor of the Cathedral of Learning, a massive stone tower done in the Late Gothic Revival style, the centerpiece of the University of Pittsburgh's Oakland campus.

Wilson hated the building.

Too overstated. Too big. Too European. It loomed. He didn't like looming. It saw too much. Like that tower with the big eye in *The Lord of the Rings*.

Wilson stepped into the classroom two minutes past the normal start time of 10:30. The phone call from his mother had upset his routine and he had missed his normal bus, the 9:37 61-A that traveled from Wilkinsburg through Squirrel Hill and then to Oakland. His normal bus usually got him to school at 10:07, with more than time enough for him to get a cup of coffee from the snack shop in the basement.

Horrible coffee, but better than anything else they sold.

For the past many months, and actually for his entire decades-long teaching career in the English department, Wilson had always been in class well before the class was to start. Students had grown accustomed to seeing him at the desk in front, his buttery-colored, well-worn leather satchel unsnapped and open in front of him, as if he was using it as a shield, his eyes on some paper or book or manuscript, barely acknowledging them until the exact proper time that the class was scheduled to begin.

It was obvious that Wilson was unaccustomed to being late and, worse, totally inept at giving socially plausible explanations as to why he was late—even though as a senior, fully tenured professor, he did not need to give excuses. In fact, the rule of thumb was that students should give a full professor at least fifteen minutes' grace before they packed up and headed out, glad to have an unexpected but excused release from class.

Two minutes was well within the margin of error, depending on the timepiece used to measure promptness.

"Sorry," Wilson mumbled as he walked to the desk. "Sorry."

It was also obvious that he was unaccustomed to apologizing.

"When one lives alone," he wrote once in an article for the *Blue and Gold*, the campus literary magazine that was briefly and actually published on real paper and not just in the electronic cloud, back in the late 1970s, "there are few things done in private that one needs to explain, let alone apologize for. Solitude does wonders for one suffering from a guilty conscience."

"It was a personal issue," he stammered, not really sure of how much to share, what exactly to explain. This was new water for him to be swimming, or floundering, in.

"Not for me. My mother. And a dog."

Then he looked up at the students. Most of them appeared befuddled and confused, as if none had really expected any sort of explanation.

"It's a long story," Wilson said, taking a breath, pausing, regrouping, "and this class is the short story."

A chuckle or two bubbled up, more out of social expectation than actual mirth.

"So if you want the entire tale, you'll have to take my 'Art of the Novel' class next semester."

Another weak chuckle followed.

Then Wilson took a deep breath, as if sloughing off whatever travails had caused him to be late that morning.

"We are reading the first draft of our first-person pieces. I have noted my comments on each. But let's see what the class has to say."

He looked down at the small stack of papers on the desk.

"Ms. Fodor, since yours is on the top of the pile, we will start with your piece."

As she began to read her two-page piece—the maximum length allowed for the assignment ("It forces a writer to be careful with words"), Wilson put his thoughts on autopilot, as it were. He never liked having students read their work. Most of the writing was not really all that good, especially in a first draft, but year after year the students claimed in their end-of-class evaluation that the comments from their peers in class were the most beneficial part of the course.

As he listened, or half-listened, something in Wilson's thoughts, deep down, deep in the back, buried, or nearly buried, startled to jangle—a shrillness, an alarm of sorts began to erupt.

It always sounded like his mother's voice, off in the distance. Shouting. Pleading. With explosions.

Wilson twisted in his seat as he tried to ignore his internal warning, a warning he had experienced on occasion before this moment, and instead he shifted his thoughts to the crisis at hand—his mother and a dog.

So my mother got a dog, he mused. *That's really odd. Even for her. I'm just glad that this is her problem and not mine. That is, if she really has a dog and it's not some elaborate hallucination.*

And that's when the warning began to sound louder, and louder, until it was the only thing that Wilson could hear, and he involuntarily shuddered.

He suddenly realized that Ms. Fodor was finished.

He took a deep breath, trying to push the warning away.

"So, who wants to give Ms. Fodor some advice, or reaction, to what she read?"

Wilson waited until Ms. Davenport, a mousy, reticent third-year grad student in creative writing, shyly raised her hand and began a long and overly polite gutting of virtually every aspect of the work just read.

Such are the ways of an unexpected ambush, Wilson thought and resisted the urge to offer a wry, knowing smile.

⌐

"Well, Thurman, Wilson will be right here after he teaches his little class at school."

Thurman growled an acknowledgment.

Gretna smiled and patted him on the head. She wasn't always exactly sure what he was saying, but she knew he was talking to her, or at least trying to talk to her.

"He'll take care of you, Thurman."

Thurman looked up, a quizzical expression on his face.

"He will, Thurman. If nothing else, Wilson is a man of his word. He'll take care of this."

She fell heavily into the couch facing the TV. Thurman walked up to her with an expectant look.

"Sure, Thurman, jump up. I've already said it was okay."

Thurman launched himself up and tumbled into a puddle of legs and paws next to Gretna, eventually maneuvering his head so it fell into her lap.

"Such a nice boy," she said and stroked his head.

Thurman growled happily, a low throaty growl, as if he was clearing his throat while trying to talk.

Gretna stopped.

"I won't be sad, Thurman, when you leave. Well, maybe a little, but you'll be with Wilson. We can still see each other."

Thurman growled in response.

"He's nice. You'll see. But he's lonely."

Thurman growled more, and longer, more nuanced.

"I know. I have told him to get married. He hasn't. He doesn't even date. Hasn't for years. He never listened to me—not about this."

Thurman growled and rasped and rumbled.

"I know. I always wanted a grandchild. Wilson should have a child. But I don't think that will ever happen. Not now."

Thurman squirmed about and eventually stood up on the couch, a little wobbly since the couch was very soft and giving. He looked directly at Gretna and rumbled, growled, mumbled.

"Thurman, you shouldn't say things that aren't true."

Thurman did say that, and growled it again.

"Thurman, are you sure? You're not making it up?"

Thurman did not speak, but nodded his head.

"Really sure?"

Thurman nodded again.

Gretna hesitated, then leaned over and gave the big black dog a very gentle but all-encompassing hug. After a long moment, she whispered into Thurman's ear, "Where did you come from, anyhow?"

And Thurman leaned back, smiled, and growled his answer.

↪

Wilson used his key to enter his mother's apartment, after signing in at the desk in the lobby. He probably did not have to, as he had seen other visitors just waltz in and wave, but the sign said ALL GUESTS MUST SIGN IN, and Wilson was a guest and not a resident, so he signed in, like he had done every other time he visited his mother in her second retirement home. Her first attempt at retirement had been in Florida, where after only two years she had declared it "too hot, too many bugs, and way too many old people."

She had returned to the punitive winters of western Pennsylvania, to a scarcity of old friends still alive, and most important, to her only son.

In the center of the rug in her living room lay a large splooch of a black dog—big paws, big frame, gentle eyes, and a lunatic's sort of grin, most likely carrying a fair amount of Labrador genetic heritage in its blood. The dog maintained his odd smile, then scrambled to his feet, growling, explaining. He took two steps, then sat down, as if to wait for proper introductions.

Gretna shuffled in from the bedroom.

"Hello, Wilson. I see you have met Thurman."

Wilson shrugged.

"I suppose. At least he didn't lunge at me and try to eat me for lunch."

Gretna hugged her son.

"Don't be ridiculous, Wilson. Thurman is a gentle soul."

Wilson slowly shook his head in disdain.

Well, at least the dog was real. That was a relief. Sort of.

"Why Thurman, Mom?"

His mother sniffed at what she must have considered an impertinent question.

"Why Thurman? I don't know. That's what the people at the animal shelter called him. I didn't think it would be right if I tried to change his name. Maybe he likes it. Hard to know with a dog, I guess. He comes when I call him, though, so he must know it by now. He smiles when he hears the name Thurman."

As if to demonstrate, Thurman looked up and did actually appear to be smiling. His tail activity increased as well.

Wilson stayed where he was. He did not want to come closer. He was not fond of dogs. He never had a dog growing up, not that he'd wanted one, his father being an otolaryngologist, specializing in allergies and sinus issues, who claimed that dogs were a boon to his practice.

"No, Mother, that wasn't quite the question. I meant, why a dog at all? Why now?"

Wilson often found himself pulling his mother back to pay

attention to the subject at hand from wherever it was she wandered off to.

"Wilson, honey, there's that ad on TV that shows all those sad dogs who didn't have homes. I couldn't resist. They are all alone. They need a home. All of them have such big eyes. And they are so...sad. Thurman wasn't, though. It was like he knew me from before. I don't know. Maybe. So I took a cab there, to that shelter over by Mellon Park, and I came back with Thurman. He's such a sweetie, isn't he?"

"He looks demented."

Wilson's mother glared at her son. As did Thurman, in a dog-judgmental way.

"He is not. He's sweet and one of God's creatures. Don't be that way. Like your father. God loves all creatures, great and small, you know. Be a Christian about this."

This was familiar ground for Wilson and his mother. He decided to remain neutral.

"I didn't know that you could have a dog here, Mother."

That was when he saw her lips start to tremble and her eyes grow watery.

"I know. I didn't know. The director came up yesterday and told me. No dogs. I can't keep him. He was nice about it—but rules are rules. That's why I called you."

"Why? Take him back. Tell them you made a mistake."

Thurman the dog warbled and growled in response, as if he was answering Wilson's remark.

"I can't, Wilson. I just can't. I can't do that. Not to that sweet face."

Wilson drew in a deep breath.

"You want me to take him back?"

Then his mother did begin to cry.

"No. No. You can't."

"Then what?"

His mother drew herself up to her full five-foot-three-inch stature, squared her shoulders, dabbed at her eyes with a tissue she always seemed to have in her hand, and shook her head.

"Well . . . he's not going back."

Wilson waited. Thurman rumbled a little.

"You have to take him home," she continued.

Wilson did not hesitate.

"No."

"Just for a day or two. Maybe three. Tops. I'll make calls. I'll find him a good home. Mrs. Berkowitz downstairs said that her son might want him. The dog can't go back to the shelter. They won't keep him. They'll . . . well, they don't want to, but they're overcrowded. I won't let them do that. I won't be party to a gassing."

It was obvious to Wilson that his mother was maneuvering, and he had already assumed that she had no intention of finding this horrid dog another home.

"No," he said with a firm tone.

"Wilson, you have always been a good boy. Just for a few days. I'll find him a home. I will. You want to make your mother happy, don't you?"

At this, as if on cue, Thurman stood, shook himself, and walked carefully and deliberately to a few feet in front of Wilson. He sat down, looked up, and warbled-grumbled-growled a long sentence.

Wilson listened, and for a moment he thought that the dog said, *I will be good.*

Wilson actually took a step backward.

What? Is he talking? It sounds like he's trying to...talk— but that's crazy.

Wilson looked first at the dog, then at the pained face of his mother attempting to radiate guilt, like a flu victim radiates germs, then closed his eyes.

It was useless to argue with this woman.

"Mom, if I agree that I'll take the dog, you have to guarantee that it will only be for a day or two. Will you promise? Or else I'll take him back, regardless of the unpleasant consequences. Understand?"

Wilson was hedging his bets—he had his mother committing to locate another home for the beast, and she was on record for acknowledging that any stay with him had to be short-lived.

Gretna nearly dove at her son, embracing him fiercely, holding him tight, murmuring that he was a good son, all the while Thurman's mumble-growling seemed to agree.

His mother let him go, offering a knowing smile.

I knew that today was not going to be a good day. I knew it.

Chapter Three

YOU ARE son of Mizz Steele?"

Wilson felt perturbed when recognized—by shopkeepers and former students, let alone cabdrivers whom he had never once seen before.

He narrowed his eyes.

Sharif Yusry climbed out of the driver's seat and hurried to the back door.

"De door, sir, it sometimes sticks."

The driver clattered with it for a moment, then managed to get the door open.

"I say son of Mizz Steele. I recognize dog. I drive Mizz Steele to animal place. I wait and she arrives out with de black dog."

That makes sense. He doesn't know me. He knows the dog.

Thurman growled and wiggled and shoved his nose at the cabdriver's hand.

"He is an appropriate dog, sir. Most friendly."

Thurman hopped into the backseat.

"Indeed. Friendly. I suppose that is an admirable trait."

"Oh, yes indeed, sir," Sharif repeated. "For a dog, most noble."

Wilson had considered walking back to his house, but with his briefcase, a half-consumed bag of dog food, two dog bowls in a plastic Giant Eagle supermarket bag, and a blanket that "Thurman just loves to sleep on," Wilson knew that the two-mile walk would be fraught with danger.

The dog could lurch out into traffic. He could attack a toddler. He could... relieve himself in someone's yard. No. The only solution was a cab ride.

Sharif pulled out of the Heritage Square Senior Apartments and Retirement Village.

Thurman braced himself on the seat beside Wilson, grinning as only a happy dog can grin, sniffing the air through the half-open window and turning back to Wilson every quarter block.

"I know your mother," Sharif said from the front seat.

At least he had waited for a red light before he started chattering.

"Sorry," Wilson replied.

"No, sir. I like her. Full of life. Tasty. Is that correct word?"

Wilson grinned in spite of his horrible mood.

"You mean testy, I think."

"Testy?"

Wilson smiled at the absurdity of it all.

"Yes. Testy is the right word for her."

Yes indeed.

⟶

Wilson paid the cabdriver, gathered up everything he carried, and escorted Thurman to the front door of his house, a tidy midcentury brick house, built in the manner of a Cape Cod style, but not really, more like Pittsburgh's interpretation of a Cape Cod house. Thurman sniffed at everything and paid close attention to every stone and bush and nuance of the front walk.

"Yes, this is where I live. And where you will live. For a day or two. So don't get comfortable. Because you are not staying."

Thurman warbled a reply.

"I mean it," Wilson replied, and he jangled out his house key. "You may have bamboozled my mother, but she is old and much easier to bamboozle. She is a bamboozle-lite, as it were."

Thurman warbled again, as if to say, *We'll see.*

Wilson stared down at the dog, who was now seated on the front stoop.

Not as if. It really sounded like *We'll see.*

Wilson unlocked the door and slowly opened it, Thurman craning his neck to peer inside, not wanting to precede his host and lunge inside like a normal canine would probably do. Thurman did not do normal.

Wilson set all his parcels down on the long table in the front hall, carefully placing the folded blanket so it would not slip off and knock something else when it fell.

"You can follow me, Thurman. And pay attention."

Thurman growled a reply.

"I know you're a dog, Thurman. No matter. You can still listen."

Wilson led him to the tidy tile-and-steel kitchen; the only modern touches were a new stainless steel refrigerator and a stove.

"This is the kitchen. I imagine that I will feed you in here. I haven't decided yet."

He walked into the small, wood-paneled "rumpus room," which held a newer flat-screen TV, a couch that looked pristine even though it must have been fifteen years old, a leather recliner next to a towering stack of books, and an old gooseneck lamp with a hundred-watt bulb in it.

"The living room and dining rooms are that way—but we never use them."

Thurman peered in that direction and nodded.

"Upstairs are the two bedrooms and bathroom. The door leads to the basement. We don't go down there either. And this door leads to the backyard."

Wilson stepped outside himself for a moment and realized how ridiculous, how absurd this all was—him leading a dumb animal around the house as if the dumb animal understood what he was saying—but even so, he gamely pressed on, aware or not aware.

He opened the back door.

Thurman's snout puckered as he drew in a large nosey breath.

The backyard was fenced, but no one could tell for sure, since the thickets of bushes and pines all but concealed the stockade fence along the property's perimeter.

And in the middle of the modest backyard ran a long reflecting pool, some thirty feet long and six feet wide and five feet deep at the far end, gradually sloping up to a depth of two feet nearest the house. The pool was lined with slate and granite with a small fountain at the far end, spouting a steady stream of water into the air and back into the pool with a dignified hiss.

Wilson, upon his return to peace and civilization, and after his stint in rehab so many decades earlier, had spent his first summer back home, back in America, back in a land devoid of the scarring realities of war. He spent it—the entire summer—digging the pool and reinforcing the walls with rebar, mixing cement, setting the stone, installing the piping, and bringing the water supply out from the house through a trench he had dug by hand from the basement.

He wasn't sure then why he had felt compelled to create such a massive serenity pool, all he knew was that he had to do it. Perhaps he was serving penance. For what he had done and what he had seen done. And even now, years and years later, he sometimes wondered why he had worked so hard to build it. And how hard he worked to forget.

Yet there were moments, slivers of moments, when he stepped outside and stared at the water and the ripples and listened and the sun caught the water just so and the noise of the outside world was muted and stilled by the gurgling water, when all else disappeared save this long, narrow strip of water lined with flinty slate and black granite—there were those slight glimpses into the why of all this.

He could smile for that brief second and feel balanced, or more precisely, feel nothing at all—nothing hidden, nothing looming, nothing lurking in the shadows.

For that one, brief pellucid moment, Wilson felt at peace, his soul and his heart and all the rest at total, restful peace.

The absence of all care.

For that one moment.

Then the world and his awareness of it would come upon him, like an unbidden wave against the shore, and he would be standing there with fists clenched.

But those small moments of peace were enough. Those moments were what kept him together.

When Thurman caught scent of the water, he tore off in pursuit and launched himself from the closest end, leaping, flying, charging into the air and coming down a full fifteen feet farther with a huge, collapsing splash.

It all happened so fast that Wilson did not even have time to sputter and curse his outrage at this horrid canine intrusion into that serenity.

"Thurman!" he shouted.

Thurman might have growled, but if he did, his splashing drowned it out. He kept dog-paddling to the far end, under the spouting water, then turned around, as if he had been practicing serenity pool turnarounds for years, and dog-paddled back toward Wilson, grinning more like a maniac this time, and less like a lunatic.

"Thurman! Get out of there. Now!"

Thurman's nails scrabbled at the slick slate surround, but he managed to get a pawhold and hauled himself out, an immense grin on his face.

Retrievers and water. Why didn't he consider that before he let him out?

"Stay."

Thurman stayed put but shook himself off, water spreading up and out in splayed rainbows as the droplets arced into the afternoon sun.

Wilson returned with two towels, old towels, from a stack of them he kept in the garage for emergencies. This was the very first time he had come upon an emergency that required two towels.

And at that, he smiled to himself, just a little, but much less than Thurman was grinning.

Wilson knelt down next to Thurman and began to towel off the excess water. The coats of retrievers and water dogs appeared to be designed to shed water quickly, so a single towel was all that was really required. But he took the second towel and grabbed at Thurman's feet, making sure the bottoms of the paws were dry.

Thurman leaned into him, his head against Wilson's shoulder, growling and rumbling as he tolerated Wilson's attentions.

Wilson stopped and leaned back.

"What?"

Thurman turned his head and re-growled.

"You like my pool?"

Thurman smiled.

"Really?"

Thurman nodded this time and tried to widen his grin.

"Really," Wilson said, his tone dry and tending to the ironic and definitely to unbelief.

As he listened, that is exactly what Thurman's growls sounded like: *I like your water.*

Thurman turned back toward the pool, and if Wilson had not held on to his collar, Thurman most likely would have launched himself back into the water to prove that he meant what he said.

"You expect me to believe that you understand?"

Thurman appeared a bit offended, or as much as an oddly grinning dog can look offended, and growled.

I understand.

Wilson stared at Thurman.

"I'm going senile," he said, "just like my mother. Two peas in a pod."

And when Thurman growled in reply, Wilson tried not to pay attention to him. But if asked, he would have said that Thurman had said that he shouldn't worry about things like that, since other things were going to happen to make all of it make sense.

Or something like that.

Chapter Four

I N PORTLAND, OREGON, at the end of a residential lane filled with tidy Craftsman-style houses and cozy bungalows, Hazel Jamison stood outside one particular house, carrying three GARAGE SALE signs under her arm. The sale was scheduled for the weekend, and that gave Hazel four more days to finish organizing her mother's worldly possessions and pricing them.

"She was a bit of a pack rat. She never married, so she never had a husband to sort of keep control of the clutter," Hazel had told her employer when asking for the time off. "I know crafters will love what she has—yarn and cloth and old clothes and antiques and all sort of bric-a-brac. A couple of sewing machines. A couple of boxes of knitting needles. A couple of bushels of yarn for future projects. Nothing all that valuable, but I don't simply want to pitch it. She had a knack for finding things that other people thought were useless and turning them into something beautiful and wonderful."

She entered the home she had grown up in and where she had not lived for nearly two decades.

Not much has changed. Still the same artwork and sofa and lamps. The rug might be new.

As she walked from room to room, she began to make a tally of what was left to process—what she would sell and what was obviously headed for the Dumpster that was coming at the beginning of the next week. Whatever did not sell in the sale and was too far gone to donate would be dumped.

"And there's a lot of junk hiding out here," Hazel said to herself. "There's still the attic and the garage and the basement."

She walked into her mother's bedroom, also mostly unchanged over the last few decades. There were a few pictures of Hazel, snapshots, tucked into the mirror—Hazel in grade school, Hazel in high school, Hazel with her college cap and gown.

She sat down at her mother's dressing table and picked up one picture, a small photo, trimmed to fit a tiny square frame. It was a photo of Hazel and her mother at a county fair somewhere—early dusk, a Ferris wheel in the background and both of them with goofy, happy grins on their faces, both holding on to large pink puffs of cotton candy.

Hazel looked at it for a long time and began to softly cry, shedding the tears she had not shed during the last brief burst of sickness that took her mother.

I needed to be strong for her.

She placed the picture back on the table.

Since there was no one else to do it for her.

There had been no one to help with any of this. Not really. Yesterday she'd watched as a pair of not-too-interested workers manhandled the stone above her mother's grave in the Skyline Memorial Gardens, overlooking Portland, although from that spot Hazel could only see a line of trees to the north, which in the summer blocked the views of the city and river.

Some plots offer better views. Hazel found that notion endearingly odd.

The setting of the stone took less than ten minutes. Both men had nodded, with practiced solemnity, as they gathered their tools—shovels, pry bars, levels, and the like—and motored off in the cemetery's golf cart. The sedate puttering as they rounded the curve and disappeared from sight was oddly suited to the sedate location.

I imagine cemeteries are pretty quiet places most of the time. How often do people visit gravesites? Or play raucous music?

She remembered looking down at the small granite rectangle containing her mother's name, her date of birth, and date of death.

Hazel had the monument company add a single Bible verse to the stone. "Make it as small as you can," she had said. "My mother would kill me if she knew what I was doing, but since I'm paying for it, not much she can do at the moment."

The monument company representative must have encountered such requests with regularity, because it had been met with not even the slightest hint of a raised eyebrow.

"What's the verse?" he had asked, pen poised in midair.

"Jeremiah 29:11."

"That's on a number of markers."

Hazel had felt obligated to repeat it. " *'For I know the plans I have for you,' declares the Lord, 'plans to prosper you and not to harm you, plans to give you hope and a future.'* That's sort of been my life verse, you know."

The agent had nodded, offered a comforting smile, then added, "We'll use an actual Bible for the quote—and we ask which version you prefer. We always do. In the past, you wouldn't believe how many people get a word or two wrong, then want us to make changes after the stone is cut."

The representative, whose name Hazel knew but quickly forgot, had leaned closer and said softly, "It's not like a computer. We can't autocorrect engraving on granite."

"No, I am sure you can't. And thank you for being thorough."

And now she sat picturing the engraved words.

They had all been there.

She looked out the window of her mother's room to the sky, the sun breaking through a dense cloud cover, shafts of light dancing along the quiet and overgrown lawn.

Now I am alone, Mother. All alone.

Just like you always wanted to be, isn't it?

Chapter Five

WILSON PACED around the house that afternoon, holding Thurman's blanket. Thurman obviously considered following him, but he must have been cognizant of Wilson's anxiety issues. Instead, he sat on the braided rug in the kitchen, enjoying the afternoon sun on his back. There were not many windows in Gretna's apartment, and none of them seemed to let in a lot of natural sunlight. There were no windows in the shelter and Thurman did not know how long he had been there, out of the sun.

So he sat, his eyes half-closed, his breathing regular, enjoying the warmth and apparently enjoying the quiet environment of Wilson's home.

At Gretna's, well, there was always the sound of televisions or doors slamming or someone calling out to someone or a phone ringing with no one hearing well enough to acknowledge it and answer.

In the shelter, there was constant barking and the metallic tang of bars being shut and locked, that clattering sound of dog nails on hard concrete.

But here, in this smallish house, in the afternoon sun, there was quiet.

And Thurman liked that quiet.

Wilson, on the other hand, seemed to grow more anxious as every potential bedding spot for Thurman was evaluated, considered, and then discarded, as Wilson found some manner of disagreement with it.

Not in his bedroom.

Too close. He'll worry me being that close. Maybe he'll bark at night.

Not in the spare bedroom.

I don't want to mess it up in case I have guests. They might be allergic.

He had not had overnight guests in over a decade, but no matter.

Not in the kitchen.

What if he gets into the pantry? Dogs do that, right?

Finally, after two circuits through the house, Wilson, frazzled, stood in front of Thurman with blanket in hand.

"Okay. Okay. So where do you want to sleep?"

Thurman looked up and growled.

"It doesn't matter? Is that what you said?"

Good grief. I'm pretending that this beast is sentient and understands English.

Wilson looked down at Thurman, who looked back up, grinning.

Just like I pretend that my students are sentient and understand English. Of which I am not always certain.

Thurman growled and walked into the room with the big chair and stack of books. He looked about and sat down.

He growled out, *Here.*

Wilson was about to ask why, but he watched Thurman look to the back of the house, then to the front, and then to the steps. From this one spot near the couch, Thurman could see the back door, the front door, and the steps leading upstairs.

Wilson turned his head.

"You want to stand guard?"

Thurman smiled and growled a yes.

As Wilson put the blanket down, and as Thurman mooshed it to fit his specific requirements, Wilson considered just how absurd and bizarre and unbalanced and disturbing these last thirty minutes had become.

"Dogs don't talk. People don't understand growls. And I'm not crazy."

Thurman sat on his blanket, looked up, and growled in agreement.

———

The next morning, Wilson woke earlier than normal, and his normal was most early, well before sunup. He sat on the edge of the bed, rubbing his face and feeling the creaks and groans of his body, the angry pings from his shoulder and back, the twists and twinges always the forerunner of a memory—a memory he had spent decades trying to ignore.

Mornings were not bright-eyed and bushy-tailed affairs. Or at least they had not been to him for the past few decades.

He stood and flexed at the waist, first to the right and then the left, a series of pops and cracks emanating from the various joints in his lower back.

He took a deep breath, walked to the window, opened up a gap in the blinds, and stared out to the darkened street beyond. A few cars slipped past, headlights glistering in the early fog.

The dog doesn't talk. I am sure of that. I'm projecting. My mother has that effect on me. She acted as though the dog was aware—and now I am believing her as well. It's all because of her. I'm susceptible to nudges like that. I am. It's probably genetic. And she's done that all her life.

He had wrestled with those truths most of the night, not sleeping well as a result.

But then, he hadn't slept well since . . . since a long, long time ago. Not that much different to last night—except this night's restlessness had a dog at the center of it. And his mother.

He grabbed his robe off the peg on the back of the door, slipped into his slippers, and padded downstairs as silently as he could.

By the time he was halfway down the steps, the beast was awake and standing at the foot of the stairs, grinning and wagging his tail in an incoherently happy manner.

Wilson waited until he was at ground level to speak.

"Thurman."

Thurman responded with a small jump, front paws only, and a warbled growl.

It might have been *Morning.* But it was most likely just a growl.

Let's face it, Wilson, dogs don't talk and you don't understand barks and growls. Let's just chalk this up to a busy day and having a horrid surprise sprung on you all of a sudden by your mother and that's all. Overwhelmed. That's it. That's what happens.

Wilson, perhaps taking after his mother, often addressed himself in the third person when talking to himself—as if he was simply an observer of the life that swirled around him.

Yes, I know it sounds ludicrous. That's what forty years of living alone will do to you.

"I suspect you need to go outside." It was a statement, not a question.

Thurman jumped again, doing a delicate half-twist as he did, like a furry ballet dancer of a sort. A smiling, four-legged ballet dancer. With fur. And a very long, relaxed pink tongue.

Wilson walked to the back door and Thurman followed at his side. Wilson had his hand on the doorknob, then turned to Thurman with a stern look.

"There will be no swimming this morning. Understand? No water."

Thurman looked up with a look of disappointment.

He growled.

"I mean it. No swimming. Not this morning."

Thurman looked down at his paws for a moment, as if thinking that literally interpreting this statement might also mean that swimming would be allowed later in the day. It was obvious that he could abide by that rule.

He smiled up at Wilson.

"Okay. Out. Don't sneak off. I'm going to make coffee. I will watch for you. Okay?"

By the time Wilson was done making his pot of coffee, Thurman was sitting by the back door, staring in, dry and happy and smiling.

I can't believe it. He does understand English.

Chapter Six

AFTER CLASS that afternoon, Wilson swallowed hard and mentally hitched up his thoughts.

Two doors down from his faculty office on the twelfth floor—a small, cramped room that he kept agonizingly devoid of all decoration, as if thinking he might be forced to pack up at a moment's notice—was the office of a Dr. Robert Limke, a small, wizened man who had some manner of doctorate in some area of psychology, a field that Wilson had long declared to be pure bunkum.

Wilson had a nodding acquaintance with Dr. Limke and occasionally had been invited to his home for some tedious manner of faculty get-together. He had attended a few of them over the last few decades and found them barely tolerable.

He assumed that Dr. Limke viewed these social obligations with the same disregard as he did.

Perhaps it was because Dr. Limke had a perpetual scowl on his face.

Wilson wondered if that was because of genetics or some sort of industrial accident.

He saw the small, shadowy figure through the frosted glass.

He tapped.

"What?" came the barked reply.

Wilson set his face to neutral and opened the door a crack, the thickness of a piece of toast.

"You have a minute?" he asked.

Dr. Limke stared at the small opening.

"Dr. Steele? Yeah. Sure. A minute. Come on in. Or at least open the door a little more."

Wilson opened it enough so that he could stand halfway inside.

"You coming to the faculty mixer this weekend?"

Wilson had no knowledge of a faculty mixer, this week-end or otherwise.

"Maybe."

Dr. Limke actually grinned after a moment.

"Yeah. Neither am I. Stupid things. An excuse to drink. Like I need an excuse."

Wilson nodded.

"So what do you want? Professional or personal?"

Wilson looked a little surprised.

"Advice," Dr. Limke explained. "The only reason someone voluntarily talks to a head-shrinker is for advice. Like we have answers to anything."

"Uhhh . . . I guess personal."

"Shoot."

"Long story . . . about a dog, sort of. My mother is forcing me to take care of this mutt—which is something she's really good at, I mean, forcing me to do things I don't want to do and . . . well, I listen to this stupid animal growling, and for the life of me, it sounds like it's trying to talk. That's crazy, right? Like the dumb beast understands and is trying to form words. Crazy, right?"

Dr. Limke leaned back and folded his hands together and placed two fingers under his chin, as if he had to supplement his neck muscles in supporting the weight of his oversized head.

"Your mother, you say?"

"Yes."

"You don't want the dog?"

"No. Not really."

"Your mother makes you feel guilty."

"She is very skilled at it."

Dr. Limke pursed his lips.

"The dog isn't telling you to do . . . anything illegal? Or dangerous, is it?"

"No. Just talking. Normal things. Like, 'When's dinner?'"

"Hmmmm."

Wilson waited, then said, "Sort of crazy, right? I'm projecting, right?"

Dr. Limke nodded.

"Probably projecting. That's normal for people with pets. And this is my five-minute, snap diagnosis. You want the real definitive answer, make an appointment at my practice. But your mother, this dog, guilt . . . that's a heady concoction for sure. Though lots of people who have dogs swear that the dog talks to them. Or at least the dogs let them know what they want. No big deal. Not crazy. Eccentric, perhaps. Not crazy. Harmless, actually. We have a dog at home that I know hates me and is plotting against me. Leaves toys on the stairs so I'll fall down and break my neck and then he can claim my side of the bed. But that's another story."

Wilson drew in a large breath.

"But if the dog tells you to get a gun or something like that," Dr. Limke cautioned cheerfully, "you come back right away and we'll talk. Okay? No appointment needed. Okay?" Wilson nodded. "Okay. Not crazy. Dogs don't talk. Projecting. No guns. Got it."

⌐

That evening, Wilson ate his individually sized take-out pepperoni pizza, while Thurman watched expectantly from a respectful distance. The dog did not whine or whimper, just stared. Wilson gathered up his plate and the empty box and looked down at the dog.

"Dogs aren't supposed to eat pizza."

Thurman looked back, appearing shocked, and growled.

"Don't tell me that they are," Wilson replied.

Thurman shook his head and re-growled his response.

"They are not. You have your food over there," Wilson said as he pointed to the half-full bowl of kibbles.

Thurman dutifully regarded the bowl, then turned back and instead of a growl, made a *Yuck* sound deep in his throat.

"Regardless, that is what you will eat."

Thurman just stared.

Wilson stared back.

"And I know you can't talk. Even Dr. Limke agreed with me. He said it was simply me projecting. Because of my mother. No dogs talk. No dogs understand. I know that, Thurman. And so do you."

Thurman lost his smile.

And then he growled out what sounded exactly like *Bunkum.*

Wilson eyed him as he placed his dish by the sink.

"Maybe. But that's the truth I am assuming to be true. That's the truth both of us are going with."

And maybe it is because I've been alone so long. Maybe it's because of that . . . and all the rest of my past. Now it comes out. Now it begins to manifest itself. After all these years. Buried memories will out, someday.

And then Thurman growled out *Bunkum* again, stood, walked into the family room, and let himself fall onto his blanket, his back toward Wilson and everything else.

"I am going to the grocery store, Thurman," Wilson said. "I need coffee and bread and half-and-half . . . And I suppose you need some dog food."

Thurman stood and smiled and growled.

Friskies.

Wilson scowled and pretended that his growl did not sound like an endorsement for a specific brand of dog food that Wilson was not even sure was a current brand, since he never traveled down the pet food aisle at the Giant Eagle supermarket.

"You have to behave while I am gone. There will be no 'accidents,' right?"

Thurman looked up, offended, and growled, *I am not an animal.*

Wilson did not want to engage in what he knew was an activity that was beginning to verge on real psychosis.

"No. I do not think you are an animal, Thurman. I think you are largely a figment of my overwrought imagination. A manifestation of repressed painful memories. Or at least some of you is. Or are."

Thurman smiled, sat down on his blanket, and growled, *I am Thurman.*

"Yes. Of course you are," Wilson replied, his thick irony beginning to dissipate, much as an early fog slowly becomes invisible over time and with adequate sunlight.

And with that, he entered the garage, closed the door firmly, and unlocked his automobile, a vehicle he used primarily to go and buy groceries.

He heard Thurman growl from behind the door, *Friskies.*

Wilson closed his eyes.

Please.

Chapter Seven

W HILE PORTLAND deserved its reputation for being wet and mostly miserable for much of the spring, the weekend of Hazel's garage sale at her mother's home turned out to be sunny and warm, which brought out a plethora of crafters and bargain hunters. She scarcely had time to sit down all morning, let alone drink the extra-strong coffee she had brought with her in a thermos.

"The nearest Starbucks is like a mile away. I can't leave the garage sale to feed my caffeine addiction," she had told herself as she poured an entire pot of "robust, full-bodied" French roast coffee into her well-worn thermos.

The insurance company where she worked as an actuary had instituted a health-and-wellness regime several years earlier, doing away with the candy and snack machine, and passing an edict—or rather a stern but pleasantly worded policy—doing away with employee coffeepots throughout the office.

"Some people cannot tolerate the percolating smell of old roasted coffee beans," the energetic human resources director had claimed in an all-company email. "And no one knows for sure if any coffee supplied by our employees is actually fair-raised and fair-traded coffee. So, rather than debate that controversial subject, if an employee must have coffee, it must be brought in from the outside, in a sealed container."

The edict had proved to be a small boomlet for local thermos sales. And for the nearest Starbucks, three blocks distant.

In the late afternoon of the garage sale, the steady flood of customers ebbed, and Hazel finally had time for her third cup of coffee of the day—the first two had come at home.

"Delicious," she said as she sipped from the red plastic thermos cup.

The house had been picked over and the garage was all but empty. Her mother had been an avid gardener up until her final year, and kept her tools cleaned and oiled and neatly hung on racks. The racks were now empty.

The lawn mower had been sold early.

Hazel wondered if she had priced things too cheaply.

I probably did, but I'm getting rid of it—and they're paying me to take it away. A win-win situation.

The furniture went quickly. There wasn't all that much of it, but it sold. Craft supplies, in boxes and priced per boxful, sold quickly, surprising Hazel.

The great majority of the for-sale items in the house now too were gone. All that was left were a few odds and ends, a couple of file cabinets, and an old desk, which was too large for Hazel's smaller apartment.

Hazel stood, folded her chair, and walked toward the GARAGE SALE sign she had placed in the front yard.

It would be replaced by the Realtor's FOR SALE sign the following day.

A young couple pulled to the curb in an old but clean Ford pickup truck, with a unicorn decal on the back window and a rainbow bumper sticker. They hurried out, holding hands, laughing.

"Are we too late?"

"No. Not at all," Hazel said, being accommodating and gracious, much as was her habit. "There's not much left. But you're welcome to take a look."

Hazel wished she could be more assertive. She really wanted to lock things up and wait for the Dumpster on Monday.

But a few more minutes won't matter . . . I guess.

And she had no idea of the impact this one simple decision would make on her life.

Next time I'll be more assertive and just say no. That would be a real change of pace for me, wouldn't it?

⟶

Thurman sat by the front door, front legs neatly together, his panting slow and steady, watching, almost as if waiting for some sort of a good-dog final inspection. He seemed to be listening intently as Wilson talked to his mother on the phone.

"Mother," Wilson said in the firmest tone he could muster, "you said a day or two. That was Tuesday. Four days have passed. It is now Saturday and the beast is still in my house."

Wilson knew he could be tougher and more rigid while on the phone. It was more anonymous, more invisible—almost as invisible as the Internet trolls and the vitriolic comments they posted on web pages and the like.

If they can't see you, they don't know how big or small you are.

"Wilson, I know what I said," his mother replied. "A couple of days. Maybe to a word genius like you, a couple means two. But I meant several. Okay? I am eighty-five years old, you know."

Wilson's mother had a master's degree in English from Carlow College and was much better at grammar and punctuation than was her son. When she called him a "word genius" it wasn't a pronouncement of fact—just a way to make him feel sorry for his less-educated mother.

It seldom worked as planned.

And Wilson noted that she was never hesitant to bring up her advanced age when it suited her purposes for gathering empathy, if not downright sympathy.

Like now.

"Two days. Four days. A week. I'm not one to quibble, Mother," Wilson stated, emphasizing the word "Mother." "You promised—within a short period of time—to have this beast removed."

At the word "beast," Thurman growled up at Wilson, looking a little hurt.

Not beast. Good dog.

Wilson stared down at him and shook his head. He mouthed the words, "It's for effect, okay?"

Thurman shook his head in return as if wondering what sort of oddly calculated game these two people were playing, neither of them being in a position to win, and both precariously close to losing.

Odd, he growled. *Too much think.*

"That is not true," Wilson hissed back, his palm over the talking-into portion of the phone.

"Wilson," his mother said, obviously hoping her flat tone would indicate hurt and pain rather than a simple attempt at manipulation, "I understand. I will make more calls. I'll post a flyer downstairs."

Wilson wanted to interject that the only people who would see that flyer would be the crotchety old people in her senior-living complex, who couldn't adopt a dog even if they wanted to.

But he didn't.

Thurman gave him that look. So he left the remark unsaid.

"Fine. You do that, Mother. I am counting on you to find a new living arrangement for this dog…"

Thurman growled again.

Better.

"…a living arrangement that does not include me."

Wilson's mother inhaled and waited a moment to answer.

"You are such a good boy, Wilson. Have I told you that recently? You are such a good boy."

To Wilson, it sounded like his mother was still talking about the good dog, Thurman.

After he hung up the phone, he crossed his arms and stared down at Thurman. Thurman adjusted his front paws just so and stared back up at him, a trace of a grin almost hidden under his black snout.

But not really hidden. Thurman had proven, over these few short days, to have an abysmal poker face.

"You should be on your way to the pound, Thurman."

Wilson had started referring to Thurman as "Thurman" on the second day of his "visit" and no longer thought of him as "that dog" or "the beast."

Thurman growled back, his growl mixed with a happy smile of subterfuge.

You like me.

Wilson shook his head and kept a mock grimace on his face.

Thurman's growls and whines and soft barks and whimpers and throat clearings all seemed to Wilson to convey something. Some of them were obvious.

Hungry.

What you eat?

Outside?

Really, what you eat?

I would like some of food you eat.

The more complicated, the more abstract—well, for those, Wilson remained unsure.

And it frightened him, just a little. Or maybe a little more than a little.

Frightened. Alarmed. Fascinated. Like a rodent is fascinated by a snake, coiled and ready to strike, unable to move because of the beauty of the snake's scales and eyes and slithery tongue, tasting the air.

Like slowing down when driving past an accident—staring, drawn to the carnage and twisted metal.

Drawn.

Wilson knew what memories were hidden and how well he had them hidden and how hard he worked at hiding them and now there's this dog who pushed whatever buttons were to be pushed and Wilson was again thinking about things that he did not want to think about—or at least blaming the effort it took to hide the memories as a reason to believe that a puddinghead of a dog could talk.

This is complicated stuff, Wilson thought, *and it is made up of things I do not want to remember.*

"You have me almost believing you can talk, Thurman. You know that?"

Yes.

"I have a doctorate in creative writing and a second master's degree in contemporary American literature—and I'm listening to a dog. Do you know how absolutely absurd that sounds?"

Thurman growled.

Yes.

Wilson knew it was ludicrous. He knew it was delusional. He knew it was perhaps the first sign of a descent into dementia, or some other horrid cognitive impairment.

But then, there it was. Thurman's ability to communicate. To talk. Sort of.

"You know, it's probably because I've lived so long by myself. That has to be a contributing factor, Thurman. I am fantasizing having someone to talk to."

Thurman growled.

Probably.

"But I'm not going to tell anyone about it."

Sure.

Wilson walked into the kitchen and Thurman followed. He reached into a shopping bag on the counter and pulled out a leash from a store in Shadyside called Petagogy. He had taken a cab there to purchase the sixteen-foot retractable leash and a plain black leather collar to replace the hideous red plaid collar with rhinestones that the rescue center had sent Thurman off with.

"What do you think?" Wilson asked.

Holding the leash in his hand, he explained the process to

Thurman, demonstrating how the leash worked, like a flight attendant on a dog airline.

"So, we are going for a walk, Thurman. No pulling or yanking. No barking. No lunging at other people."

Thurman growled yes.

Wilson, on occasion over the years, took walks around the neighborhood. But not often. When he walked alone, he knew people would be watching and evaluating, obviously thinking that he had no business being out and about with no purpose or destination in mind.

He had tried walking at night, but the shadows unnerved him, and the sweep of headlights brought back troubling memories, or at least let them edge closer to his consciousness, and he wanted no part of those nighttime terrors, not anymore, not ever.

"But with a dog, Thurman—that's you by the way—I have a reason to be out. And it will allow me to get exercise without resorting to using that disgusting faculty health center."

Thurman smiled and nodded.

Wilson snapped the leash onto the collar and tested the resistance of the retractable section of the leash.

Thurman barked and smiled.

We go.

Chapter Eight

THE YOUNG COUPLE exited Hazel's mother's house holding a large ceramic vase, orange and blue, that might charitably be called kitsch.

Hazel saw it as simply ugly.

The couple was laughing, as if now in possession of a decorating practical joke.

Then they came upon the large desk that had been placed in the garage.

"Twenty dollars? Really? For the whole desk?" the young man said. "Wow."

Apparently he had not attended the garage-sale negotiating seminar, Hazel thought, smiling.

The young woman ran her hand over the surface and pulled out each drawer, making sure that every one worked. She stepped back and tilted her head in appraisal.

"It's perfect," she said.

"We'll take it," the young man said, "and this cool vase. That's like thirty dollars for both, right?"

Their excitement was nearly palpable. Their energy made Hazel smile—and grow a little wistful as well. Or maybe jealous.

"Tell you what, I'll take a twenty-dollar bill for both items. I'm just glad to see the desk gone, to tell you the truth. It won't fit in my condo and it's too heavy for me to move any farther."

The pair looked at Hazel, then each other, grinning. "It's a deal. Thanks. Really. Thanks so much. We're trying to fill our place and neither of us has much money. And we have to save up for wedding rings as well. The preacher said it was okay not to have rings—but we want them . . . you know . . . so people know. God knows, which is all that matters, really, but we still want rings."

The young woman hurried to the truck, stashed the vase on the front seat, and lowered the tailgate while her husband, or husband-to-be, paid the twenty dollars.

The two of them hefted the desk up and carried it to the truck, Hazel offering directional advice as they did and a helping hand as they maneuvered it into the open back of the truck. The young woman jumped up with it and shouldered the desk into place, surprising Hazel with her dexterity and strength.

She didn't look like she weighed more than a hundred pounds.

She then busied herself by removing the drawers and stacking them securely, so they wouldn't fly open on the way home.

As she pulled out the last drawer, a brown envelope fell out onto the truck bed.

The young woman picked it up.

"Are you Hazel? This must be yours."

Hazel stepped closer and extended her hand.

"I am. The desk was my mother's."

"Well, it doesn't feel like money," the young woman said, fingering the sealed envelope. "But it obviously belongs to you. It must have been taped to the bottom of a drawer or something."

Hazel took it and saw her name printed on the envelope in her mother's handwriting, plus a date written in large block letters—a date decades earlier.

"Hey, like a time capsule, huh?" the young man said as he closed the tailgate.

Hazel slid her finger under the flap; the adhesive had all but disappeared, offering a crinkled rasp as it released.

A picture fluttered out and fell to the ground. And then a key fell out with a brassy, metallic clink.

Hazel reached down and picked them both up.

The black-and-white tones of the photograph had turned sepia. The picture depicted her mother, carrying a handful of flowers, and with a halo of small flowers—violets, perhaps—circling her head, holding hands with a young man in a military uniform. They were both smiling, but the young man had a guarded, apprehensive look in his eyes. Haunted, perhaps.

Hazel turned the photo over.

Written in her mother's expansive, flowery handwriting were two words: *Our Wedding*.

The brass key was just as enigmatic. Etched into the key, in small type, was the following:

#349-H

And on a small, metal-ringed paper disk, clipped to the key with a small chain, were the words, written in her mother's handwriting, *Umpqua Bank*.

⌁

Gretna shuffled toward the brightly lit dining room of the senior citizen complex, joining a handful of other seniors all shuffling toward the same destination. Had they been able to travel at full walking speed, a traffic jam, or even a collision or two, would be the result of their combined fixation on finding a "good" table. But as it was, most of them moved at not much faster than a shuffle, and they seamlessly merged into one relatively docile line of hungry diners.

Gretna was one of the fortunate ones: Her hearing was still adequate, her vision was decent—not enough to drive, but decent—and her mobility, while compromised slightly, still allowed her to travel faster than most of her fellow seniors. She made a beeline to the farthest table from the entrance and the one closest to the kitchen.

"Food is warmer at this table. You sit by the entrance and you get icicles in your stewed prunes."

She found her favorite spot at her favorite table, looking out to a mostly unused courtyard that was filled with trees on the verge of green and gold.

Gretna liked the spring. Rebirth. Renewal. New life.

And she could sneak outside from time to time and smoke a cigarette.

She had a pack of Lucky Strikes that was now a year old, and only three cigarettes remained in it.

I wonder if the Giant Eagle still sells them? I don't see them at the checkout counter anymore. Maybe I could get that nosey cabdriver to buy me some. I certainly couldn't ask Wilson. He'd have me locked up, for sure.

A few minutes later, as the slow tide of old folks ebbed into the dining area, one of Gretna's hallmates wrinkled her face like a raisin, squinting with great effort.

"Gretna?"

"Yes," she replied. "Sit down, Mavis. I'm friendly today. Won't bite . . . much."

Mavis laughed and waved her hand, as if dismissing Gretna's semi-brittle greeting. They often shared a table at lunch.

Mavis took several minutes maneuvering her walker into exactly the correct position, then sort of launched herself at the chair, causing it to slide a few inches from the hard landing. She then set about attempting to fold her walker, complete with angry muttering in Yiddish under her breath. One leg of the walker folded in easily, but one leg remained obstinate and erect. After more than a few minutes, Mavis's Yiddish became more inflammatory, and even though Gretna did not understand much of the language, she could easily guess the meaning from the harsh, angry tone and brittle inflection.

In the end, Mavis shoved at the walker with a Yiddish curse, and it fell to its side. Then she kicked it once and dragged it closer to her chair, making sure that the walkway around the table was clear.

"And a good day to you too, Mavis."

Mavis waved off the sarcasm with a weary sigh.

"A pain in the tuches, this getting old is."

Gretna nodded, then realized that Mavis might not see the nod, so she added loudly, "It certainly is. Getting old, I mean. A pain."

"In the tuches," Mavis added, grinning.

"Among other places," Gretna replied.

The server—a twig of a young girl from the Philippines, Gretna had heard—came up with glasses of water and the xeroxed lunch menu.

Mavis squinted.

"What they got today?" she asked, holding the menu up-side down and peering over at Gretna.

"Get the chicken soup. And the tuna salad sandwich."

Mavis replied with a practiced scowl, "That means the other choice is either Salisbury steak or chicken à la king."

"The first one. It's probably left over from last week."

The pair sat in silence for a long moment, Gretna peering about the dining room, Mavis fiddling with her necklace, which had become tangled.

Suddenly, Gretna brightened.

"Did you hear the news?" she asked.

"What news? They fired the cook?"

"No," Gretna replied, then paused. "They did?"

"Did what?"

"Fired the cook?"

Mavis waved her hand again in dismissal. It was a familiar gesture. "No. I was just guessing. But they should."

"Oh. No, that wasn't it," Gretna said, a smile returning to her face. "I'm going to become a grandmother."

"Really?"

"Yep. After all these years."

"I didn't know your son was married."

"Oh. He isn't."

Mavis leaned back, trying not to appear judgmental. When one squinted most of the day, it was difficult not to look judgmental.

"So . . . is he getting married?" she asked.

"I don't know," Gretna replied. "I don't think so."

Mavis leaned back as the young Filipina server placed a bowl of soup in front of her.

"But he might? There must be a woman, yes?"

"No."

"So then... how..." Mavis asked, apparently not sure of exactly what she was asking.

"I don't know. But I know."

"But... how...?"

"Oh... how do I know?"

Mavis shrugged and nodded.

"Thurman told me. Just before he left."

"Thurman?"

"Yes," Gretna replied, crushing two packets of unsalted saltines into her soup. "And Thurman wouldn't lie."

↩

In a daze, Hazel waved as her last two customers left the garage sale, driving slowly, not taking chances with their new twenty-dollar desk. On autopilot, she pulled the GARAGE SALE sign from the parkway in front of the house and wandered, as if she had no specific destination in mind, to one end of the block and then the other, retrieving two other signs.

Once back in the garage, she let the signs clatter to the concrete floor. She took her foldable chair and unfolded it, poured out another cup of coffee from her thermos, and sat with a world-weary sigh, holding the coffee in her left hand and the old photograph in her right.

The brass key, which she assumed was for a safe-deposit box, was in the right front pocket of her jeans. She could feel the jagged edge against her thigh.

She sipped at the coffee. It was no longer hot, but drink-able.

She closed her eyes for a moment, then opened them and stared at the picture. The participants had not changed. Her mother was still there, looking very young, very angelic, and very hopeful. The soldier was still there, at her side, a little more distance between them than would be normal for most brides and grooms, but perhaps it was snapped just before they hugged.

Or something like that.

The soldier, whom Hazel assumed was in a uniform of the U.S. Army, remained enigmatic. Not happy. Not sad.

Troubled, maybe.

And her mother's handwriting. Definitely her mother's script.

Our Wedding.

A car slowly rolled past, perhaps looking for garage-sale leftovers to scavenge. There were none, none that Hazel wanted to deal with at this moment, so she did not look up.

Looking up would have been an invitation of sorts, and Hazel wanted no one to intrude on this odd, disjointed moment.

She stared at the photo.

"She was never married. That's what she told me," she said aloud.

She tilted her head and squinted, hoping the picture would reveal something to her, something hidden, something carefully placed out of view.

It did not.

"She said that I was born and that event was the result of

a short affair," Hazel said. "She always claimed that she did not know where my father went or where he might be. She wasn't even positive of his last name."

She felt a tightness in her throat.

"'It was the seventies, dear,' she'd said. 'Things like that happened,' she'd said. 'I'm not proud of it,' she'd said. 'But it happened,' she'd said. 'And I had to deal with it,' she'd said."

Hazel looked over the photo to the first reds of sunset.

"She never once mentioned a wedding. Never. Not once."

Chapter Nine

WILSON TOOK confident steps to the end of the walk. Then he stopped, and Thurman stopped. And then the dog sat and looked up at Wilson, as if trying to determine what rhythm a walk with this person might take.

Thurman had walked with Gretna, and with her he'd paced so slowly that he could have navigated his way with eyes shut. In fact, he had tried that once, walking to the end of the block, trying to guess when they were close to the curb by the sound of traffic, judging the distance using Gretna's shuffled steps as a measuring rod.

Thurman had come close that day to counting it out exactly, opening his eyes only two small shuffle steps from the curb on Wilkins Avenue.

But with this person, Thurman did not possess the same manner of assuredness.

Wilson stopped. He looked both ways several times. He then looked down at Thurman and shrugged his shoulders.

"I suspect it doesn't matter which way we go, does it?"

Thurman growled in response, not being able to shrug like a person, but almost saying that he wished he could. It often seemed like the most fitting gesture in certain circumstances, situations where there was no right or wrong but only equally vague choices.

Wilson turned left, heading away from the house, heading east.

Squirrel Hill at one time was old Jewish, and Jewish old money. The houses were not what anyone might call palatial, but they were large and solid and brick and substantial, making a statement as to their owners—that they had arrived, that they had come to America from the old country and had made it and built a big brick home on a big lot and there was even a room for a garden in back, if so desired, or a gazebo or a patio with electric lights strung out over the expanse.

Wilson knew that the sumptuousness of the houses in this neighborhood could never match the sumptuousness of newer homes in trendier, more up-and-coming neighborhoods, but he liked it nonetheless. While the demographics were in a state of flux, to Wilson the area recalled a simpler time, a time when there was truth and beauty and permanence and solidness.

Now there was no solidness.

He walked along with some purpose. Thurman growled a bit as they trotted along, as if he was endorsing, or enjoying, the pace.

They turned a corner five blocks later and headed north.

Wilson must not have been used to the spring sun just yet and felt beads of some small perspiration on his forehead.

He was not fond of sweating, not like this.

The beads of sweat on his forehead were tangents of past memories.

He reached up, swiped them away before the salt and the sweat fell into his eyes. He slowed down, Thurman keeping pace, a step to his side and a half-step behind, like a well-trained dog should walk with a person, exactly how they should walk.

Wilson wiped at his forehead again.

"Maybe we'll do this at dusk, Thurman. It will be cooler."

Thurman growled *Okay* and added that he didn't mind the warmth.

Wilson turned another corner and headed back west.

From the corner of his eye he saw a man at the top of a driveway. It was a slight incline—Pittsburgh was a city built on hills, after all. The driveway wasn't all that steep, but a car might have trouble climbing the expanse if snow were packed into a layer of ice.

Thurman saw the man too. He must have, because he slowed and offered a bark. Thurman had yet to bark in Wilson's presence. He did growl a lot, and mutter and whisper just under his breath, but this bark was new, and it took Wilson by surprise.

The bark was a friendly bark, a bark of greeting, if Wilson had been asked to classify the bark on some sort of dog/ English translation grid.

The man at the top of the driveway was seated.

Wilson now felt obligated to stop and look, which he did not want to do—not with anyone—but Thurman did bark and that required something.

Wilson waved. Well, sort of waved. He reached up, palm out, and acknowledged the man.

"Dr. Steele," the man called out. "Good to see you. It's been a while. How's your mother?"

Thurman looked up and growled.

You know man?

Wilson leaned forward, as if three inches of a closer view would bring anything into closer focus. He noticed then the wheelchair. And then he remembered.

"Dr. Killeen, how are you?"

"Just fine, Wilson. Your mother?"

"She's fine too," Wilson responded, hoping the conversation would not go on much longer.

"Tell her I said hello, would you?"

"I will."

There was silence.

Then the man in the wheelchair spoke.

"I see you got a dog."

Wilson nodded.

"I guess."

Silence.

Then Wilson waved and set off walking again. Thurman's leash grew taut before he began to follow.

Then the dog growled.

Who that?

Wilson wiped at his forehead again.

"It's a long story, Thurman. And not one I want to get into. Not now."

⟶

Fog blanketed Portland in the morning, muffling and concealing, and to Hazel the outside environment perfectly mirrored how she felt. She padded about her smallish apartment, drinking only a single cup of coffee, unusual for any morning, even more unusual for a Sunday morning. She left the *Sunday*

Oregonian newspaper on the kitchen counter, still wrapped in its protective plastic sleeve. She had not even bothered with toast this morning—again exhibiting a most unusual behavior.

Hazel never skipped breakfast.

She had the TV turned on and then off and then on and then finally off. The chatter of the Sunday press reports made no sense, and she was in no mood to sit down and attempt to concentrate.

The small sepia-tinted photo remained where she had placed it the previous evening, on the small desk that occupied a corner of the kitchen and from where Hazel managed all her finances and correspondence. A small laptop sat there as well. It was also dark.

She could not imagine trying to access Facebook that morning.

What would I post? "Oh, by the way, my mother was really married once. Sorry for the elaborate, decades-long façade."

To complete a circuit in her apartment took a few dozen steps. The space was not large enough for a serious, soul-searching walk. That sort of activity had to be done outside.

Hazel didn't really want to go outside, not in this thick fog and mist, but the walls of the apartment grew inward, making the space even smaller, and any cogent thought had become much more difficult.

She pulled on a pair of jeans, a sweatshirt, a mostly waterproof jacket, a wide-brimmed hat she had bought from L.L. Bean that promised to keep all rain off the back of one's neck. She slipped on her waterproof duck boots, grabbed her phone, and hurried down the steps to the street below.

Where to?

She did not stop to think, just turned right and began to walk. That direction was more level and therefore more conducive to contemplation.

Harder to think when you're panting up a hill.

The fog, thicker than she had anticipated, really did muffle most of the sounds that morning. Traffic was always light on Sunday, but what traffic there was appeared to be mostly silent.

That's good . . . I guess.

She kept walking, thinking about that photograph, that snapshot, and all that it entailed—or rather not thinking about that snapshot, pretending that it did not change a thing in her life, and then thinking that her life had just exploded and there was no one left to place the pieces even in close proximity to one another.

She walked on, feeling the fog sort of creep into her sleeves and under her coat and drip off the brim of her hat. The air was not exactly cold that morning, but the dampness and the fog and her sense of temporal dislocation gave her a severe case of the chills.

Hazel looked up and tried to figure out exactly where she was.

A pool of light illuminated the sidewalk on the next block.

A pool of light meant one of two things: a restaurant or a coffee shop.

She was hoping for the latter.

And it was. As she neared it, she recognized the place, having been there once before—Stumptown Coffee.

Coffee, lots of varieties, all fair trade, of course; hand-made, mostly organic pastries; a hip, urban vibe, with hipsters in plaid and ironic camouflage—just the sort of place Hazel felt most out of place in.

But she was cold now and wanted to sit.

And perhaps think.

Or not think.

She ordered a medium-sized coffee.

The barista waited for extras and further instructions about the coffee, and hearing none, she shrugged and poured a reg-ular cup of coffee into a regular paper cup, no markings on the cup, no foam, no flavors—just like Hazel liked it.

She planned on adding the half-and-half and the artificial sweetener at the mixing station and avoiding the possibility of any arched eyebrows from an anti-milk or anti–artificial sweetener barista.

There was an empty chair facing out to the fog-clogged street.

Hazel sat down with an audible sigh.

Loud, poignant sighs were probably not unusual in a place frequented by disparate hipsters offended by most of what goes on in the world. Certainly no one that foggy Sunday morning turned around to notice, or paid attention to Hazel's sigh.

She sipped at her creamed and sweetened coffee, feeling the warmth in her chest and stomach.

And then it was back to that photograph.

She almost wished that it had remained taped to the drawer, or wedged in the back of the drawer, so that she would never have had to deal with the fallout of its discovery.

But it did exist.

And the carefully constructed history of her life was now upended.

While it had been painful to think that her existence only occurred because of a fleeting affair with an almost nameless man, it was a history that she had inured herself to long ago. That history had become comfortable over the years, like an old pair of shoes or a well-worn shirt. The people who knew her best, her closest friends, knew that she had a gap in her genealogy—and they loved her in spite of it.

Perhaps their love was tinted with sympathy. Hazel suspected that of some of them, but sympathy was okay.

Now her version of the past, and of herself, had suddenly been irrevocably altered, changed in a twinkling, in the blink of an eye, and she was unsure of what direction to proceed.

Do I get angry with my mother?

She shook her head.

A little late for that now.

But I am no longer a foundling . . . but I guess I never really was. A foundling, I mean.

She sipped at her coffee again.

The fog was slowly burning off.

I wonder who he was.

And then it hit her.

Is he still alive?

Was I born when they were together?

Did he ever see me?

Was he my father?

I suspect he was.

He could still be alive, couldn't he?

And at that, she sat up straight. She pushed the hair off her forehead and stood up, put her hat back on. Stepping outside, she wondered what route would get her home in the least amount of time.

Chapter Ten

WILSON MADE his way downstairs, holding on to the banister as he did.

How long have I been holding on to this just to make it downstairs without falling and breaking a hip?

Thurman had been up, Wilson surmised, ever since the garbage truck rattled down the street at 4:30 in the morning, crashing down the empty bins with an echoed din. But to Wilson's surprise, Thurman left the truck and driver alone, or rather, unbarked at. From the bay window at the front of the house, Thurman had a commanding view of the sidewalk and street. Wilson watched him sit there, observing traffic, wiggling and growling if a pedestrian walked past—especially a pedestrian with a dog in tow.

But no barks.

Must have been well trained before . . . before he came here.

Thurman wiggled at the bottom of the steps, not at the very bottom, but a few feet away, as if intentionally leaving room for Wilson to get on solid, level ground first.

When that happened, only then did Thurman rush over and rub his head against Wilson's thigh. Wilson accepted the gesture begrudgingly, unwilling to tell him to cease and desist, although he was certain Thurman would stop it if bidden, but the dog also seemed to view this greeting as one of the most important rituals of the day. Only food seemed a bit higher in the dog's hierarchy of important events.

Wilson leaned over and stroked the dog's forehead.

"You want out, right?"

Thurman growled, *Yes*.

When Wilson's hand was on the doorknob, he added, as he had done every day now, "No swimming."

Thurman, on cue, looked back over his shoulder with a disappointed look, and growled in reply, *Okay*.

Then Wilson went back into the kitchen.

By the time his coffee was ready, Thurman would be standing by the back door, staring in, as if he had been locked out for hours instead of a moment, overjoyed when he saw Wilson return, with cup in hand.

Thurman bounded inside, growling *Breakfast* as he rushed past.

While Wilson sat in his recliner with his coffee and the local news on the TV, he could hear Thurman's rustling crunch-chew-rustle-swallow routine with the fresh bowl of Friskies laid out next to the pantry door.

As Thurman ate, Wilson wondered if all of this—Thurman talking, him talking to Thurman, all of this—was simply a precursor, as it were, to some serious malady, some degenerative brain withering, some "slipping into the vast unaware."

From the kitchen came an interruption in the nibbling and crunching.

He heard Thurman shake his head, his ears flapping like soft leather straps whacking on a wooden post. Then he growled, *No. No worry*.

Wilson smiled, then shut his eyes, and began to worry, just a little, and then a little more.

⌐

"You're not supposed to be here this week," Henry Karch, an insurance auditor at the agency where Hazel worked, whispered as Hazel appeared in front of his desk, as if her being there while on vacation was some manner of corporate disobedience that might involve him somehow.

And Henry did not want that at all.

"I'm still on vacation, Henry," Hazel said with some patience. "And I've already said hello to Mr. Shupp. So they know I'm here. It's okay."

Henry glanced in the direction of the corner office, and, seeing no security guards hurrying toward them, not just yet, he relaxed, if only a little.

"Henry," Hazel said calmly, "you know a lot about military history, right?"

Henry wore camouflage ties on occasion, and often mentioned, unbidden, his involvement in a war-gaming group that met in a basement room of the civic center twice a month.

"Maybe."

Hazel reached into her purse, and Henry's eyes followed her hand closely.

She pulled out the photograph.

"What branch of service is this uniform?"

Henry leaned in closer, then leaned back, opened his desk drawer, and retrieved a rather large magnifying glass.

Why would he have a magnifying glass at work? Hazel thought and was about to ask, but decided against it.

He did not actually touch the photo, but simply leaned closer and peered at it with intensity.

"That's easy. Army. Regular issue. Vietnam time frame. He's wearing a Vietnam campaign ribbon. Can't see his nametag. Well, maybe that's a W there. Could be. He's a corporal. No big deal there. Everyone was a corporal."

Hazel's eyes widened.

"Wow. You can tell that much?"

"And he's from the 25th Infantry Division. The Army called it 'Tropic Thunder.' See the divisional ID patch there? The soldiers called it the 'Electric Strawberry.' I guess it does look like one, sort of. An electrified strawberry, I mean."

Hazel turned the picture back to herself, hiding her mother's handwritten note, and stared at it again, as if hoping to see something different this time.

"Did they see much combat? The 25th?"

Henry shrugged.

"A good bit. The division was among the last to leave the country . . . when the war, such as it was, was ending. So, depending, this soldier could have seen a lot of combat. Or not."

Henry looked up.

"Who is he?"

Hazel slipped the photo back into her purse. She looked at Henry. Her eyes were weary.

"I don't know exactly. Someone my mother knew, I guess."

Henry nodded as if such requests were a regular

occurrence at the sedate insurance agency, which they were obviously not.

"You could check with Facebook. I bet the 25th Division has a page. There would have to be some sort of veterans' group, somewhere. Maybe someone will recognize him. I mean, if you really want to find out. But Vietnam happened a while ago now."

Hazel offered Henry an honest smile and then hoped he wouldn't interpret it as something else, and hurried toward the front door.

She was pretty sure he had already started misinterpreting it.

Chapter Eleven

*H*AZEL WALKED out of her office building, modern and glass and sleek and antithetical to all that transpired within the walls—which involved business intricacies of a turn-of-the-last-century insurance company rife with arcane evaluations and formulas and policies and products and a staff nearly chained to their desks during the day, unwilling to risk being seen enjoying the work by a boss with no apparent happy emotions in him. She stopped for coffee, her fifth cup of the day so far. Her nerves were already jangled to their maximum, so another serving of caffeine would not make much of an impact. And it would provide a moment's respite, to think, to collect her disparate thoughts. She sat on a stool at the window, with the photo on the counter, staring at it, her finger light on the corner, as if to make sure that it all would not disappear. The sun was out, and the bright light glistered off the photo. She slipped it back into a new envelope and placed that back into a zippered pocket in her purse.

She had one more task to complete that morning.

The key that had been in the envelope with the photo hidden in the desk now rested in the coin pouch of her wallet. She assumed that it was for a safe-deposit box.

What else could it be?

A branch of the Umpqua Bank was only two blocks distant. She had driven to her office but left her car in the parking lot.

Don't want to worry about parking places. And the sun feels good.

The cheery receptionist took a look at the key, then pointed to her left.

"One of our personal bankers can help you with this."

I don't really want a personal banker, since I don't do business with this bank.

—

Charles Harnett showed her to a chair in front of a non-descript desk with absolutely no personalization on it—apparently used by other "personal" bankers at other times. Other than a computer keyboard with a monitor, and a little metal stand with a sheaf of business cards, the desk was empty.

"An old key, right? One of ours, right?"

Hazel passed the key to him.

He pursed his lips and hummed.

Then the young Mr. Harnett began to tap away at the keyboard, swinging the mouse into action, clicking three times, then typing some more, much faster than Hazel could ever have hoped to have done.

Finally he stopped, took his hands from the keyboard, looked up with his best personal banker smile, and said, "Yes. This is current. The key is still good."

Hazel exhaled.

"I was hoping it wasn't out of date. This is sort of a mystery to me."

"And a Ms. Florence Jamison...three years ago...paid $250 for another ten years of use," he said, glancing at the monitor.

"She was my mother. She passed away."

"Oh, I am sorry to hear that."

Hazel waited a moment, not sure what to ask next, or if Mr. Harnett was going to take her to the place in the bank where these secure boxes were kept.

He did not.

Finally, she asked, "Is this box number here? Wherever it is you have safe-deposit boxes, I mean."

Mr. Harnett shook his head. "No. I'm afraid not. This number was originally from an older branch that must have moved or was closed. Back in the day, the bank did that often. Move, I mean. Close small branches. Consolidate and all that. All the safe-deposit boxes from the closed branches were moved to the big location on Columbia."

"Downtown?"

Mr. Harnett nodded.

"Is it open? I mean, do I need to make an appointment or anything to go there and see what's inside?"

"No. Just show up with the key and ID. During regular business hours. That's all there is to it."

Hazel hurried back to her car. Perhaps the box held some answers. Perhaps it held nothing—but that would be an answer as well.

↢

Wilson taught three classes that day, "The Craft of the Short Story," "Readings in Contemporary American Fiction," and "Writing the Screenplay."

He disliked the latter class the most of all his classes.

Posers, all of them. Like some Hollywood agent is sitting in some neighborhood tavern in Pittsburgh just drooling over their insufferable "coming of age" story set in some hardscrabble western Pennsylvanian neighborhood. Well, I think not. I know not.

Three classes meant a long day, and that happened twice a week. He got on the bus, actually looking forward to getting home that evening.

Before Thurman, going home was not something he always looked forward to. To be sure, it meant leaving work, and leaving behind a slew of mostly untalented writers, and getting to spend time in silence. But with Thurman, there was a body at home now—a warm body of sorts, a creature who appeared to be ecstatic when he returned.

Maybe Thurman was so excited because he wanted to go outside.

But Wilson thought it was more than just that, although he was sure that it played a part in the dog's exhilaration.

Wilson stepped off the bus and the doors whooshed shut behind him with a wheeze. He almost said goodbye to the driver—the same bus driver had been on this route for several years now—and Wilson watched others call him by name and inquire as to his family, but he never did that, or had not until now.

And yet even though he thought about saying something, he did not.

Maybe next time.

And as he walked the two blocks to his home, he wondered why this sudden occurrence of interest in the bus driver.

He scowled to himself.

Thurman.

—

The downtown location of the bank looked exactly like a bank should look: sedate, secure, and traditional.

Hazel was not sure what a "traditional" bank looked like exactly, but this one boasted of marble and walnut and high ceilings and a hushed, monetary feel, with muted lighting.

She walked up to the information desk, key in hand, and instead of pointing, the young woman receptionist stood and escorted her past a series of open offices and to the open, very thick circular metal door of a massive safe, with a floor-to-ceiling metal fence in front and a young man seated inside.

"Clark will show you to your box. Will you need a private room?"

Hazel tried not to look totally unaware, totally naïve in the way of safe-deposit box protocols, even though she was.

Am I supposed to keep whatever is in there hidden? Are there cameras? Or snoops?

"I don't think so. Really, I'm not sure what's in here. It was my mother's. She passed away."

"Oh, I am sorry," the young woman replied. "If you need anything, just let Clark know."

Clark took a look at the number and escorted Hazel into the vault, past the large boxes that looked like they could hold a small fortune in gold bullion, past the medium-sized boxes that might hold half a fortune, to the smaller boxes that could hold a few envelopes and a deed and perhaps a dance card from a long-ago prom.

I wonder if she ever went to a prom in high school? We never talked about that, did we?

"Right here," Clark said, gesturing to a small box, in much the way that one of the models on a game show gestures to a grand prize.

With that, he stepped back.

"I'll be at my desk if you need anything."

Hazel began to worry that there would be nothing inside . . .

But why would she have paid for it, then?

Or perhaps something complicated and mysterious . . .

But that wouldn't be like her, not at all.

She unlocked the box, pulled out the inner metal box, and gingerly opened it. The only thing inside was a standard mid-size mailing envelope. She took it and then felt around the metal interior to see if there was something else, but there wasn't.

The envelope was not sealed. She lifted the flap and pulled out a thin sheaf of official-looking documents. She turned them right side up.

On the top was a familiar image of an apple with a single bite missing.

The forms were Apple Computer stock certificates.

Ten certificates were inside the envelope, each claiming to

represent the ownership of two hundred shares of common stock.

Hazel stared at them for a long moment, not sure what to think or what to do next.

Stocks? Mom never bought stocks. She never said she bought stocks. She barely knew anything about stocks or financial matters.

She looked around, wondering what she was supposed to do now. She waited another moment, thinking that some plan of action, some path might open up and tell her what the next step would be.

No such thought occurred.

She slipped the certificates back into the envelope, tucked it under her arm, closed the box, and relocked it, not sure why she needed to do that since it was now empty.

Clark looked up as she approached.

"All done?"

Hazel shrugged.

"I guess. There wasn't much in there. Just this one envelope. Some old stock certificates. I doubt they're worth anything."

Clark stood and unlocked the gate with the key that was attached to his belt on a metal string of some sort.

"Well, miss, you never know. I would check with Mr. Hild, one of our personal bankers..."

They all must be personal bankers. The bank is lousy with them.

Hazel smiled, mostly to herself. Her mother often said that about any excess.

"He knows all about stocks and things like that. He could quickly determine if they have any value or not."

Hazel thanked him and made her way back to the information desk to find Mr. Hild, thinking that little would come out of this and she would be no further to getting to the bottom of her mother's . . . other life—her former, secret, hidden life—than she was when she first discovered the photograph.

—

From half a block away, Wilson could see that all was not well at his home. Or at least it was not how he had left it earlier in the day.

Sort of.

His mother stood at the start of the walk, almost on the sidewalk, holding what appeared to be a leash.

It is a leash.

No doubt Thurman was at the other end of the leash, and Wilson refrained from calling out, thinking that if he did, Thurman would get excited, lunge toward him, pull his tottering mother over, and she would break a hip. She would never forgive him for it and she would be forced to move into his house so Wilson could provide round-the-clock medical care.

Not that. Please, not that.

Instead, he waved silently. He was nothing if not cautious.

And careful. And often worried about what might happen, even if those things never did happen as he imagined them occurring.

There was another figure standing near his front door: a woman—a woman whom Thurman was seated next to. The dog was obediently sitting still, grinning, his hindquarters vibrating in anticipation of seeing Wilson again. The woman

was not young, but neither old—younger than Wilson by
perhaps a decade, with short, straight black hair, near lumi-
nescent in the sun, cut in a stylish manner, Wilson assumed,
a style that required some hair fashion awareness. She had a
hint of Middle Eastern about her, with a slight darkness to the
tone of the skin on her face and her bare arms—perhaps Is-
raeli, perhaps some other ethnicity.

Not Nordic for certain.

"Wilson," Gretna called out. "I missed Thurman. Emily
drove me over. I hope you don't mind that I used my emergency key."

*Mother, that emergency key was for when I fell down the
steps and was lying in a pool of blood—not because you
missed a dog you only possessed for two weeks.*

"No. That's okay. But be careful. Thurman could easily
knock you over."

His mother waved away his objection with a sweep of her
hand.

"Nonsense. We've already walked around the block and
Thurman has been a complete gentleman the whole time.
Right, Thurman?"

Thurman was up now, bouncing, doing little canine cha-
cha steps, awaiting Wilson's greeting. Now within the radius
of the leash, he did jump up and rush at Wilson, obviously
excited, and obviously fully aware of the limits of the leash
and the stability of the woman who currently held it.

Wilson bent down and patted his head, Thurman bouncing and grinning and growling, *Where were you?*

Thurman had asked that question every time Wilson returned home, and no matter how often Wilson explained that

he had to go to work, to school, Thurman seemed to be unable to grasp the concept.

Wilson was fairly certain that dogs would not be able to understand the convoluted process of work and money and all the rest of the abstract ideas that capitalism involved.

Or perhaps it was that Thurman just enjoyed posing the ritual question.

"Good dog, Thurman," Wilson said. "Good dog. I'm home now. It's okay."

Thurman beamed at the praise.

"See?" Gretna said, now beaming as well. "He grows on you, doesn't he? He is a good dog."

Wilson stood back up and sniffed. He was unwilling to fully commit to this arrangement, at least to his mother.

"I suppose."

Gretna knew posing when she saw it, and she probably knew Wilson was simply being obstreperous for show.

Wilson looked toward the front door.

"That's Emily," Gretna said. "Emily, this is my son, Wilson."

Both offered the standard "Nice to meet you" response.

"Emily's mother is at Heritage Square too, isn't she, Emily?" Gretna said. "Mother-in-law. I meant mother-in-law." Then she added in a softer, lower voice, "But the poor woman can't get out much. Being in a wheelchair, you know. And she gets confused sometimes. So I asked Emily if she could take me here for a few minutes and Emily said she would be happy to. Right, Emily?"

Emily smiled and shrugged.

Wilson recognized the look of capitulation. Not a horrible forced-under-pain-of-death capitulation, but still...

"I wanted to see the dog," Emily added. "Thurman, I mean. Your mother goes on and on about him."

Wilson arched his eyebrows.

"No doubt she does."

Thurman appeared to follow the conversation, then growled toward Gretna.

"Are you going to invite us in for coffee, Wilson?" Gretna asked. "Thurman likes company."

Emily looked socially horrified, a little bit.

At least she has manners...or good sense, Wilson thought.

Obviously, Gretna noticed the look and waved it away.

"Nonsense. He's my son. He can offer us a cup of coffee."

She started walking toward the front door.

"Seeing as how you've already been inside, Mother, I guess coffee would be fine."

Gretna offered a knowing grin to Emily.

"Such a good boy. Didn't I tell you he was such a good boy?"

———

Mr. Hild looked exactly like an old-school personal banker should look, Hazel thought, wearing a very sedate gray suit, an old-school striped tie, wingtip shoes—all of which was in opposition to the standard blue blazers the rest of the personal banking crew probably had been forced to wear.

They look like they work at an upscale McDonald's—and wear better uniforms, Hazel thought.

"Old stock certificates, you say," Mr. Hild said, folding his hands and placing them on the desk. He had a nameplate on a little rack on the desk, obviously a subtle sign of seniority.

Hazel held her purse in her lap, with the envelope in one hand, and explained about the desk in the garage sale and finding the key and finding just the one envelope in the box and the fact that her mother never once mentioned owning any stock, or any investments of any kind.

She slid the certificates out of the envelope as Mr. Hild explained that very few companies offered paper certificates any longer. "It's all electronic now. I miss these. Some certificates were like works of art."

He saw the one-bite-from-the-apple logo and his eyes widened a little.

And his hand shook, just a bit, as he took them from her. Hazel thought it was because he was elderly, after all.

He laid them on the desk, staring at them.

Then he turned to the computer monitor and began to type. He was much slower and more deliberate than any personal banker she had been with up to now.

Hazel chattered on, nervous, without being sure why exactly.

"It would be nice to have a little inheritance. After I settle all her debts and sell the house, I may have a few thousand dollars, if that. I mean, I'm not looking for anything, nor am I expecting anything, and I don't really need anything, but a little cushion would be nice, you know what I mean? Maybe I could get my condo painted or something. That would be nice. It's been years since I could afford to do that."

Mr. Hild did not look at her but murmured, "Uh-huh."

He stopped typing and looked up.

"Did she . . . your mother, I mean . . . did she have any other investments?"

"No. None. Or none that I know of. She had a little over six hundred dollars in the bank when she passed. She still had a mortgage. She lived pretty simply. She was sort of an old hippie, you know, nuts and berries and wanting to live off the land—that sort of person. Not in a bad way. But she never wanted much and seemed to be very happy all the time—even with the little she had. She was a very nice person. Very content. Happy. Mostly happy, anyhow."

"Uh-huh."

Mr. Hild spread the certificates into a fan shape on the desk and entered each number into the computer, very slowly and very carefully.

He waited a long moment.

Then he moved the keyboard aside and refolded his hands.

"You should probably thank your mother. I mean . . . however you do that . . . you know . . ."

"It's okay, really," Hazel replied, almost apologetic that her mother had died and couldn't be thanked, and now she was wondering why he would say such an odd thing.

Mr. Hild seemed to grow more flustered—for a personal banker, that is.

"Are they worth anything?" Hazel asked, breaking the tension. "It must have been years and years ago that she bought them. Probably not worth much, right?"

Mr. Hild responded with a tight financial grimace, then allowed himself a smile.

"These are real, Ms. Jamison."

She waited.

"And that's good?"

"Yes," Mr. Hild said, exhaling politely, "that is good. Very good."

"Are they worth anything?"

He looked at the screen again.

"As of the close of trading yesterday, these stock certificates, in total, were worth in the neighborhood of $1.26 million."

Hazel stared back, a blank look on her face.

"Dollars?"

"Yes. These were purchased in 1981. The stock was trading for a few dollars a share. They would have cost her roughly $12,000. Since then, there have been a few splits, buybacks, and what have you, and as of now, their value is $1.26 million."

Hazel blinked.

"You are talking about American dollars, right?"

"Yes."

Mr. Hild smiled his best, cordial, we're-a-nice-bank-to-do-business-with smile and added, in a somber, responsible tone, "And we at Umpqua Bank certainly hope that if you decide to sell them, you'll use our bank to help you with the transaction. No fees involved. We would waive all fees for this size transaction."

Hazel leaned against the padded back of the chair and exhaled.

"American dollars. You're sure, right?"

"Yes. I am sure. You must realize that I seldom joke about money. It's sort a personal banker motto here at Umpqua."

Hazel stared at him, not knowing if laughter or tears were appropriate.

—

The four of them were in the kitchen and Wilson began to feel a bit claustrophobic. It had been a long time, decades really, since so many people were in that one room at the same time. Wilson did have people over on rare occasions—not recently, of course—and they never gathered in the kitchen. He kept them in the formal living room.

Gretna was offering a tour of the kitchen, explaining to Emily what changes Wilson had made over the years and which appliances had been updated.

"The sink is still the same," she said. "Don't make them this way anymore. Like a battleship, it is."

Trying not to appear perturbed, Wilson switched on the coffeemaker to heat the water and pulled out three varieties of coffee and one of tea.

Thurman sat near his food dish, watching, looking a bit confused as well.

It seemed as if he was trying to follow Gretna's conversation and maintain eye contact with Wilson at the same time. And obviously he was not eminently successful at either endeavor.

Once their coffees had been brewed—Emily had chosen tea—Gretna insisted on showing Emily the backyard and Wilson's massive reflecting pool.

"He built it entirely by hand and all by himself. With just a shovel. Isn't it beautiful?"

Emily appeared to be impressed.

"It is. I never would have imagined such a serene view back here...I mean, looking at the house from the street."

"Like a hidden jewel," Gretna bragged. "An undiscovered gem. Overlooked."

Wilson was fairly certain his mother was dropping hints, but what she was hinting at eluded him.

Thurman stood next to Gretna and growled up at her.

"Of course you can, you sweet dog. Of course."

And with her permission, Thurman took off at a run toward the pool and launched himself into the water.

Wilson was no more than a second from shouting at Thurman, telling him he was a bad dog for jumping in the water and didn't he remember that Wilson expressly forbade him from swimming and that these water hijinks were not allowed, but then he realized that his mother had given the poor beast permission to swim.

Emily laughed at the sight of Thurman's energetic grin as he paddled about.

"Retrievers and water," Wilson muttered, setting his coffee cup on the stone step and hurrying back into the garage for towels.

When he stepped back into the house holding three emergency towels, his mother was halfway across the room.

"Isn't Emily nice?"

Wilson shrugged.

"Well, she is. And she's a widow. With children, Wilson. You know what that means."

Wilson shut his eyes for a second and considered what to say in response. He quickly decided not to say anything at all.

"She has children, Wilson. Young children. Younger. Young-ish. I could be a grandmother. Isn't she nice?"

Wilson scowled in her direction.

"I am sure she is a lovely person, Mother."

Gretna nodded firmly.

"And Thurman promised me, Wilson. And Thurman would not lie about grandchildren."

Wilson looked at his mother, then at Thurman, who was joyously dog-paddling in the water, then at Emily, who indeed was attractive and pleasant, and then back to his mother, finally making the connections that she had been implying, and then trying to determine if they were both sliding into the same memory abyss at the same dizzying rate of descent.

At that moment, in the afternoon, on a warm spring day, he was pretty sure that they were.

Chapter Twelve

*H*AZEL HAD two more official days of her much-longer-than-customary-at-this-office vacation, and only a few more things to attend to . . . before she had to come to some sort of decision . . . about what to do . . . now that everything had changed. Everything in her life was now different. Changed. The old had gone and the new, the "now," wasn't here just yet, but it certainly was about to arrive.

Hazel hoped she would be ready for it.

Her mother's house had been broom-swept, and then some, in accordance with the Realtor's request, and the windows had been professionally cleaned by a van's worth of workers, each carrying a bucket, a rag, and a squeegee—perhaps clean for the first time in decades. Her mother's eyesight at the end had been failing, so a smudgy window was the least of her worries.

A landscape crew had come in and spruced up the small lawn, trimming shrubs and edging around trees and beds. They had planted two new shrubs by the end of the walk and placed flowers into two large terra-cotta pots on either side of the front stoop. Hazel had had the front door repainted.

The house appeared as nice as Hazel could recall ever seeing it. But it was empty, and her steps echoed as she made one more pass through.

I could have painted a few of the rooms . . .

The Realtor had waved off her offer.

"This paint is okay. A little faded, and that's not bad. People will repaint anyhow. Everyone wants to make a fresh start when they move in."

There were no tasks remaining in her mother's soon-to-be former house, nothing left for Hazel to do, so she locked the front door and drove to the cemetery. Cemeteries are quiet places, maybe more so on Thursdays, she thought.

Unless there's an active funeral taking place.

She drove to where her mother's grave was located, stopped the car, and walked slowly over the grass to the recently set headstone.

She stared down at the marker.

She read and re-read the Bible verse.

Maybe those plans God had were for me, she thought.

Then she looked up, cleared her throat, and narrowed her eyes.

"I don't get it, Mother. This money could have been yours. And it was almost lost. I didn't know it was there. You could have told me."

Hazel folded her hands and prayed, one of her standard prayers, for peace and wisdom and for God to be merciful to her mother.

She looked up into the clouds.

"She did the best she could, God. She tried her best. And she was a good person. I told her about you. I did. Like I was supposed to. She listened. She nodded at the right times. She said she understood. She did. She said she understood. That means she believed, right? I suppose she could have just been humoring me, but God, this is all I have to hang on to. Those few nods. A smile. I thought she understood."

Hazel could feel a tear forming. The first tear always came from her right eye.

"I don't know if that's enough for you, God. But it is all I have. If you're merciful, she's there with you now. She really did do the best she could."

She looked down at the stone.

"And Mother, you could have told me about the stocks," she said aloud. "You could have least hinted at it. Now, all of a sudden, I'm rich."

She took a deep breath.

Over the crest of the hill to the west, she caught the reflection off the windshield of a hearse as it slowly made its way into the cemetery. Only a single car followed.

She looked back down at the headstone.

"So what do I do? Really, Mom, what do I do now?"

⟶

Wilson and Thurman stood on the front step as Emily and Gretna drove away. Wilson offered a half-wave and Thurman barked—twice.

Wilson sighed loudly and Thurman looked up at him, a puzzled look on the dog's face.

"It's hard, Thurman, that's all. I don't know what she wants me to do. I don't know what I want to do."

Thurman appeared to nod in agreement, then he shook his head, his ears making flapping noises as he did so. Then he growled up at Wilson.

Hungry.

Wilson stared back at the dog.

"You know, I am simply projecting all this talking onto you, right? You know that, right? You know you can't talk. I know you can't talk. Let's be honest here, Thurman."

Thurman smiled and nodded again, or looked like he nodded. Then he growled again.

Hungry.

Wilson stared for a moment, as if waiting for some spark of clarity, or understanding. None occurred. So he shrugged and entered his house, Thurman a step or two behind, his nails clackering on the wooden floor. Wilson measured out a generous serving of kibbles, poured it into Thurman's dish, and made a second cup of coffee as Thurman nibbled, with great canine daintiness, at his evening meal.

Wilson sighed again and Thurman interrupted his eating to walk over to him and gently butt his head against his thigh. Without growling, without saying anything, he stared up at Wilson.

Wilson reached down and patted at the dog's head. Thurman smiled and returned to his dinner.

After a few minutes, Thurman had finished eating. He sat down, facing Wilson.

Hungry.

Wilson shook his head.

"No. We do this every night, Thurman. I even called Dr. Stansing about this."

Not vet, Thurman whisper-growled, almost under his breath, muttering in a dog growl, dismissing Dr. Stansing, but doing so politely.

"I know he's not a vet. But he has dogs. And he's a doctor. He should know. He said a cup and a quarter, maybe a cup and a half, is all a dog your size needs."

Bunkum.

Wilson smiled. The two of them had gone through the very same thing before, holding the same discussion, at least a few times a week.

Wilson decided that Thurman might be intelligent, but he had a problem with short-term memory.

Or perhaps he just liked to repeat things, like a toddler relishing the hundredth time a storybook is read to them. *Safety and security in repetition.* Wilson recalled that truth from a psychology class he took decades ago.

Thurman looked back at his bowl and snorted, as if finally realizing that it was not going to be refilled. Then he looked back at Wilson and smiled.

Then he growled.

"What?"

He growled again.

"Emily? Is that what you're trying to say? Emily?"

Thurman grinned and stood and walked to Wilson, raising up and placing his front paws on his thigh.

Pretty.

Wilson shrugged.

"I suppose. But young. Much younger than me."

Thurman tilted his head as if what Wilson said made no sense.

He growled again.

Pretty.

Then he bounced back to the floor and trotted over to the back door.

Wilson sighed.

"You want to go for a real walk?"

Thurman bounded up and ran to the front door, nails machine-gunning on the floor.

"I could use some time to think," Wilson said.

Walk, Thurman growled happily. *Walk. Walkies-walkies-walkies-walkies.*

—

Emily insisted on walking Gretna back upstairs to her apartment.

"I can manage," Gretna objected. "Really. I'll be fine."

Emily smiled her best long-suffering smile. "I know. But I would feel so much better if I see you get home safe."

Gretna shrugged in submission.

"I guess taking care of your mother-in-law is hard, isn't it?" Gretna said. "This is what it's like, isn't it?"

Emily's smile did not evaporate, not really, but it did wither.

"It is. But I don't mind."

She pressed the elevator button and it clicked as it lit up.

Gretna let the obvious lie go unchecked. At least Gretna thought it was a lie.

Maybe she doesn't mind. Maybe she's okay with it. After all, there are people who want to be podiatrists and urologists. Go figure. Or dentists.

Gretna fumbled with the key, then held it close to her eyes, checking to see which side had the ridges.

"I can do that," Emily said, gently reaching for and taking

the keys, inserting each into its lock before finally opening the door.

"There you go," she said as she handed Gretna back her keys.

Gretna stepped inside, then quickly turned back.

"You believe in God, don't you?" she asked, peering a little at Emily's face, watching her expression.

Emily hesitated only a few heartbeats.

"I do."

Gretna leaned closer.

"Which one?"

It was obvious that Emily wanted to laugh, and her smile broadened, but she quickly drew herself to a serious look again.

"The only one."

Gretna remained questioning.

"Not just the Jewish one?"

Emily's mother-in-law was Jewish and had mentioned once, when she had an episode of clarity, that Emily, who was "such a good daughter-in-law," had been born in Israel.

Emily reached out and took Gretna's hand in hers.

"They are actually the same God, Gretna. But I believe in the God of the New Testament."

Gretna looked down at her hand.

"That's the same one as me, right?" Gretna asked. "The real one, right?"

"It is."

Gretna nodded.

"Good."

Emily's smile had a wistful, almost sorrowful tilt to it.

"Though there were times...after my husband...when it was hard. It's still hard. But I believe. I do."

Gretna pulled Emily closer.

"Then I can tell you this: I think Thurman talks to God. Or maybe it is vice versa. I can't tell for sure."

Emily's surprise was more than obvious.

"He does?"

"He does. And he told me today that you're not supposed to be worried anymore. That it will all work out."

"He did?"

Gretna's nod was firm and decisive.

"It will all work out, he says. For me. For you. And for Wilson."

Emily's face bore...well, not a laughing-at-you look, but one of tenderness and understanding. It was apparent that she had faced the same manner of statements from her mother-in-law on more than one occasion.

"I'm glad, Gretna. That makes me feel good."

Gretna squeezed Emily's hand.

"Good. We believe in God. And I believe in Thurman. And that settles it."

Gretna's door latched with a metallic finality.

And Emily walked back toward the elevator, smiling and shaking her head just a little, obviously exhibiting equal measures of pity and amusement and skepticism, if not downright disbelief.

Chapter Thirteen

*H*AZEL WOKE UP an hour earlier than normal—for a workday, that is. For nearly the past month, while on her first
extended vacation in years, the time needed to handle all the
details after her mother's death, she had lived without the
tyranny of the alarm clock, and she had enjoyed that freedom
immensely. This morning her early awakening provided extra
time and allowed her to have two additional cups of coffee as
she glanced at the newspaper—"glanced" was the operative
word, since none of the stories seemed to make any sense to
her today.

The jumble of thoughts and emotions kept her from thinking clearly, or focusing on the news from the Middle East.

She dressed carefully, wearing one of her more sedate
outfits—dark pants and a dark blouse with a matching jacket.
It was old and loose and comfortable. She did not want to
think about her outfit, at least not today. Instead of catching
the bus, she chose to drive her car to the office.

Parking was a bit of a problem, and expensive if one had
to park in one of the area's parking garages every workday.
But for once, Hazel did not factor into this week's budget the
dollars spent on parking.

She arrived ten minutes before her usual ten minutes early
and went to her desk and just sat behind it, waiting for the
rest of the staff to arrive, waiting without looking around

or adjusting her computer screen or cleaning out the break room.

Today, she just sat.

On the one bookcase in her office was a framed picture of her mother, a picture Hazel had taken several years ago. Her mother was seated in her backyard, sunlight illuminating her smile.

Hazel had never realized, or perhaps never saw it, but her mother's smile was somehow incomplete, a half-smile, as if she was happy, but knew that she could have been happier, as if there was something holding her back from truly being lost in happiness. Or that her life wasn't totally complete. Something appeared to be missing.

You can tell a lot from a smile. Or a half-smile, I guess.

Perhaps that was just what Hazel saw in the picture this morning as she sat and waited.

Mr. Shupp, the owner, was a stickler for promptness. His office looked out on the main entrance to the agency, and anyone who came in late would get a baleful glare from the owner. If one's tardiness became commonplace, like several times in a single week, the lateness marked that employee as a "short-termer" who might well be replaced at the next opportunity.

Hazel was never late. And on those few occasions when cars broke down or bus drivers went on strike, she notified Mr. Shupp immediately, always offering to make up the lost time after 5 p.m.

He always accepted her offer to work a full eight hours regardless of the starting time.

Hazel smiled.

I should have strolled in ten minutes late this morning. Just to see what would happen.

Too early for pretending to be late, she gave Mr. Shupp ten minutes to get his coffee or whatever it was he did in the morning, then she stood up, tugged her jacket into place, took a deep breath, and marched slowly, with even steps, toward his office.

"Mr. Shupp?"

The older man, wearing a tailored three-piece suit, the kind of suit that no one, other than undertakers, perhaps, wore anymore, looked up. He was not smiling. He seldom smiled.

"You're back. Good. What?"

He was a man of few words as well.

"Mr. Shupp, I am leaving the agency."

Mr. Shupp looked at her the way a dog looks at complex machinery—with little to no comprehension.

"What?"

Hazel was afraid that her resignation would be difficult. She had never quit anything before, other than her job as a waitress in college, but that was decades ago, and she remembered it as being difficult as well.

Hazel did not like to disappoint anyone.

"I am resigning. I wrote out a resignation letter," she said as she looked down at her empty hands, "but I must have left it in my office."

"What?"

"Resigning, sir. Quitting."

The color in Mr. Shupp's face went from a cold pallor to a somewhat more crimson hue.

"Why? What? Resigning? You've been here forever...Ms. Jamison. This seems like a most rash decision. Jobs don't grow on trees, you know."

His features grew sharper, his angular jaw growing more angular as he thrust it out at her decision.

"You're not going to another insurance agency, are you? Not the Gibson Group, are you? That might be problematic, you know. Noncompete clauses and the like. You did sign one of those, right? You all did, right?"

Hazel closed her eyes for a moment, then opened them and smiled.

"I might have, Mr. Shupp. But I'm quitting...and not going anywhere. Workwise, that is. At least for a while."

That surprised the old man more than anything else that morning.

Hazel turned her head, just for a moment, and stared out at the beige walls of the office, and the beige fabric on the walls of the cubicles, and the beige-tinted fluorescent lights overhead, and the beige window blinds, and the beige carpet.

My mother never left Portland, not really, but said she wanted someday to travel the world. And now I can do what she wanted to do. And maybe look for some truth out there. Isn't that what they said on the TV show, The X-Files? *"The truth is out there"?*

"Not work? That's insane, Ms. Jamison. That's for millionaires and people who win the lottery. You didn't win the lottery, did you?"

Hazel shook her head. "I've never played the lottery, Mr. Shupp."

"Then are you sure you're feeling all right? It's not because of one of those female problems, is it?"

Hazel laughed to herself, mostly at the agency owner's inelegance with a phrase, or his ineptitude.

"No, Mr. Shupp. I feel fine. But I'm leaving. I have made up my mind."

Mr. Shupp stood, trying to look more august and somber than he typically did.

"You know that you have to work two more weeks. In order to get your last paycheck, that is indeed what you have to do. Otherwise, you will not get any vacation pay due you."

He was no longer smiling, and he let his non-smile curve into a semi-frown, semi-sneer. Hazel had expected as much.

"Fine," she replied, and she walked back to her office, took the photograph of her mother off the bookcase, slipped it into her purse, looked around the rather spartan interior of her small office, her home for the last several decades. She knew, right then, without a shadow of a doubt, that she could never return to this place again. Not with the world waiting for her. She touched her desk with a fingertip, then walked out, and walked past the desk of Henry Karch, who offered her a hopeful, almost leering smile, and kept walking, through the front lobby, and out the front door, and into the sunshine, smiling broadly now, feeling suddenly free, if not freer than she had ever felt in her entire life.

⌒

Gretna sat in the large, open foyer of the senior apartment complex and watched two old women, each holding a magnifying glass, working on a massive jigsaw puzzle—a picture of a seaside village, probably in New England some-where. The picture included a large swath of blue sky and blue water.

The puzzle had remained half-completed for the past several weeks. Gretna scowled as she watched. That same puzzle had been put together several times over the course of her residency—put together, admired in its totality for up to a week, then returned to its box, and brought back out after most everyone forgot that they had once put it together.

"Like Sisyphus," Gretna mumbled to herself. "But he remembered how useless his task was. No one here remembers."

She sat in one of the upholstered chairs, feeling the afternoon sun on her face. Her apartment only caught the morning sun.

"The afternoon sun is better," she said, self-narrating again, and closed her eyes, just for a few seconds. "Just to rest them for a bit."

A moment later, a wheelchair wheezed closer. Gretna could hear the familiar squeak of the wheels.

She opened her eyes.

"Lucille," she said loudly, knowing Lucille's hearing was not very acute.

"But then no one here can hear worth beans," she said quietly, again self-narrating. "Lucille," she said with more volume, "I was with your daughter-in-law yesterday. A lovely person."

Lucille, a small frail woman, appeared to brighten.

"Emily? Yes. Yes. She told me. Thurman. That's the dog,

right? She said she met Thurman. She liked him, she said. A good dog, she said."

Gretna leaned closer.

"She did. Thurman is a good dog."

Lucille looked over Gretna's shoulder as if remembering a time long ago when perhaps some dog was in her life and when things were good and memories were still being made and remembered.

"Emily is a very nice person," Gretna said.

Lucille nodded.

"She is so good."

Then Lucille's face grew somber. Her eyes reflected pain.

"Emily is married to my son, isn't she?"

Gretna was not sure where Lucille was at that moment, but she decided to stay positive.

"Yes, yes, she is."

Then Lucille sniffed.

"He's dead. Isn't he? My son. He died."

Gretna reached over and took Lucille's hand.

"I believe he is gone, Lucille. You told me that before."

Nodding, Lucille replied, "Yes. It was the war. Not in the war. After. He came home. It was after. Something was wrong. After the war, that's when it happened. Even I could tell something wasn't right. Poor Emily."

Gretna was at a loss for words, unsure if offering comfort was the right response, or if simply listening would offer some small amount of solace.

"I don't remember what happened. But he doesn't come here anymore. I have his picture. He was handsome. Did you see it? The picture."

Gretna had not, but she said that she did.

"Poor Emily. Maybe God will help. Do you think God would help?"

Gretna leaned closer and hugged the woman.

"I'm sure he will, Lucille. I am sure he will. Have you asked him?"

Lucille looked at Gretna for a long time.

"About what?"

Chapter Fourteen

WEDNESDAYS WERE Wilson's late-start days at the university. And his first class today was even later. He had given his first class, a graduate short-story-writing class, the day off to work on their final projects—a complete short story (of at least seven pages) that they would submit to various journals and magazines for possible publication.

In the past, one or two students with actual writing ability would get picked up for publication right away, and a few others of the more middling skills would find an audience in more arcane, smaller university "literary" publications, while the majority of students would simply get rejection notices.

Most of these rejections would be chalked up by those writers who had been rejected as grievous errors made by shortsighted and elitist editors who wouldn't know good writing if they tripped over it.

Wilson knew that to be untrue, but he no longer felt the need to set everyone straight, no longer felt the need to burst dreams and make students wonder why they had spent thousands of dollars on a graduate education.

The publishing world will take care of that, he told himself, *and it doesn't need me to protect it from inept and immature writers.*

Today, during a wonderful late spring morning, with a warm breeze and the first full greening of the maple tree and its welcome shield between his house and the insufferably cheerful Heasleys, Wilson luxuriated in spending most of the morning in the kitchen, with his electronic tablet and multiple cups of coffee as he read through an entire issue of the *Pittsburgh Press*, the formerly preeminent Pittsburgh newspaper, now published only online.

Thurman wandered into the kitchen several times that morning, mumbling to himself, looking up at Wilson, tilting his head, snorting on occasion, all in an effort, Wilson surmised, to get his attention.

Up until now, Wilson had resisted the dog's efforts.

The last time, Thurman walked away, back toward his bed in the den, mumbling *Boring* to himself over and over.

Thurman seemed to latch on to words, Wilson discovered, and repeat them over and over, as if in an effort to memorize them, or memorize how they sounded or how they were formed in a dog's mouth.

Around 11:30, Wilson heard Thurman get up, stretch and yawn loudly, shake himself awake, his ears doing their usual flapping against the top of his head, then with methodic, careful steps amble back into the kitchen.

Wilson thought he saw a more resolute look on Thurman's face, as if this would be the time he was successful in rousing the seated person to do . . . something. Go for a walk. Maybe make lunch. Maybe share his lunch.

Thurman seemed to stop at that idea—or at least Wilson thought he was stopping at that idea.

Hungry.

Wilson shook his head back at the dog.

"You had breakfast. The Internet says that dogs should only eat twice a day."

Thurman appeared hurt.

Bunkum.

Wilson shrugged.

"Maybe so, but that's the truth I'm going with."

Thurman sat down, a little deflated. Perhaps a little peeved as well.

Then Wilson stood up, the chair squealing just a bit on the tile floor of the kitchen. Wilson had replaced the rose-motif linoleum decades ago with a very sturdy dark slate tile.

"Do you want to go for a walk?"

At this, Thurman lit up, bounced to all fours, did his back-end-moving-first cha-cha dance, pranced, and jumped with the joyful enthusiasm of a newborn goat.

"Okay. Once around the block."

They got to the front door.

"Leash or no leash?"

Thurman looked up, and appeared to give the options some thought.

No leash, he grumbled, grinning.

Since Wilson and Thurman had been going for walks, Thurman was nothing short of a miracle dog on a leash, never pulling, never straining, never trying to run ahead of Wilson's pace. A few weeks prior, Wilson had experimented with Thurman off the leash, and he'd behaved the same as on it. Walking without a leash was easier for Wilson. He did not enjoy being tethered together, being tied to someone or something else. It felt so constricting.

"All right. No leash. But no chasing things. No running into the street. Okay?"

Thurman looked up, still grinning.

Okay, he growled. *Walkie-walkie-walkie.*

And they set off, Thurman all but prancing at Wilson's side, head butting his leg every few paces, growling happily, not really saying anything, but Wilson could tell that the dog was in a good mood.

And Wilson was in a similar mood.

That doesn't happen all that often. To have a living creature here with me, and for me to be evenly modulated and almost happy. It has been a long time.

Thurman bounced and sniffed and growled his greeting to a bevy of pigeons clutching onto a set of overhead wires.

They must not have understood "dog," because instead of chirping back, they all turned their eyes to Thurman, making sure that this was not one of those dogs that could climb trees—or fly.

The two walked on to the end of the block and turned to the north.

Midway down the block, Thurman stopped and looked to his left. Actually it was more than a look. It was as if Thurman was pointing, ready to go retrieving, following the millennia-long instinctual path of all retrievers.

Wilson turned to look.

At the top of the driveway was a figure in a wheelchair.

Thurman barked, then turned back to Wilson.

Wilson did not want to stop, did not want to engage in any conversation, but Thurman appeared so earnest, so wanting.

"Go ahead," Wilson said softly.

Then he looked up and waved.

"He wants to say hello, Dr. Killeen. He won't bite. At least he hasn't so far."

Thurman was already at the top of the drive as Wilson finished, and he bounced around the wheelchair, growling happily, sniffing, and grinning.

Dr. Killeen leaned forward as best he could and extended his right hand. Even from the street, Wilson could see the tremors. Thurman stopped and let the man put his hand on his head. He began to stroke the dog and Thurman growled his happy, contented growl.

Wilson walked up and stopped a few feet away.

"Thurman, right? That's his name, right?" Dr. Killeen said.

Wilson nodded.

"You've got a good memory."

Dr. Killeen grinned.

"It may be the only thing that still works. And I'm not so sure some days."

Wilson nodded.

"You and me both."

"I saw your mother again a few days ago. Walking Thurman."

"She had him for all of two weeks and she still considers him to be her dog, I guess."

Thurman bounced and growled, *That's right.*

But Dr. Killeen did not appear to understand him.

Must be like developing an ear for a foreign language, Wilson thought.

Dr. Killeen drew his jacket closer around his chest, despite the fact that the temperature was in the mid-seventies. Wilson was not sure exactly what condition or disease or malady Dr. Killeen had. All he knew for certain was that he had been in a wheelchair for at least ten years, maybe more. He had retired from full-time pastoral work at the large Presbyterian church in Shadyside a few years before his...infirmity appeared. Wilson's mother had attended his church for a long stretch following her husband's death, and she had told Wilson that she liked the teaching and preaching, disliked the music. Gretna Steele did not suffer through many services where "something was off-kilter."

"The music sounds like medieval caterwauling," she'd said.

Wilson himself had never attended.

"And Emily Gold was with her," Dr. Killeen said. "That was nice to see."

Wilson did not show his surprise, but he was surprised.

"You know Emily?"

"I do. Not as well as I knew her husband. I mean, I knew them both. But more her husband."

Thurman paced down the driveway and then back again, sniffing virtually every square inch of the bushes that lined one side.

"He was in the military, wasn't he?"

Dr. Killeen nodded.

"Special Forces. An officer. I forget which rank. Served several tours of duty in the Middle East. Maybe in Afghanistan as well."

Wilson listened and remained silent. He simply did not know how much to probe, how much to let happen, how much people were willing or able to tell others. So as a matter of course, he seldom asked follow-up questions, questions his mother would have had no problem in asking and re-asking until she was satisfied. Wilson guessed that it was because he'd lived with the ambiguity and uncertainty of his past, he could accept both in his daily life now.

"He's dead, you know."

Wilson nodded as Thurman padded up to them, his tongue lolling out to one side, appearing like a deranged participant in some manner of frat-house bender during spring break. At least that was the image that flashed in Wilson's thoughts.

"I do. Well, my mother said she was a widow. I guess that means the same thing."

Dr. Killeen nodded.

"It was one of the most painful experiences in my work as a pastor."

Wilson reached down and patted Thurman, having absolutely no idea if he should ask further questions or simply look like a sympathetic listener.

"He came back to the States damaged. Not physically. But something broke. He couldn't readjust. And I couldn't help him. I tried. We tried. Emily. Me. And others."

Dr. Killeen raised his left hand to push an errant wisp of hair off his forehead. His hand trembled the entire time and it appeared to Wilson that it took a great effort just to raise it up.

Then Dr. Killeen looked up at Wilson.

"You know what that's like, don't you, Dr. Steele? Coming back from a war."

Wilson stepped back. In the span of a second, his heart

lurched and sped up, and he could feel a bead of sweat at the back of his neck.

"Maybe," he finally said. His voice was less than a whisper. "Maybe."

Dr. Killeen offered a weary smile in return, as if he had heard such equivocations before, as if he knew the certain futility of pressing the issue, then he looked at Thurman. "Thurman, look at me."

Thurman did as he was asked, staring at the old man with a focused intensity that only dogs could exhibit.

"You tell him, Thurman. It has been too long. It's time."

Thurman appeared to nod, looked back at Wilson with a look of great compassion, then back to the old man.

He growled.

Wilson knew he said, *I will.*

But Wilson knew that only he and Thurman heard it.

⌐

Hazel walked down the street to her car, feeling lighter and more unfettered than she had ever felt in her adult life.

Maybe it was like this when I was a little girl. Maybe.

She got her car keys out of her pocket.

But I don't remember it. Not really. Not this way.

She paid the parking fee with a twenty-dollar bill and drove toward town. The safe-deposit key was in her right pocket. She could feel the ridges. It was a most comfortable feeling.

She retrieved her stock certificates and asked to see Mr. Hild.

I guess I have a personal banker now.

Mr. Hild was all smiles when he escorted her to his desk.

"I didn't expect to see you so soon," he said.

Hazel wanted to shrug but thought that shrugging was not a proper way to deal with financial matters.

Instead, she laid the envelope on his desk.

"I want to sell it."

Mr. Hild raised an eyebrow.

"The stock, you mean."

"Yes."

"All of it?"

Hazel had been sure, almost since finding out that she was now middle-class wealthy. It had not been a difficult choice. In truth, she had discovered that making a million-dollar decision was easier than making a choice of breakfast at Denny's.

"Yes."

Mr. Hild waited a moment, as if the waiting was a personal banker sort of behavior to ensure that clients were telling the truth.

"If I hold on to some of it, then I'll worry about it. I'll keep asking myself if it's time to sell or not. And that's not a problem I want to have. I wasn't worried before I knew that I had it, and I don't want to be worried now."

Mr. Hild nodded gravely, if one could nod with a grave attitude.

"I understand."

"I want you to sell it for me. You said no fee, right?"

"That is correct. However, it would be our hope that you may keep some of that money here at our bank. But there would be no restrictions to our offer."

Hazel found herself smiling.

"I will keep most of it here," she said.

"Thank you," he replied, his relief most evident in his thanks.

"But I would like to put some of it into a checking account. Like maybe fifty thousand dollars?"

Mr. Hild appeared to breathe a great sigh of relief, without wanting to, without wanting to express his true emotions, which were obviously delight and relief.

"I want to buy a new car. And I want to sell my condo."

"Well, fifty thousand dollars would buy a very nice car, Ms. Jamison."

Hazel began to grow more comfortable with the whole stock-rich-personal banker sort of feeling.

"Actually, I just want to get an older delivery van. Reliable. But used."

Mr. Hild nodded and probably would have asked why, but that also might be a question that personal bankers don't ask their newly wealthy clients.

"I'm not going to make deliveries, of course. But I want to put a bed in back, and maybe get a little stove where I could make coffee."

"So you'll do some camping, then?"

"Heavens no," Hazel replied. "I just want a place to rest. If I get tired driving. I plan on doing some traveling. My mother always said she wanted to travel and never did, not really."

Mr. Hild looked a little jealous, or envious, as she spoke of her plans.

"So you'll go out and explore America?"

"Something like that," Hazel said. "I want to look for the truth."

And after a moment, Mr. Hild took the envelope with the Apple stock.

"Let me get you a receipt for this. And then I'll call the bank's stock traders. We'll have an accurate amount of the total for the sale within a few hours, probably. This sort of stock sells quickly."

Maybe I don't know what's it is like coming back from a war, Wilson thought as he stood by the coffee maker waiting for the little light to show up that would tell him the unit was ready to brew coffee. *Maybe I've forgotten. Maybe I never remembered.*

He jabbed at the button on the coffee maker, missing it on his first attempt.

Maybe I don't want to remember.

Thurman continued eating as Wilson spoke his internal dialogue. Obviously, he had watched Wilson as he stormed about the kitchen that afternoon.

Wilson would not have called it "storming."

Something much less than storming. Maybe a little disturbed. But not tempestuous. Or raging. Perturbed. That's it. That's the word. Perturbed.

Thurman was having none of it, apparently, and as he finished his dog treats he sat by the refrigerator and stared at Wilson, a most . . . disappointed look on his face, if disappointment was a possible emotion for a dog to exhibit.

Thurman appeared to have that ability, however, to reflect whatever emotion he was feeling, from disappointment

to joy, from melancholy to choleric, from unctuous to felic-
itous.

Wilson pretended to glower at the dog, and wondered if a
less literate owner would attribute any of those complex emotions to a mere canine companion.

Probably not, he thought and slumped at his usual chair
at the kitchen table.

Thurman simply stared at him.

Then he growled, *Emily*.

Wilson's glower did not abate.

"Emily? You're asking about Emily?"

Thurman growled again.

Maybe.

Wilson pushed his coffee cup to one side.

"I don't see why you're asking about that. Or her, I should
say."

Thurman shook his head, then snorted, and whisper-
growled.

Past, he growled, looking over his shoulder. Then *Not
past*, staring hard at Wilson.

"What? What are you talking about?" Wilson said, his voice
more forceful than it had ever been since Thurman's arrival. And
louder. Not a shout, not yet. Wilson was not a man who shouted,
but these words were hard-edged, and louder than Thurman
liked. But Thurman was not cowed, not in the least. He would
not slink off thinking he had done something bad, because he
had not. He met Wilson's glare with his own focused stare.

"What? What do you want from me?" Wilson asked, gesturing wide with his left hand, something he seldom did—
gesturing at all, with any hand.

Thurman waited a long time. Then he stood and growled a long, nuanced growl, with stops and starts and peaks and valleys.

Past. Now. Move. Deal.

Thurman stood up and walked to Wilson. He butted his head against his thigh.

Hiding.

Wilson looked down at the dog. He didn't want to soften, but there was something about those big golden liquid eyes that drew the truth out.

"But I don't want to remember. It's too...hard. Too much pain."

Thurman nodded as if he understood.

Then he turned his head up and stared, not at the ceiling, but at the heaven beyond the ceiling. The dog's eyes seemed to focus on something far away, something that reflected peace and calm.

Wilson knew what he was looking at. He could tell from the tilt of his head and the comfort he could see in those dark eyes.

"God?" Wilson said. "You're talking about God now? Some sort of comforting divinity?"

Thurman smiled. It was not a joyous smile but a smile of comfort.

Wilson shook his head this time.

"No. Don't you start on this go-to-church-and-find-peace bunkum too. My mother has mentioned that I should just go ahead and take advantage of some manner of divine relief more than enough times over the years. I think she actually believes that it could happen—that I would suddenly be 'better' if all I did was turn to Jesus. That's not going to happen."

He stood up and left his coffee on the table, a half-cup remaining.

"I don't want to remember, Thurman. And I won't."

Thurman had not backed away. He waited until Wilson was out of the room, but still within earshot.

He ambled to his bed in the den, growling. Growling louder than he normally did, in order that someone else in the house would hear his admonitions.

Remember. Talk. Remember. Talk. Remember. Talk.

⌐

By the time Hazel had lunch at Denny's, walked down to the park along the Willamette River, and came back to the bank, her stocks had been sold.

They actually sold for more than what Mr. Hild had first quoted only a few days before.

"Stocks go up. Stocks go down. No one really knows why," Mr. Hild said. "You happened to sell when they were up. Good news for you."

She signed all the paperwork, set up a checking account with a small portion of the proceeds, and placed the rest into a series of certificates of deposit.

"They're insured, aren't they?" Hazel asked. "Just in case, you know..."

Mr. Hild nodded.

"We actually use an outside insurance group for sums of this level. A little more expensive for the bank, but these agencies do not set limits on the amount insured. So all your funds will be safe... in case something untoward was to happen here at Umpqua. Which it won't."

Hazel had no idea if any of this was standard protocol. And she had no idea of what an "untoward" event meant in the world of Umpqua banking. But she had not worried much about banking and finance and the security of deposits before this moment, and probably would not start worrying about any of those things in the future.

Hazel was not a worrier by nature.

She now had a *personal* personal banker, who knew her name and who had fetched, or had some other lesser personal banker fetch, a chilled bottle of water for her so she would stay hydrated during the process of signing her name many multiple times.

And now, after all that, after all the newly rich financial dealings had been concluded, she returned to her small condo, dropped her purse on the dining table, and looked around—this time with a more critical eye. It was not as if she was finding fault with where she lived, or looking now with disdain on her modest dwelling or modest possessions in particular. It was that she now had the freedom to leave this place... forever, if she wanted, and not have to worry about coming up with the means of financing another place to live.

She walked to the window in her living area, which also contained her dining area. The window faced west, toward the ocean, sort of, though the ocean was more than two hours distant. What she could see most clearly was the parking lot of a strip mall with a convenience store, a branch bank, a dry cleaner, and an outpost of a chain sandwich shop.

She had her couch placed facing away from the window.

Sunsets were usually pleasant, until you came close to the window and were faced with too much local detail.

"Maybe I could find a place on the ocean. Or the river. Something small. I don't need much."

The sun was midway to setting.

"When I come back, that is. When I come back to Portland."

A large semi truck pulled into the parking lot below, sounding its horn several times, for no apparent reason.

"If I come back to Portland."

She thought about making coffee, but decided against it. She thought about having a glass of wine, as a celebration, but realized that the one bottle of wine she owned was nearly three years old and left over from a "buy some of our overpriced jewelry" party that she had cohosted with an acquaintance from work.

She didn't take that idea any further, realizing that she did not own a corkscrew. And she had never developed a taste for wine.

Instead, she decided on tea.

"Something to calm my nerves."

She rummaged about and found a dry, wrinkled, probably old chamomile tea bag.

"Better than nothing," she said as she switched on the electric kettle.

The tea brewed and Hazel sat at her dining table, looking to the west. Her computer sat on that table as well.

On the wall facing her was a framed diploma, representing her two-year stint at the Portland Community College.

From there, she had migrated to the insurance agency, which brought her to today.

"Not much of a life's arc, is it?" she said, with a touch of regret.

Hazel was not a person who let regrets fester. She considered herself a realist. Maybe an optimistic realist.

There had been a boyfriend, right after her community college days, a boyfriend of almost four years. There must have been reasons why they drifted apart, but Hazel could not recall any of them at the moment. There were other dates, and a few other ill-suited suitors over the years.

"You don't encounter many options working at an insurance agency."

The computer sat there, dark. She had resisted going online to meet a man. She resisted being set up—or at least resisted the few times a friend asked her about going on a double date with "a really nice guy," as they would tell her. "And he's almost done with his parole and/or community service and/or anger management counseling and/or contentious divorce proceedings."

She wondered if she had been described as having lots of "spirit" and being "loyal," like a middle-aged dog put up for adoption.

She sipped at her tea.

"So what do I do now?"

Whatever closed doors and out-of-reach options had existed before this moment were now open. Finances? No longer a problem. Dead-end job? Not any longer. Confusion over her past?

"Well, that's still there."

Hazel slipped around to her computer, switched it on, and waited for the machine to whirr into life.

Why didn't you sell that stock, Mom? You could have had such an easy life.

The screen blinked once and Hazel tapped in her password, which was "HAZEL."

How many people are named Hazel these days? I think not too many.

Were you doing some sort of penance for having an "illegitimate" baby? But you were married, right? Surprise, surprise. Or maybe there was someone else?

She tapped at the keyboard and Google came up.

"I don't get it. Not at all. None of this makes sense, Mom. None of it."

She sighed, then began to type "f-a-c-" . . . and Google decided that she was looking for the Facebook website, almost before Hazel knew it.

⟶

Darkness had settled over Squirrel Hill by the time Wilson came back downstairs. He had spent the last several hours lying on his bed and staring at the ceiling, not thinking, not being angry, not being sad, not being scared, just staring. Just being, no feeling, no thought.

That skill of being "nowhere" had been developed over the years, and Wilson had grown adept at it.

Thurman was sitting in the kitchen when he entered.

Hungry.

"I know, Thurman. It's after dark and you haven't eaten.

I was afraid that you might have passed out from hunger by now."

Thurman looked at him with a squirrel-tight face that Wilson interpreted as showing that the dog did not appreciate his sarcasm.

Thurman simply growled *Hungry* again.

"I get it, Thurman," Wilson replied. "You hold grudges. Okay, I get it. You don't want to laugh and make up."

Thurman shook his head and bounded to Wilson in a flash and had his paws on his chest before Wilson could react, and his tongue was out, trying to catch Wilson's face, an activity that Wilson did not really enjoy, which Thurman knew, but most often he could not help himself.

"Okay, okay," Wilson said, running his hand over Thurman's head. "It's okay. We're okay. Now let me get your dinner."

With that, Thurman hopped back and sat by his bowl, waiting with smiling joy for his usual kibble dinner.

He was not disappointed and set into it with enthusiasm.

As the dog ate, Wilson peered inside the refrigerator, wondering if he was hungry and wondering if he had any easily consumable food in there.

He did not.

But the search gave him the time to decide he really was not hungry, not really, so he took an apple from the fruit basket on the counter and sat at the table and began to eat.

Any biting or chewing brought Thurman to attention—that is, any biting or chewing that did not originate with Thurman. The dog stopped eating, looked up, and sniffed. He stared at Wilson, then decided that the thing Wilson was eating was not worth his effort to stop eating his real meal and investigate.

Thurman had tasted apples before and had decided that they were not proper food for dogs, or at least not for him, so if Wilson wanted to eat the entire thing and not share even a nibble with him, he was okay with that.

They both finished eating at about the same time. Wilson made coffee while Thurman ran his tongue over his mouth and nose and tried his best to remove all kibble crumbs from his snout.

When Wilson was seated back at the kitchen table, Thurman walked a little closer and sat down.

Emily, he growled, or at least that was what Wilson thought he growled.

"What about her?" Wilson asked. "And why are you so interested in her?"

Thurman tilted his head to the side as if concentrating.

Then he smiled and growled, *Pretty*.

Wilson shrugged.

"I guess. In that Middle Eastern way. She's from Israel, you know. At least that's what my mother said. I think."

It was obvious to Wilson that Thurman wanted to shrug at that information, but he lacked the proper shoulder blades and bone structure to do it well. Instead he simply stared back at Wilson. Wilson was fairly certain that dogs were not all that interested or knowledgeable about international geography.

Sad, he growled.

Wilson looked at the dog.

I am going crazy, Wilson thought to himself. *I am. Having conversations with a dog. I know it's just me...talking to me. Like Dr. Limke said. Pressure. Guilt. It's a toxic stew and I'm just reacting to that by talking to myself using the dog as a substitute for my own subconscious. I'm making this all up. To exorcise my demons. Right?*

Thurman growled, *Not right.*

Well, Thurman, it's just me talking to me. And so what if it is?

"Why is she sad?" Wilson asked. "And how can you tell?"

Thurman made a point of lifting his snout into the air and sniffing loudly, for effect.

"You can smell sad?"

Thurman smiled, a half-smile, and nodded.

"It's all because of my mother, you know."

Thurman smiled anytime Wilson mentioned his mother.

"When I came back...way back then...my mother tried her best. She thought an aspiring writer and a future college professor had to be matched up with someone. She thought it would help. You know...with adjusting. The first few years were difficult, Thurman. And she thought a wife would be a good anchor. Someone to mediate my problems. So, Thurman, there have been other 'Emilys' over the years."

Thurman appeared puzzled.

Emily, he growled.

"They were all nice. But it never lasted. My fault, it has always been my fault."

Thurman growled, *Yes.*

"Then my father died and my mother moved to Florida to escape the cold and came back a few years later to escape the heat."

Why? Thurman whisper-growled.

"She said it was too far, too buggy, and too old."

Thurman smiled, but Wilson was pretty sure he did not know why he was smiling.

Probably just because I'm talking about my mother.

"Then I got tenure. She moved to her apartment at the Cranky Old Jewish People's Heritage Square, and that was that."

Thurman walked over and bumped his head into Wilson's thigh. It was his way of introducing a change in conversation, Wilson surmised.

Remember.

"No. Thurman, you don't understand. It is simply too hard. And I don't want to."

Thurman's face tightened.

Emily.

Wilson could not help but smile at the dog's prunelike visage.

"Thurman, you are not a dog that discourages easily, you know that?"

Thurman's tail began to twitch and wag, leading Wilson to think that he had no idea of what "discourage" even meant.

Chapter Fifteen

*H*AZEL SLID the paperwork, after carefully signing her initials multiple times by the little yellow sticky-note flags indicating where they should go, back across the table to Mrs. Charlene Mason, a real estate agent she had met while working at the insurance agency.

"Mr. Shupp has been acting apoplectic since you walked out, Hazel," Charlene said. Charlene, a middle-aged woman who could be best described as flouncy—in dress as well as mannerisms—waved the paperwork with a flourish. "He said you'll have to take him to court to get your vacation pay now, since you abandoned your position with not even a proper fare-thee-well."

Hazel did not want to smile, but she did, and broadly.

"Apoplectic? Really?"

"I was at your office because of a claim on one of the agency's rental units. The receptionist...what's-her-name...the tiny blond woman with the squeaky voice..."

"Margie."

"Yes, that's it. Margie whispered to me that Mr. Shupp had been storming about the office for days now and muttering to himself."

"Really?"

Charlene leaned close.

"Didn't anyone ever quit before?"

Hazel tilted her head in thought.

"I guess. Maybe. They retired. They got fired. But not many people quit. Only one or two that I remember."

Charlene nodded, adjusting her necklace.

"So you just walked out? No farewell party? No two weeks' notice?"

Actually, Hazel had given this whole leaving-at-that-very-moment some thought for much of that morning—the morning before she had taken action and walked out.

"I hate goodbye parties. Should you be sad that they're leaving? Or happy, because you never liked them to begin with?"

"True," Charlene replied, and slipped the sale documents into her briefcase.

"And," Hazel continued, "two weeks' notice is only 'customary.' There's no legal standing for it. And while he does owe me for vacation time . . . I am not going to bother with going after it. And during those last two weeks, what do people do with you while you're still at work? It's like you're dead—but not just yet. A lot of sad, fake smiles. And then someone steals your stapler and tape dispenser."

Charlene laughed. She knew that a good real estate agent does not probe too deeply, but could hardly help herself. There were a lot of whispers at the insurance agency—from early-onset dementia to a winning lottery ticket—as the cause of Hazel's unusual departure.

Charlene leaned closer and with an extended finger beckoned Hazel to lean closer as well.

"Was it the lottery?" she whispered as if a fellow conspirator.

Hazel had prepared an answer.

"Something like that," she whispered back, with just a trace of an enigmatic smile. "Something like that."

Charlene appeared to be only partially satisfied with the answer, but she also realized that it was all she would get.

"Well, then," she concluded as she stood. "Your condo should sell quickly. Good location. Good condition."

Hazel stood as well.

"And a good price."

Hazel had priced it below market value. It was the only anchor that was holding her to Portland. Once it was sold, she would be free.

"There is that," Charlene said. "I bet no more than a couple of weeks on the market. If that."

"Let's hope," Hazel replied, feeling more relaxed than she felt she had a right to be, but she was not about to let that delicious feeling evaporate too quickly.

The two women shook hands and Hazel walked out with a little smile, leaving Charlene, who forced her own smile, with a few unanswered questions as well.

⌒

The next four mornings, after Thurman greeted Wilson, after Thurman made his circuit around the backyard, after he came back into the kitchen, after he sat down and growled *Hungry* and just prior to setting into his breakfast kibbles, he would look at Wilson with some intensity and growl, *Emily*.

Wilson would respond by scowling perfunctorily and

waving the dog's whispered growl off, as if batting away an errant but persistent moth.

Halfway through breakfast, Thurman had been given to stopping for just a moment, turning toward Wilson, and again growling, *Emily.*

Wilson usually met the second *Emily* with just a grimace.

And Thurman would respond to Wilson's grimace with a whispered *Pretty.*

"How do you know if Emily is pretty? I never thought of that before."

Thurman appeared to seize up for a moment, then grinned. *Good.*

"So good is like being pretty?"

Thurman's grin expanded, and he nodded. *Good. Pretty. Good.*

When Thurman said *Pretty*, it stopped Wilson for a moment. Then he would shake his head in some manner of disbelief and return to the morning copy of the *Pittsburgh Tribune-Review.*

This morning proved to be no different than the preceding four.

Thurman stared at Wilson and growled, *Emily.*

Wilson appeared pained.

"I know, Thurman. My mother called again yesterday. She said the same thing. That I should call Emily. That we have so much in common. As if trauma and social disorders are some manner of bonding agent. I have to call her, she said, like she was expecting it. Maybe demanding it. Maybe my mother told Emily that I would call, and now I have to act to fulfill her end of the bargain—which I was not part of."

It took Thurman a moment to digest the information, unexpected as it was. Then he stood and cha-cha'ed over toward Wilson, growling, *Good, good.*

Wilson did not appear to be nearly as happy as Thurman.

"She is a lot younger than me, Thurman. I told my mother the same thing. Ten years is a lot of years."

Thurman appeared puzzled.

"I know you don't get time, Thurman. Years and hours aren't part of a dog's understanding. Dogs don't get time. I know that."

Thurman appeared to be a little hurt by that assessment, making his face tighten up and his eyes narrow.

"It's true, Thurman. You don't care about years and oldness and age gaps. But I do. She is from an entirely different decade than me. More than a decade. That's a big difference in personal experiences."

Thurman sat back down, making sure he was in the wide square of sunlight that filled a portion of the kitchen. Thurman loved the sunlight. It often warmed his black fur to a toasty, well-done temperature. Wilson wondered how he stood it.

And today, while he was sitting in that warm sunlight pool, Thurman's face slowly uncoiled, slowly relaxed, as if new ideas and concepts were gradually being understood, like a young man coming to faith, his eyes finally open to the glory all around him. That's what Thurman looked like. At the end, he was all smiles and acknowledgments and relief and happiness.

Think, he growled. *Think. Emily.*

Wilson twisted his face in response to this comment.

"What do you mean, Thurman? 'Think'? All I do is think."

Thurman stood and walked out of the sunlight.

He closed his eyes as if trying to remember some arcane fact, some almost buried truth.

Not think, he finally whisper-growled. *Stop think*.

Wilson leaned back in the chair, the metal legs making that scratchy metallic sound on the tile.

A very long moment passed, Thurman staring hard at Wilson, Wilson staring back, a little less hard, their eyes trying to communicate the uncommunicable.

Wilson took a deep breath.

"Maybe you're right, Thurman," he said, his voice on the edge of relief, on the edge of acceptance of a sort.

Thurman wiggled, smiling and grinning and trying hard not to bounce and dance, his nails making small clickery noises on the floor, a hesitant yet happy sound.

"Maybe I should stop thinking and just do it. Maybe the years have changed me."

With that, Thurman did bounce up, and his front paws landed on Wilson's thighs, the dog's mouth open, tongue lolling out, trying to make contact with Wilson's face.

Stop. Think, Thurman growled, then added in a quiet whisper-growl, *Not think, do*.

Wilson put his hand on Thurman's head and looked into his eyes.

"Maybe, Thurman. Maybe I will."

He looked at Thurman with a critical eye.

"And maybe you can stop sounding like Yoda. I never did like that movie, you know."

Thurman responded by jumping back down and doing

his happy dance, where his backside would slowly turn in a circle.

Not think. Do, he whisper-growled, looking happier than Wilson thought a dog had the right to appear.

⟶

Hazel's small condo overlooking the parking lot was littered with boxes—a veritable jungle of boxes, box tape, wide-tipped markers, and a sense of urgency.

She had been correct: a low price brought out plenty of lookers, and two quick offers within the first week. The first was for asking price. The second was for a thousand dollars more than the asking price.

Hazel toyed with the idea of accepting the first offer, "Because they were first." Charlene quickly disavowed her of that notion, and the condo sold, and a closing date in two weeks had been requested.

That date did not provide her much time, but she wanted it over and done with, and this would accomplish that.

In truth, Hazel owned much less than her mother had. Her condo was much smaller than her mother's house; the only true storage area was a closet-sized cage in the basement that contained mostly Christmas decorations and an artificial Christmas tree that never stood quite perpendicular.

As the packing progressed, Hazel only packed up three larger cardboard boxes marked prominently with the words HAZEL JAMISON/KEEP written in bold block letters on the top.

Those few boxes, containing items with some sentimental

value, were being sent to an indoor storage facility—licensed, bonded, fire-rated, and insured.

"This is just stuff that I would have stored at my mother's house," Hazel explained to Charlene, who had brought over a sheaf of paperwork to be signed and initialed. "Nothing of real value. A few sentimental things. A couple of yearbooks. A few things I had when I was a child. Things that belong in a parent's attic or basement. Which are two locations I don't have."

Charlene actually gave Hazel a hug after hearing this.

"I know it's hard, Hazel. It's hard doing this alone."

Hazel accepted the hug but did not want to tell the Realtor that it wasn't really all that hard. She had been alone most of her adult life. She had been doing things alone for over two and half decades. This did not feel all that different.

True, my mother is gone...but we didn't spend all that much time together, did we? After I moved out, I mean. It was her choice, after all. She liked being alone.

Box after box had been filled with things that Hazel really didn't like all that much, or had seldom used, and now that they were soon to be on their way to her church's resale shop, they would soon fill someone else's home.

The church that Hazel had attended, on and off, promised to send a few sturdy men to take all the filled boxes away, once Hazel gave the call.

She was close to giving the call.

"Be sure to keep a list," the director of the resale shop had cautioned her. "So you can claim all of this on your taxes."

Hazel did not tell her that she was keeping no list at all. A truckload of used merchandise was not going to substantially impact her tax expense this year.

Her personal banker was already at work attempting to shield as much money as legally possible.

"As long as it is legal," Hazel had instructed Mr. Hild at Umpqua Bank.

He had nodded knowingly.

"We will keep everything legal," Mr. Hild assured her. "But we do not want you to pay any more than what you legitimately owe. There are very legal maneuvers that we can take advantage of. Nothing gray or esoteric or exotic. Just run-of-the-mill tax strategies."

She assumed that the knowing nod and his explanation were indications that all such maneuvers would stay well within the tax code.

Hazel did not like worry and did not want to add a tax liability to her short worry list.

The day after setting up all her new bank accounts and deposits, she spent an unpleasant day shopping for a van or "some sort of used delivery truck." She had never been a car person, so even knowing what to ask for was a problem.

She discovered that delivery vans are at best a no-frills means of transportation—a box with an engine. A vehicle that drove hard and loud was not what she had envisioned as a comfortable cross-country driving machine.

After realizing that a delivery van was not suitable, she had been steered to conversion vans, either offering multiple seating arrangements with some form of audiovisual entertainment system, or a camper van, with refrigerators and stoves and bathrooms and that cost more than the amount she had kept back from the sale of her stock—sometimes almost twice as much.

She could not imagine spending that much on a car—even a big car. Even a new car.

Instead, she settled for a used Nissan Quest. "A quest for the truth, get it?" she had told herself.

There wasn't really space for a bed, but if she folded down the backseats she could lie down.

And there wasn't really a place for a stove inside the vehicle for making coffee. That bothered her at first, but she then decided it was okay. "When am I going to be so far off the beaten path that I can't find a Starbucks . . . or a Texaco station selling coffee?"

Her mother may have been a hippie at heart, willing to sleep on the ground and eschew showers and morning coffee, but Hazel was not her mother—not at all.

"I'll stay at hotels. Maybe not expensive hotels, but I don't think I'll ever have to sleep in the car overnight."

She walked through her condo—it didn't take more than a few dozen steps—taking a mental inventory of what still needed to be boxed, and what would be sent along unboxed, like the couch and bedframe and large lamps. She was close to being done.

She returned to the kitchen, made a cup of instant coffee; her fancier pod coffeemaker had already been scrubbed clean and packed up, ready for donating. She sat at her computer. The computer would go as well, but not until she figured out how to get her email on the new electronic tablet she had purchased.

She typed in her password and checked her email account.

Most were several ads from stores where she shopped.

But one was not.

The email listed as sender a name she did not recognize, but the name was followed by the words "Tropic Thunder Veterans 25th Division."

She felt her heart thump in response, and she waited a long moment before opening the email—worried, excited, and anxious all at the same time.

⤙

"I hear you. I have heard you. You haven't said much else to me for the past two weeks."

Wilson stood in the front alcove of the house, in the more official telephone-answering spot, ignoring his reflection in the mirror, and ignoring Thurman, who sauntered about the entryway with cheerful energy, looking up at Wilson every few steps and whispering-growling some matter of encouragement. Wilson wondered how the dog could tell it was his mother on the other end of the line. When the call was a telemarketing call, from a window-cleaning business, for example, Thurman hardly opened his eyes or raised his head.

Maybe he has good hearing and can actually hear her voice.

Wilson stared at the dog, then offered a world-weary scowl. It was obvious that Thurman viewed it as a good-natured, well-intended scowl, because he grinned and growled, *Bunkum.*

Or maybe the mutt is psychic.

Wilson listened to his mother go on, without really listening.

Or maybe he's tapped into the power of the underworld. A demon dog.

One of Wilson's students had read several pages of his Stephen King–wannabe novel, which Wilson had disliked thoroughly, but it did get him thinking in odd directions that afternoon.

"Okay, Mother, I said I would call. And I will. But remember, you were the one who promised her I would call. I didn't."

There was a gap of several moments of silence. Wilson's mother apparently was deciding if she could risk showing offense at the comment, and thus risk having Wilson change his mind, or if she should show some small amount of umbrage over her son's caustic response.

"I can hear you thinking, Mother."

There was a snort on the other end of the line.

"I will call her. I said I would. And I will. Today. This afternoon. Okay?"

With that, Thurman bounced up, put his front paws on Wilson's chest, and growled out, *Good boy*, all the while grinning like a toddler in a toy store.

Gretna responded loudly, "That's a good boy."

Again, Wilson was sure she was talking to both of them, but probably more to Thurman than to her own son.

Chapter Sixteen

_H_AZEL'S QUEST had been packed with two bags of red licorice, four average-sized suitcases, and three bottles of water she had left in her refrigerator.

None of the suitcases held cold-weather gear.

"If it gets cold, I'll buy a coat," she told herself, giving herself permission to travel light, or lighter than one would expect for someone going on the road for an indefinite period of time.

If I get tired of traveling, I'll stay at one of those suite hotels for a week. Do laundry. Watch TV all day. Normal things. That's if I get tired of traveling.

Her first objective, after leaving Portland, was to drive south along the Pacific Coast Highway, a road she had read about and seen pictures of but had never once visited. Once in California, she would head east, into Arizona and on to Phoenix.

The email about the 25th Division had come from a man in Phoenix who was the current head of the division's reunion committee.

"I might have a lead on who this is," the man wrote. "I have a couple of pictures here that might be him. Any chance you could travel to Phoenix? My traveling days, unfortunately, are over—and I don't want to let any photos out of my possession."

Hazel wondered why he just didn't scan them and send them electronically, but if he was a Vietnam veteran, he could easily be close to seventy now, and Hazel also knew that some technological solutions might seem insurmountable to that sort of person. He would not have been a digital native.

Scanning might be beyond his pay grade, she thought, smiling.

The closing on her condo was taking place tomorrow, and while she could have skipped the signing and left it up to the attorney that Charlene had recommended, she thought her being there would be a definitive closing act to her life in Portland.

It meant that she had to stay at a hotel that last night.

Might as well get used to it.

She'd booked a room at the Embassy Suites. On her way there that afternoon, she'd stopped at St. James Lutheran Church. Inside her coat was a sealed envelope. Wondering if she should have called and made an appointment, she'd opened the massive wooden door and walked inside, the quiet enveloping her like a thick, dark shawl. The offices were off to one side and she'd walked slowly and as quietly as she could, not wanting to shatter the cloaking, intimate silence with the sound of footsteps.

I should have come more often, she thought to herself at the time.

She stopped and peered in at the sanctuary. The deep red carpet, the ornately carved wooden support beams of the ceiling, the gleam of the pipe organ even in the dim light, the glistering, fractured afternoon sun coming through the stained glass windows . . .

It is so peaceful. And so...reverential...if that's a real word. Like God lives here, sort of. I mean, I know he doesn't, but he could. It would suit him.

She stepped into the office and blinked, the bright fluorescent lights a sharp contrast to the sanctuary.

The woman at the first desk looked up, smiling.

"Yes?"

Hazel hesitated for a second. She had never spoken to one of the pastors, other than to offer a "Good morning" if she happened to get stuck in the aisle where he stood shaking hands at the end of a service. She usually tried to guess which section of the pews would be pastorless at the end of the service, but it still happened occasionally.

"Is the...the pastor here?"

The woman did not stop smiling.

"You mean Pastor Coggins?"

Is that his name? I thought it was something else. I should have checked. Or remembered.

"Uh...sure."

The woman at the desk waited for just a beat.

"May I tell him who you are? And what this might be in reference to?"

I hadn't considered that. They probably get all sorts of wacky people in here. I should have thought of something that doesn't sound wacky. Or deranged.

Hazel looked as if she was attempting to decide just what to say. She took a deep breath.

"I'm Hazel Jamison. I come here...not often, but I like it. And I'm leaving the area. And I wanted to give the pastor something before I left. Like a donation. It will only take a minute."

The woman's smile did not change or slip away or shift into a questioning grimace.

"I'm sure he has more than a minute, Mrs. Jamison."

"It's sort of . . . Miss. I mean, I'm not married."

The woman's smile did shift, just a bit, and she nodded.

"I'm sorry. I mean, not that you're a Miss or a Mrs. I guess we're all guilty of making assumptions, aren't we?"

"I guess we are," Hazel agreed.

"Wait here. I'll let Pastor Coggins know you're here."

I should have called. Or just mailed this. I knew it.

⌒

Wilson stared at the phone.

Thurman ambled into the vestibule of the house and took it upon himself to stare at it as well, but it was very apparent that he had no idea of just what he was looking at, or why. He sniffed loudly, his nose in the air, thinking that perhaps a mouse or a squirrel or some large morsel of food had become lodged behind the thing that Wilson talked into.

But nothing moved and Thurman did not detect a food scent. Yet Wilson continued to stare, so Thurman happily sat down next to him and kept him company as he did so.

He whisper-growled, *Dogs do this.*

Wilson did not pay attention to his remark.

He looked at a slip of paper in his left hand. A number was written on it. He took a deep breath, picked up the receiver, and slowly and carefully tapped the numbers on the keypad.

He did not want to make a dialing mistake, which would

then entail trying to build up the courage to redial all over again. He took a deep breath and held it for a long moment, exhaling loudly as the phone made a connection.

Thurman must not have noticed Wilson ever doing that before, and tried to mimic him, but dogs are apparently not skilled at holding their breath unless they're in the water, and Thurman, while a water sort of dog, was skilled at swimming and retrieving; holding his breath on dry land was a novel and untried behavior.

Instead of holding his breath, Thurman sort of gulped and coughed and shook his head, knowing that he had done it wrong, then looked up at Wilson to see if he might get more instructions on this. None were forthcoming. Wilson was not paying attention to him, at least not at this moment.

"Hello?"

Wilson shut his eyes tightly, for just a moment, and Thurman responded by trying to do the same thing.

"Hi, Emily?"

There was no pause on the other end.

"Yes. Is this Wilson?"

Wilson let out another long breath, one of relief, and hoped it was not audible over the phone.

"It is. I guess my mother has covered all her bases, hasn't she?"

Emily did not laugh loudly, but the lilt of her voice told Wilson that she must have been smiling.

"She has. Your mother can be . . ."

"Tenacious?" Wilson suggested.

"Well, yes, but I was looking for a kinder word."

Wilson was smiling, which he had not expected to do.

"Pleasantly persistent, perhaps."

At this, Emily did offer a small laugh.

"Yes. That fits better. She means well, right?"

Wilson was nodding, then realized that Emily could not see a nod over the phone.

"Indeed," he said. "Which is one of the refuges, or a moral high ground as it were, of an obstinate old woman who likes to meddle."

"But . . . after all, she does mean well."

Wilson offered a small laugh in reply.

"And we'll leave it at that," he said.

Then he took another deep breath, which Thurman tried to imitate as well, unsuccessfully, much to his consternation.

"Emily," he said, trying not to sound as if he had rehearsed this, which he had, but did not want it to sound that way, "since my mother has put us both on notice, would it be okay with you if we actually met . . . and went out?"

"Like a date," she replied, both restating his request and turning it, just a little, into a question.

"Like a date. I guess it would be a date. Not like a date."

He sighed loudly.

"Semantics. It drives everyone other than rhetoric professors crazy."

Emily paused.

"I thought you taught rhetoric."

Wilson snorted.

"I did. For two semesters when I first started at the university. I hated it. Since then, just creative writing. And the occasional survey of American literature, old and new."

Emily waited and Wilson waited.

Wilson thought the pause went on for a very long time, but time and the duration of this phone call had already been distorted by his high level of anxiety.

"Sure. That would be nice. The date thing, I mean. Not the rhetoric thing. And from what your mother tells me, and from what I know about myself, this will mark the end of a long period of 'not dating' for both of us."

Wilson nodded again, then quickly agreed.

"Yes. It will."

"Okay."

"Okay."

There was a pause, then Emily added in a small voice, "I guess I should ask when and where."

Wilson actually smacked his forehead with his palm.

Then he said, "That was me smacking my forehead with my palm. It has been a long time."

Emily laughed.

"I understand. They do say all of this is like riding a bicycle."

"I was never good at that either. I crashed a lot as a kid."

He waited for her to laugh again, and she might have, quietly, but perhaps she was simply trying to be sensitive to the memory of an oddly coordinated child who was prone to running off curbs and into trees.

"I have tickets to a play at the university this Friday night. It's a Shakespeare play. *The Tempest*. It is supposed to be good—for a student production, that is."

"Wilson, that sounds wonderful."

"I have your address already—thanks to my mother. The play starts at seven. I guess I will pick you up at six-fifteen or so. Parking can be a problem."

"Six-fifteen on Friday. Got it. I'm looking forward to it."

When Wilson put the phone down, his hands were trembling, he was sweating profusely, his heart was pounding, and his breath came in shorter and shorter gulps.

He looked over at Thurman, who had watched the entire conversation, and who looked a little alarmed, if Wilson was reading his expression correctly.

"If I die from a heart attack right here, tell my mother it was all her fault. Okay, Thurman?"

And Thurman grinned and bounced and growled-whispered, *Okay. Okay. Okay.*

⟶

"Ms. Jamison?"

Pastor Coggins appeared to be shorter, older, and kinder than he did when he was on the platform on Sunday mornings.

Even when Hazel had been forced to shake hands and say hello, she did so in a hurry, not wanting to bother him, not wanting to be yet another congregant with some deep-seated emotional problem that required solving in the thirty seconds spent together in the narthex of the church.

"I recognize you. When you stand up front week after week, you get good with faces. And you can tell who's there and who isn't—within a couple of faces. You don't stick with one pew. You play pew roulette—avoiding handshakes at the end, right?"

Hazel hoped she wasn't blushing at being caught, but she knew she probably was.

"Don't worry, Ms. Jamison. A lot of people don't like me standing back there either. A third of them think they need to say, 'Nice sermon.' Another third want to fight with me about some scriptural interpretation that I missed. And the other third don't want to talk to me at all."

Hazel tried not to laugh, but she did as she agreed. "You're right."

Pastor Coggins gestured for her to come into his office.

"No. That's okay. I just wanted to say goodbye. I'm leaving the Portland area. And I wanted to drop something off with you. I don't want to interrupt your busy schedule."

He leaned a little closer to her. He smelled of Old Spice and coffee.

"Ms. Jamison, I'm stuck on point two of this week's message. Your interruption is a godsend, actually."

Hazel tried to think of something to say in reply, but nothing came to mind that wasn't sort of silly or awkward.

"So, then," he continued. "Where are you moving to?"

And again, Hazel was not sure of what to say. She had not formulated a concise answer to that question.

"Well, I'm going to be traveling for a while. And I'm not really sure where I'll stop."

Pastor Coggins's face warmed and his eyes seemed to be alive with compassion and understanding. Hazel realized how corny that sounded in her head, but that was how he looked.

Maybe I should tell him a bit more than that.

"You see, my mother passed away a little while ago . . ."

Pastor Coggins reached out and took her hand.

"I am so sorry to hear that. Did she ever come here to church with you? Had I ever met her?"

Hazel glanced into his office and he read the subtle sign.

"Please, let's sit for just a minute," he said.

He did not sit behind his desk, with a stack of open books piled in several mounds, but instead took the other guest chair in front of the desk.

"She was not a churchgoer, Pastor," Hazel began. "She never seemed to have any sympathy for it. I told her about it—faith and all that—but she sort of dismissed it. I mean, she listened to me. She said she understood. But when I'm being cynical, I think she was simply placating me. But maybe she did get it. Maybe."

Hazel felt the hint of tears and pushed them aside.

"She was kind of an old hippie...Mother Earth and nuts and berries and all you need is love, you know?"

The pastor nodded.

"I have a brother much like that. A free spirit, he claims, but he is the least free of any person I know, because he keeps having to find freedom again and again. Nothing stays. He's always searching."

Hazel nodded.

"But that's my story, not yours," he said.

Hazel wiped at her cheek, preventing the one tear that escaped from streaking down her face. "Then you understand."

The pastor did not say a word but waited for Hazel to speak, and then she did, and in a torrent she told him of her life and her mother's death and finding the stock and quitting her job and finding the picture of her mother's wedding when all these years she had been told that she had never married, and about Hazel's quiet...no, boring life at the insurance agency, and now that she had money, she was going to travel like her mother always wanted to and maybe find out more about the man in the wedding photo, and if she could do that, then maybe she would come back, or maybe she would just settle down wherever that happened to be and start over.

The pastor listened, his eyes not condemning or judging, but just listening, the hint of an understanding smile on his face.

"So I sold my condo—it closes tomorrow—and then I'm driving down the Pacific Coast Highway. I can't believe it is so close and I have never seen it."

Then Pastor Coggins did smile.

"You'll love the drive. It is beautiful."

And Hazel reached into her jacket and pulled out the envelope.

"I want to give this to you. In memory of my mother, I guess. She wouldn't have done it, but I want to do something for her. Maybe you could use it for those apartments you have for . . . is it . . . the homeless?"

"Low-income, actually."

"Yes, those."

He took the envelope and slipped his finger under the flap. Hazel hadn't expected that, but he would have found out soon enough.

His eyes widened when he saw the amount.

"Fifty thousand dollars is a very, very generous gift, Ms. Jamison. I'm almost speechless. And you never hear those words from a pastor."

"I want her money, some of it, to do some good. She loved this city. And she did have a heart for those who were down on their luck."

Pastor Coggins put the envelope on his desk.

"You're sure she wasn't a believer?"

"I told her about church...and the Bible. She was kind and didn't disagree, but I think she didn't really want to hear. I don't think she wanted to change."

The pastor let silence fill the room. Hazel took a few deep breaths.

"I've taken up enough of your time, Pastor Coggins. I should go."

He reached out and put his hand on her forearm, gently holding her back.

"You seem unsettled. If there is anything I'm good at, it's spotting an unsettled soul. Probably because I recognize my past self in that condition."

Hazel looked on the verge of being lost, a little lost—not completely, but a little.

"Maybe. I don't know if leaving everything and being a gypsy is the...you know, the 'Christian' thing to do."

"You want me to pray with you?" the pastor asked.

"Really? But I'm not a member here or anything."

Pastor Coggins put his other hand on Hazel's other arm, holding her.

"Do you know God? Do you know Jesus?"

It was obvious that Hazel was scared, scared of being asked that question, those questions.

"I do. I do. But maybe...maybe not as well as I should."

Pastor Coggins waited and then spoke, carefully, softly, and slowly.

"While you search, continue to search for Jesus. He knows you're looking. Keep searching. Keep praying. You'll find the truth."

"I will. I really will. Pray, I mean."

And then Pastor Coggins began to pray, about safety, about traveling mercies, about blessings...and many other things, of that Hazel was certain, but by the time she reached the church door, she could not remember a single word.

Yet she felt totally light and free and clean and hopeful, for the first time in a long time, perhaps ever. Hopeful.

That is such a wonderful word. Hopeful.

And as she opened the massive front door of the church, the pastor handed her a Bible.

"My name and cell phone number are written in the front. Anytime, day or night, call me if you have a question. I mean that."

Hazel turned and gave him a quick hug, then hurried down the steps to her Quest and then on to her two-room suite at the Embassy Suites, thinking about the hotel's complimentary chocolate chip cookies.

Chapter Seventeen

WILSON LEFT his house earlier than required and drove around Emily's block, past her house four times, taking some solace in the fact that Emily did not yet know his car and would not think him odd, or slightly deranged, for arriving seventeen minutes early for their "date."

"People my age don't date," he'd explained to Thurman as he'd dressed that evening. Thurman had sat in his bedroom, watching intently, smiling, as he'd put on a light blue shirt and debated over wearing a tie.

"People my age 'see' people. We have dinner. We don't date. Dating is for teenagers."

He'd held two ties up for Thurman to look at. Thurman had sniffed at each, then had shaken his head, perhaps trying to say no, or perhaps shaking some manner of lint from his sensitive nose.

Wilson had taken it as a no and had decided on just wearing a blue sports coat instead.

"Dressy, but not in an overcompensating way, right, Thurman?"

Thurman had looked as if he wanted to shrug again and was trying to figure out a way to do that, given his canine physiology.

Now in front of her house only a few miles from his own, Wilson pulled to the curb, finally, and switched off the engine. He took several deep breaths. He knew he couldn't just sit in the car until his nerves quieted down. That might take hours, or days, and he did not have hours, let alone days.

"Why did I agree to this?" he said aloud as he exited the car and walked up to the house.

The porch lights were on, and he could see a blue glow from inside; someone was watching TV. He could hear the pleasant chatter . . .

"A sitcom," he decided, "and not the news."

He did not see a doorbell, so he rapped at the door three times, trying not to sound insistent or aggressive.

The door swung open almost immediately, as if someone was waiting within arm's reach.

Emily stood in the doorway, wearing a . . . Wilson was not sure what it was, exactly, but a dress of some sort, with long sleeves, and a regular neckline, if women's dresses could be described as having a "regular" neckline.

Wilson had been a solitary creature for a long time, with not much of a feminine influence on his existence, or human influence, for that matter.

"Hi. I'm ready."

Wilson found himself nodding and thinking that he shouldn't be.

"Okay, then. We can go, right?" he said, unsure of doorway protocol among adults who weren't really on a "date."

Emily, who Wilson thought would be calm and composed about all of this "dating" or "seeing" someone, appeared to him to be as nervous as he was—perhaps even more so. She put her hand on the doorknob, turned, and, facing inside, called out, "I'm leaving now. Please lock the door."

She turned back to him, smiled, and pulled the door shut.

Wilson had no idea if she was supposed to take his arm going down the walk or if they should walk side by side, or if he should lead the way, just in case of Indian attack or the threat of being set upon by highwaymen.

Emily solved his quandary by slipping her hand into the crook of his arm as they headed to his car.

When they got to the car, which was not all that distant, Wilson pulled out his keys and unlocked her door.

"I have to tell you, Emily . . ." he said.

"Yes?" she replied, as if wanting to not be accused of not upholding her end of their conversation.

" . . . I am so far out of practice being with someone . . . anyone . . . that I'm going to apologize right now for any social blunders I make this evening."

Emily smiled in reply, then reached out and put her hand on his forearm.

"I'll forgive you if you forgive me. It has been a very long time. And regardless of what they say, it is not like riding a bicycle."

"No. It is not. It is definitely not."

⌒

Hazel took a single canvas duffel bag, a small one, with her into the Embassy Suites.

If I always had access to a washing machine, I could get by with only a satchel. It's boring wearing the same clothes all the time, but it would solve a lot of what-to-wear problems.

She placed her bag at the foot of the bed.

Not that I really worry that much about what I'm wearing.
She looked out the window over downtown Portland.
Am I going to miss anything . . . or anyone here?
Growing up, she had friends. Not a lot of friends, but friends. After high school, some of them moved, some of them married and moved, some of them stayed and grew distant. They stayed in touch, sort of, on Facebook. She liked some of the people she worked with . . . well, a few of them. But she would place none of them into the "good friend" category.

Maybe it's because I never had a father.
Some of her high school friends came from "broken" homes, as they called them back then, and they seemed normal.

Maybe it's because my mother was sort of strange.
A few of her high school friends had mothers or fathers who were strange individually, or together, so that wasn't it either.

Maybe it's because I felt as if I never really belonged.
She took one of the chocolate chip cookies off the nightstand and sat on the edge of the bed, thinking about Pastor Coggins's prayer and the start of her life after Portland.

Plays are good, because you don't have to talk.
During the single intermission, most of the time was taken up by Wilson struggling through the crowd to get a drink for both of them, all the while thinking of what he might say after the play was over and they were once again alone.

The thought of normal conversation unnerved him.

Why am I doing this? She doesn't want to be here. Does she? And if she does, what does that say about her?

The house lights came up, the cast took their multiple bows, and the applause ebbed and slowed and stopped. Emily and Wilson stood and slowly shuffled their way out of the theater building and back onto the street into a mild, nearly warm late spring evening.

"Did you enjoy it?" he asked, thinking that was one of the more innocuous questions he could ask, or should ask, following a performance.

"It was good. It has been a while since I have been at a play, let alone a Shakespeare play. The language is so poetic, I guess. You have to develop an ear for it."

Wilson nodded. He did not like old plays, plays hundreds of years old, because no one talked that way and the impact and import of the dialogue—much of it at any rate—was lost on contemporary audiences. Even though he had studied Elizabethan literature in college, it had never been a field that he enjoyed.

"They were all so earnest about it," he said.

"Youth, right?"

Wilson nodded. "The bane of every old cynic."

She laughed, not a lot, but politely, as if she was not exactly sure of what response was expected, so a laugh was a safe reply.

"Would you like to get something to eat? It's not that late, is it? Or do you have to get back...you know. I mean, are people waiting up for you?"

Wilson knew she had children, of course. He did not

know ages or the requirements of babysitting relief times, or expenses, or any of that, but he did want to be sensitive.

She looked at her watch, then held it closer.

"Women's watches are too small for anyone to read," she said, trying to catch the watch face in the light of a streetlamp.

Wilson slipped out his cell phone and tapped at it.

"Nine forty-eight."

"Thanks."

She looked over at him, as if she was making a decision of some import.

"No. I mean, yes. Something to eat would be fine. I said late. They'll be okay."

Wilson navigated them back toward his car, which he had parked in the faculty parking lot nearby.

One of the few privileges of a tenured professor. Glad there was an open spot.

He opened her car door and she slid in.

This is going okay, he thought as he hurried around to the other side.

But where do I go from here? I should have planned ahead.

He started the engine.

"Any place you have in mind?"

She turned to him. The streetlight lit her face in silhouette.

A classic profile.

"No. Not really, Wilson. I . . . it has been so long since I've been to anyplace that doesn't focus on hamburgers or pizza. Teenagers have a very narrow dietary range. I am afraid I don't really know any . . . adult sort of restaurants. There were a few . . . from before . . . you know. But that was a long time ago."

Wilson did not put the car in gear. He was not one to drive about aimlessly. Aimless made him anxious. It reminded him too much of . . . other times.

He turned to her, a half-turn.

"How old are your . . . kids? Is it okay to say 'kids'? Or is it 'children'?"

" 'Kids' is fine. Are fine. Whatever. I guess I should be careful when talking to an English professor. But . . . there are three. The oldest is twenty-two and a senior now at Penn. Business major. Whip-smart. Like his dad."

Her voice caught, just a little.

"The next, Audrey, is nineteen. She is between colleges, she tells people. Went to Pitt for a year and didn't 'find' herself. She's applied to several others. And to nursing school. And the youngest is Sam. He's fifteen. Still in high school. And a champ at nihilism and eye-rolling."

She appeared to catch herself.

"Is this too much? I don't know anymore. What's the limit on sharing? Too much?"

"No. It's not."

They both looked away from each other, looking forward, out into the darkness.

"And I have Thurman, who will be waiting up for me and will expect a full report on this evening."

Emily grinned, and she put her hand on Wilson's arm again.

"Pick a place, Wilson. It won't matter where. The kids are fine at home. They have my cell phone in case the place catches on fire. I just want to forget for a little while."

Wilson nodded and put the car in gear, then headed out of the lot and away from the theater.

⸺

At that moment, Thurman was pacing back and forth between the back door and the front door, with stops at the stairs and the big window in the front of the house with the soft thing in front. To this point in their living arrangement, Wilson had never been gone from daylight to when it got dark, and it was obvious that Thurman was concerned. There were no lights left on in the house—not that Thurman needed lights to see his way about. There was the streetlight down the block that provided more than enough illumination for him to avoid running into things. And there was the little light that was always on by the box that got hot and where food came out. But that was always on. Thurman looked upstairs to the darkened second floor, perhaps thinking that Wilson should have left lights on for him, since the sun was down and he was here all by himself.

But there were no lights. And there was no food left. Thurman had eaten when Wilson left, but that was a long time ago, and much before he normally ate dinner, and now he wondered if that had not been an early half-dinner like he thought, but his entire evening meal, which if it were true would have disappointed him greatly.

He climbed up onto the soft thing by the front window and stared out. Cars drove past on the street—they always did that—but not one of them stopped and not one of them contained Wilson.

Then Thurman brightened a little.

Wilson had told him something before he left...something important.

Then Thurman smiled, and he placed his chin on the back of the soft thing by the window, so he could keep a watchful eye out for Wilson.

He softly whisper-growled to himself, *Emily*.

⌒

Gretna sat in the rocking chair near her television set and rocked slowly back and forth in a steady rhythm, nearly matching the pace of her breathing. She did not sit in that chair often. "Rockers are for old people," she had once explained. "A rocking chair makes them think they are being active."

The TV was on and muted, as usual. Some manner of police investigation show was on, the lead characters peering into microscopes and holding fuzz-filled tweezers up to the light.

Gretna disliked those shows.

"Nobody is that smart. Especially policemen."

Gretna had developed a distrust of virtually all manner of authority figures over the years.

She had been unsettled all evening.

Of course, she knew that Wilson and Emily were out together this evening, but "not on a date," her son had explained.

"I know what it is, even if they're not calling it a date," Gretna said to herself. "I don't see the need to hide from the truth."

Then she stopped rocking and began to worry, just a little. She closed her eyes.

"I know hiding from the truth. And so does Wilson."

She rocked, then planted her feet on the ground and stopped.

"But Thurman doesn't lie. He doesn't hide from the truth. Does he?"

And she sat there for a long time, worrying about Wilson and his ability to face the truth, and was not willing herself to face certain truths as well.

"And I don't want to bother God with this. Since I've already asked him so many times. He doesn't want to hear me complain about it anymore."

She started rocking again.

Then she stopped to smile, if only to herself.

"And that's why he sent Thurman to us."

⌐

Thurman spent five minutes totally apoplectic upon Wilson's arrival back home, unable to curb his enthusiasm long enough to go outside to complete his necessary evening constitutional.

Wilson waited at the back door, the door half-open, Thurman bouncing and wiggling and yipping and nudging his head against his legs.

After a long, forced bout of remaining patient, Wilson pretended to close the door. Still, Thurman bounded about.

"I am not going to tell you a word about Emily until you go outside, Thurman."

At that, Thurman snorted, appeared to take in a deep breath, and pulled himself together—at least together enough to run outside in a rush. He spent only a moment or two out there, not worried, for once, about locating the perfect spot and attempting to determine who else had visited the yard in the past few hours, a process that could take upwards of twenty minutes, on a good night.

A very cursory run around the perimeter of the yard was all Thurman required that night, and then he was back inside, bounding and half-jumping again. His half-jumps were characterized by him pushing off with his front paws, and he would balance a moment on his back legs, even taking a few steps. He looked like a semi-inebriated amateur stilt-walker, if there was such a character, teetering on two uncertain legs that were not accustomed to bearing the full weight and balance of an adult canine.

Wilson took off his sports coat and carefully placed it over the back of a kitchen chair. Then he switched on the electric kettle and found the jar of instant coffee in the pantry. He considered using the pod coffeemaker, but it took too long to warm up and he really wanted a third cup of coffee that evening, this one at home, in addition to the two he'd had at the restaurant.

Thurman snorked at his empty food dish while Wilson puttered about getting a spoon and cup.

"No more food, Thurman. You ate. Early, but you ate."

Thurman growled, *Bunkum.*

That appeared to be one of his favorite words.

Wilson measured out the coffee, water, cream, and sugar and stirred it, standing next to the sink. Then he sat down at the chair closest to the counter.

Thurman stared at him, a most curious look on his face.

Move, the dog growled.

"Thurman, I can sit at any chair in the kitchen. Just because I always sit over there, that doesn't mean I can't sit here on occasion."

Thurman growled *Bunkum* again, then readjusted his spot so he had a clear look at Wilson's face. Then he grinned and waited.

"You really want to hear about tonight?"

Thurman wagged his head up and down.

"Before I begin, I simply want to say that this is ridiculous—me thinking you want me to talk to you. Like you understand."

Thurman appeared at first confused, then hurt.

"But it seems to help, Thurman. I mean, it seems to help me. To talk about things. Talking out loud is different than just thinking. The words feel different when you say them out loud. The meanings change when you add sound to thoughts. And emotion. Thoughts stay relatively unemotional. At least in my head, they do. So . . . that's why I'm talking to you. Not because you are some super-sentient dog creature that really understands."

Bunkum.

"Well, regardless. Or as most of my students say, irregardless."

Thurman smiled and waited.

"The play was fine . . . for Shakespeare. Never liked any of them. His plays, I mean. Pretentious, now. And a little elitist, if you ask me. The play was written for the masses, but now only the educated get him, the Bard. Or over-educated, I would say. But it was tolerable. They cut a lot out. Otherwise we would still be there. The actors were most energetic."

Thurman nodded, attempting to appear sage and wise, but Wilson knew that he had no idea of what a play was, let alone a Shakespearean play.

He sipped at his coffee.

Thurman growled, some nonsense growl, as if he was impatient for the story to go on.

"She said she enjoyed it. Emily. I think she did. And then we went to the Elbow Room for food."

Thurman perked up at the word "food."

"No, I did not bring any home with me, Thurman. And besides, we just had a few appetizers. No bones in anything."

Wilson turned and looked out the window for a moment.

"Now I remember why I sit over there. So I don't have a window at my back. Bad luck... but you don't know about bad luck, do you, Thurman. Bad luck and death and stray bullets and a split second between being alive and being not alive."

Wilson stopped talking and closed his eyes for a long moment. Thurman sat, silent and still, and let the memory happen, and almost overtake Wilson. Wilson opened his eyes, a faraway, lost look in them for a second or two. Then he looked over to Thurman with a fading smile.

"I haven't thought of all this in... well, decades now. Having my back to an open window. In the dark."

Thurman did not grow impatient. He just sat and listened.

The kitchen grew quiet, save for the rhythmic hum of the refrigerator.

"He killed himself."

Thurman looked up. His eyes appeared to comprehend the words, a sad look edging onto Thurman's usually happy face.

"Emily's husband. He killed himself. After he got back."

Thurman stood and walked to Wilson and put his head against his leg, then rested his chin just above his knee, his eyes focused on Wilson's face.

"She didn't say a lot more than that. I didn't ask. I said I understood—as much as anyone can, really. She nodded at that, and it looked like she was trying not to cry."

Thurman rose up and placed his front paws on Wilson's thighs.

"I know, Thurman. No one can really know what that is like. And I don't. But then...well, I do. I know. How close it can come. How hard it is. To never feel normal again. To know that you will never find 'normal' again. That's paralyzing, Thurman. You're always different. Broken. But no one can see. And no one can help."

Wilson took a deep breath.

"Don't you see, Thurman? The fact that it's me...and her...that fact...that death, his death, will always be right in front of us. Because it's me and not someone else who never knew what all that is like firsthand. How could it not be? With what I saw and did and lived through. She would look at me and there would be a reflection of her dead husband in that. I could tell that she saw that in my eyes. What happened to me...back then. I didn't want her to see that, but she did. I know that she did."

He put his hand on Thurman's head.

"I don't think I can do that to her, Thurman. I don't think

I can do it to myself. I don't want to remember. It took too long to bury it all."

He stood up and left the half-filled coffee cup on the table and walked toward the stairs.

"I just can't do it, Thurman. I can't."

Chapter Eighteen

H AZEL TRAVELED west until she reached the ocean.

She loved the ocean, even in Oregon, where the seawater was only a step above frigid and the skies blustery most of the time and no one went swimming unless they were from Canada or wore a wetsuit.

She had vacationed there several times, in little hotels along the coast. The towns were small, the restaurants few, and the crowds minimal.

She considered it all so perfect.

And with the ocean in front of her, the sharp tang of salt and the scent of seaweed filling the car, she turned left, heading south, and would drive with the expanse of water on her right shoulder the whole way to California.

And with each mile she drove, with each mile more distant from Portland, she grew lighter, she felt more at ease. Leaving the town of her birth had not felt traumatic, not at all. Nor would it in the future, she imagined. She felt a momentary tug over leaving her mother's grave, but told herself quickly that her mother was not there, and there was no one to judge her for not visiting the cemetery a prescribed number of times.

"No one will miss me," she said aloud as she drove through Waldport on the coast.

"Well, maybe there are a few people, but I can stay in

touch with Facebook," she said aloud as she drove through Coos Bay.

She stopped at Sharkbites Café for lunch and ate three fish tacos while staring out at the main street that ran through the small town. There was chatter and conversation all about her, and she didn't listen to any of it. She simply let the voices and the words and the laughter and the clatter of dishes and silverware flow over her, like a noise rainfall, not letting any of it penetrate, not hearing any specific word.

She felt immune, for that moment, from being connected.

As a child, and as a young woman, she often was at the edge of things, at the edge of a group, at the edge of a lunchtime gaggle of girls, at the edge of a school dance—not in the shadows, exactly, but not in the spotlight either.

And when that had happened in the past, standing alone on the fringe of something, there was a part of her that yearned to be closer to the circle, to be inside the circle, but that was not usually the case, or it happened very infrequently. And years ago she had given up on wanting that inclusion. It was not hard. She did not suffer because of it.

Being alone is not the same as being lonely.

And now today she had deliberately placed herself adrift, floating free, much like a lost buoy would drift in the ocean, unanchored, letting the water carry her, not worried about where the end might be, where the final safe haven would be—or even if there was a safe harbor at the edge of the horizon.

It doesn't matter now. I'm free.

Hazel smiled at the thought of the lost buoy. There was a small snug of a bittersweet feeling as well, but all of it, all her former unhappiness, her former feelings of estrangement, her sense of being alone . . . had vanished.

No, not vanished, she thought. *But gone. I let them go. And they're gone. And I feel . . .*

She paid her bill, left a generous tip, and walked out into a sunny afternoon, squinting and smiling.

I feel reborn.

And she walked down the street to her Quest . . .

I love that name.

. . . and started the engine, and headed south, toward golden California and then to the heat and the sand and the clarity of the desert city of Phoenix.

A phoenix gets reborn, she thought. *And maybe that's what will happen there.*

She drove on, and after a few minutes a less pleasant thought came to mind.

But don't phoenixes have to crash and burn before being reborn?

She felt a chill.

I should have read more Roman mythology . . . way back then.

Or was it Greek?

⟶

Gretna watched three weather reports on three different television channels, each relaying the same basic facts: warm temperatures and no chance of rain. She looked out her window several times and decided that for once, those overpaid script readers had been telling the truth.

She did not want to get caught in the rain.

She laced up her running shoes.

"They're running shoes?" she'd exclaimed when she bought them at the Payless shoe store across the river. Wilson had taken her there for the express purpose of finding a pair of cheap shoes. "I'm not planning on running," she had sputtered, trying to unlace them.

The clerk had convinced her after several minutes that walking, not just running, in the shoes would be perfectly fine.

"Lots of people buy running shoes," she said, "and they never run anywhere."

Gretna had eyed the short salesperson sporting a nose ring with head-tilting suspicion.

"Why don't they call them walking shoes, then?" she asked.

The clerk smiled wearily. "We have lots of walking shoes, but all of them are more expensive. I don't know why," she added preemptively.

So Gretna wore a pair of semi-high-tech running shoes anytime she went for a longer walk.

Today she had a long walk planned.

And had even called in advance of her journey, to make sure people would be where they were supposed to be when she got there . . . or rather, the person would be there.

She knew the way. After all, she had lived in this neighborhood all of her life, save for the few years spent in that horrific, blisteringly hot place—Florida.

"Pardon my French," Gretna would sometimes add if she used harsher words when describing her exodus into the apparent retirement capital of the universe. "Never should have moved. Should have come back right away. Learned my lesson."

Despite having grown up here, she looked at the local map she kept in a desk drawer. She wore her glasses and traced her route with a finger, naming each street that she would take to get there.

Other residents of the retirement complex had gotten lost walking around the block, completely baffled by how to get back to where they came from. Gretna did not want to become one of those enfeebled seniors who appeared confused over simple matters like directions.

She set off with a determined lift in her steps, estimating that the walk there would take perhaps twenty minutes, maybe less.

It took seventeen minutes.

She timed it so she could estimate the return trip.

Probably take ten minutes longer. Gas in the tank will be lower then.

She saw him before he saw her.

His eyesight is probably going as well as everything else.

She waved from half a block away and he did not respond.

She waited until she was at the bottom of the drive. Then she called out, in a gentle, welcoming voice.

"Pastor Killeen."

His head bobbed up and he leaned forward, lifting himself slightly, painfully, from the cradle of his wheelchair.

"Gretna, is that you?"

She walked up to him and took his hand.

"It is. It's been a while."

The old man nodded.

"I saw you with Thurman...When was that?"

"Over a month ago. Maybe longer."

Pastor Killeen nodded again.

"And how is Thurman? And Wilson, of course."

"They are both fine," Gretna replied. "Thurman is doing better than Wilson, by the looks of things. But you probably guessed that."

She grabbed a lawn chair that was leaning against the corner of the house and unfolded it, the legs screeching out a rusty complaint. The webbing appeared sturdy enough, but Gretna sat down carefully, making sure that she would not be deposited on the asphalt in an undignified heap.

"Dogs have the edge on humans, Gretna. They seem only to have the present—that is, the only thing they truly know is right now. Whatever happened to them in the past, painful or happy, doesn't follow them about like a boomerang, or as if some cloud of past mistakes hovers over us, always threatening to drench us in cold reality."

Gretna smiled.

"Hey, that's good, Pastor Killeen. You should write that down. Write a book or something."

"Thanks. But, no. My days of thinking that I can write a book have faded. Nowadays, if I can get one good idea out, I'm doing well."

She laughed.

I think he meant that to be funny. Didn't he? It didn't sound like a complaint. But then, I was never that good at reading these religious people.

They sat together in the warm sunlight, Pastor Killeen turning his face to the sun as if trying to absorb as much warmth as he could. Gretna sat and thought about her reason for being there today.

She finally broke the silence.

"I know I was not the best churchgoer," she said, her tone as much explanatory as apologetic.

Pastor Killeen shrugged. It appeared that it took him some effort to do that—at least to make the shrug an obvious gesture and not simply a slight roll of his shoulder.

"I was cranky," Gretna added.

"Faith comes in all sorts of packages, Gretna. I never minded different behaviors in people who came to church. At least they were there and could hear the truth."

Gretna scowled at his insinuation that she was a "package," but let it go.

"You're here on a mission, right? You have an issue, don't you?" Pastor Killeen asked, an empathetic tone to his question.

Gretna snorted. "Don't psychoanalyze me, you old goat. I'm not the problem."

She tried to add a laugh at the end, as if she was pretending to bluster—which she wasn't—hoping it would be enough to mollify any umbrage that Pastor Killeen might have dredged up over her former criticisms, now years and years old.

"Okay, Gretna. I'm old enough to know what battles to pick. It's not you. Then who?"

She looked at him, then away, then stared at the black asphalt.

"It's Wilson."

Pastor Killeen waited.

"I'm worried about him."

Pastor Killeen waited.

"He's damaged."

Pastor Killeen waited.

"Is he too damaged?"

Then Pastor Killeen spoke. His tone was soft, understanding, yet solid, as if this was not his first time dealing with people who had suffered and could not or would not let that suffering go, would not release the pain. Or could not.

"Has he talked about it? With you? Or with anyone?"

"No."

Pastor Killeen waited.

"He talks to Thurman. That's what Thurman said. Or was trying to tell me. I think. Something about the past. I'm sure. Maybe Thurman isn't sure what war means. Dogs, even a dog like Thurman, do not understand everything, do they?"

If Pastor Killeen thought it odd, or peculiar, or alarming that Gretna had been in conversation with a dog, he made no mention of it.

"When did he come back . . . Wilson, I mean? How old was he when he returned?"

"Twenty-four."

Pastor Killeen took a deep breath.

"I was there too, Gretna."

She turned to him, obviously surprised.

"Where? You?"

"I was a chaplain in the Army. For eight years. I did three tours in Vietnam."

She looked into his face, trying to see into his eyes, now a little cloudy, a little less penetrating than they had been when he stood in the pulpit.

"So you know? I mean, you understand?"

Pastor Killeen shrugged again.

"Maybe. No one really knows what another human goes through. Some soldiers can do things and simply box them up and never think on them again. Others can't. So they find ways to cope. By not getting close to anyone. By hiding behind alcohol or some other substance to self-medicate. By blaming others. No one likes pain. No one enjoys terror. Or horror."

Gretna shook her head.

"Wilson doesn't blame anyone, I'm pretty sure of that. And he doesn't drink, more than a glass or two, once in a while, if that. In the beginning, maybe then. But that was a long time ago. Maybe he doesn't drink at all anymore."

Pastor Killeen waited.

"But he is alone," Gretna said, her voice now small and mouselike.

Pastor Killeen waited.

"He came back damaged," she said. "I didn't know what to do. Then he went to school and became a professor and everything seemed fine. That's what I told myself."

Pastor Killeen waited.

"But maybe it wasn't."

Pastor Killeen nodded.

"Gretna, war is a terrible thing. Terrible. Horrific. Seeing people cut in two by bullets. Or firing those bullets that cut people in half. It squeezes on your soul. It is hard, Gretna. It is very hard."

Gretna sniffed. She might have been fighting back a tear. She was not a woman who shed tears freely, or easily, or often.

"Is he too badly damaged? I don't have that much time left," she said, her hands open to the sun. "I want him to be normal."

"I know, Gretna. I know."

She waited a long moment, anticipating.

"Do you ask God about this?" Pastor Killeen asked.

"No. Well, I did. Back then. A lot. And nothing happened. So I stopped asking. I figured that maybe he's broken, Wilson, I mean . . . and that maybe God was okay with that."

Pastor Killeen reached out and took Gretna's hand.

"Start praying again. God does not want that. Ask him again."

She waited.

"Can I ask Thurman to help him too?"

Pastor Killeen did not hesitate.

"You can, Gretna. And you should. Where one or two of us are gathered . . ."

She smiled back at him, a wan, weak, hopeful but not totally hopeful smile.

"He's a good boy."

Chapter Nineteen

W HY DID I never take this trip before?" Hazel said aloud. "The scenery on this road has been absolutely breathtaking."

Hazel, in her Quest, was just north of Crescent City, California.

A drive that could have taken four hours and change was taking double that time. She kept stopping and pulling to the side of the road and staring out at the ocean, watching the waves and the gulls and the clouds and the sun glistering off the water. By the time she arrived in California, the sun had set, and Hazel never liked driving after dark on roads she did not know. She found a modest, unstylish motel almost on the beach . . . well, it had a road between it and the water, but still.

She fell asleep to the sound of a foghorn sounding occasionally and woke to the same foghorn sounding almost incessantly. She opened the drapes in her room to look out and saw nothing, nothing at all—except a cocoon of white. Fog enveloped the hotel, and perhaps much of that section of the California coast.

Hazel prepared for the day, then walked down to the breakfast area, poured a cup of coffee, and joined two other hotel guests who were intently staring out the front doors of the motel, staring at the white nothingness that surrounded them all, everything gone from view except within a few

yards' radius of a person. Beyond that, it was as if an indi-
vidual simply walked through some manner of a space-time
portal to be transported to another dimension.

"They say it'll burn off by noon," one man said. If Hazel
had to guess, he went with the semi truck and trailer that she
had noticed in the farthest part of the parking lot when she
arrived. She looked over to that area and saw nothing.

Maybe it's gone. Vaporized. Teleported, perhaps. Can they
teleport big trucks?

"I hope so," the other guest said, a middle-aged man in a
crisp white shirt that was too snug on his belly and a sports
coat with sleeves an inch short. "I need to be in San Fran by
tonight."

Hazel had read somewhere that no one who lives in San
Francisco ever calls their town "San Fran." So she assumed
that he was some sort of traveling salesman who was not
from there. And she surprised herself for not feeling sympathetic to his plight.

It's beautiful out there. And here. In the white. And all he
sees is an inconvenience.

The truck driver nodded to Hazel.

"Which way you headed, miss?"

Miss? Well that's nice...I guess.

"South," she replied. "I have to be in Phoenix eventually...
but I'm not on any schedule."

The truck driver nodded again.

"Nice not having a schedule."

"It is," Hazel replied. "It's only been a few days, but I'm
getting used to it."

"Vacation?" the traveling salesman asked.

"Something like that," Hazel replied, and then wondered if being semi-mysterious and enigmatic about what she was doing was fair to others.

It might not be. But I have never been mysterious and enigmatic in my life. Feels good, in an odd way.

"I have seven more years until I stop driving," the truck driver said. "After that, I'm never driving anywhere ever again. I'm buying a condo somewhere that is within walking distance of everything. And if there's a place I can't walk to, then I ain't going there."

Hazel wanted to say, "Amen, brother," but didn't. She smiled instead and said, "I hear you."

The traveling salesman was having none of it.

"At least the Wi-Fi here is fast. I gotta send some emails. Let people know I'm going to be late. You know, places to go, people to see."

And with that he took his paper cup of coffee and trundled off back toward his room, apparently.

The truck driver and Hazel stared at the whiteness, and watched as it billowed and sailed in and around itself, like milk coursing with milk, like smoke mixing with smoke, where all is hidden, nothing remains, and everything has disappeared from sight.

Hazel thought it an apt analogy to her life.

What will I see when the fog clears?

"Pretty, ain't it? If it wasn't such a pain in the butt, that is," the truck driver said.

"You're right about that."

Coming out of the fog . . . is like being reborn, reborn out of blindness.

Hazel smiled at the whiteness.

I should write that down. I'll never remember it if I don't.

And even as she made her way to the front desk to ask for a pen and paper, the words were already slipping away, being rearranged, much like life itself.

That's good too.

Thurman followed Wilson around the house over the next few days, growling, almost to himself, as if offering a commentary on Wilson and his behavior, all the while speaking in a more arcane canine language that Wilson was not privy to.

Wilson often stopped, midstep, as it were, and stared at the grumbling-to-himself Thurman, asking sharply and pointedly, "What?"

Thurman would then respond by looking up with his curious face, as if asking, *Whatever do you mean? I didn't say anything*.

Wilson knew better. He figured that Thurman was making some sort of snide comment but keeping it to himself.

The afternoon sun on this day was bright, but little sunlight reached the kitchen, since it faced the east. Reflected sunlight off the pool in back danced on the kitchen ceiling, an ever-widening trapezoid of shadows and light. Wilson often saw Thurman staring up at the mirrored show, as if trying to determine the source of such animation.

He was certain that dogs, even Thurman, did not understand the physics of sunlight glistening off the surface of a liquid.

Thurman looked up when Wilson entered the kitchen.

Thurman smiled and growled, *Swim?*

It struck Wilson as a reasonable request, for once. Thurman often asked, and up until now Wilson had always said no. Thurman's requests had grown less frequent, but they did not stop altogether.

Anything to keep him from muttering to himself.

So Wilson smiled back.

"Sure. You can go for a swim, Thurman. If you really want to."

Thurman appeared astonished, and it took him several seconds for the positive reply to be made manifest in a wiggling, dancing, smiling dog. He shimmied all the way to the back door, and when Wilson opened it he hesitated another moment.

Swim? he growled again.

"Go ahead, Thurman. I said it was okay. It's a hot day."

With that second reassurance, Thurman raced toward the water and again leaped into the air, sailing with grinning abandon through the void and coming down with a furry, explosive splash. Once his head bobbed to the surface, he set off, paddling away, to the far end of the pool and then back again. He had made two entire circuits of the long reflecting pool by the time Wilson came out and stood at the shallow end, closest to the house.

Wilson watched as the dog so thoroughly enjoyed the experience, as if this was the pinnacle of all canine pleasures, or at least the apex of all retriever pleasures. Wilson took a deep breath and let it out slowly. Then he slipped off his shoes, reached down with a groan, and pulled off his socks.

He hitched up the bottoms of his trousers and sat at the edge of the pool, lowering his feet and calves into the tepid water.

Thurman neared the shallow end, where he could stand on the bottom, with the water level at midchest. He stopped and stared incredulously, like a bird stares at a snake, readying to strike.

You wet, he growled.

Wilson tilted his head, more amused than anything. "I'm allowed to do this, Thurman. It's my house. And I built this pool."

Thurman grinned and turned and paddled back to the far end, splashing as much as he could, reveling under the fountain that pumped out in a gentle arc. When he turned back, he was still smiling.

And Thurman had stopped muttering.

For that, Wilson was eminently grateful.

Thurman paddled about, doing four more complete laps, climbing out and diving back in three times, shaking and re-shaking himself, creating a rainbow of water droplets each time. He lolled into the water, falling in sideways, now breathing a bit more deeply than usual, then paddled back to the shallow end, where he could stand, and instead of standing, he sat down, just his head, neck, and a portion of his shoulders out of the water. He bobbed a bit, as if his natural buoyancy kept him from being more firmly planted on the slate bottom. If that were the case, it did not appear as if he minded the slight, watery rocking one bit.

He looked up at Wilson, his tongue out, a huge smile plastered under his wet fur.

Good water, he growled.

Wilson nodded.

"It is good. I don't think I have ever sat here like this. I mean, with my feet in the water. I sat on the back steps a lot and watched the water. But I don't think I ever felt it."

Good wet. I like wet, Thurman growled.

Wilson nodded in agreement.

Thurman's smile slowly evaporated, replaced by a more serene look, then his face morphed into one of concern, if Wilson was to guess the changeable expressions of a dog.

You should talk, Thurman finally said.

Wilson closed his eyes for a long moment, knowing that this was a discussion he was having with himself, between two fractured facets of his own personality, and that Thurman, as a dog, was not speaking but merely growling in an odd way that Wilson chose to interpret as real words with real meaning.

He knew all that.

He reminded himself of that fact every time Thurman spoke.

And yet...and yet Thurman spoke sometimes—not always, though—in a way that Wilson would never speak, on subjects that Wilson would never discuss, even with himself. He would never say to himself...that is, one part of Wilson would never say to another part of Wilson that he "should talk."

That's what threw Wilson, that's what perplexed and confounded him.

He didn't want to talk. He never wanted to talk. None of him, not any of the parts of him, ever wanted to talk. Not now. Not ever.

Thurman did not act like a part of Wilson. He didn't. Thurman was not merely a Wilson-formed projection, a carefully arranged figment of Wilson's overwrought psyche.

That's what confused Wilson. That's why he carried on these conversations with Thurman.

Because under all the layers of his degrees and schooling and trappings of academia and sophistication, he thought, at least at times, that Thurman was actually and really talking.

And Wilson did not want to take the chance that all of this was simply a figment of his imagination or the outgrowth of a decades-old psychosis or trauma or a severe, long-term manifestation of some horrible, long-buried post-traumatic stress disorder, a condition that he thought mostly contrived.

And what's the harm, really?

"Talk about what?" Wilson replied, opening his eyes and squinting into the afternoon sun.

Past things, Thurman growled.

Wilson thought about it.

"Why?"

That appeared to take Thurman by surprise, a little. He blinked several times, but maybe he was simply blinking at drops of water falling from his waterlogged eyebrows.

Then become human.

Wilson thought he had him.

"Why? I'm already human."

Thurman shook his head slowly.

Bunkum, he snorted. Then he went on. *Broken. Past broken. Not human now. Not all human. Part human.*

Wilson felt close to peace, at least at the moment. The sun felt good on his face. For once, sunlight glinting off the water did not tighten up his chest, reminding him of afternoon patrols, flying low over the Mekong River. For once warm water did not remind him of the bathwater-warm swampland. For once, water was just water again, and sunlight was just sunlight.

"Why? What do you know about being human?"

Thurman did not look upset or angry or hurt. He stared back, unflinching.

Dogs are dogs, he growled. *I good at dog. You not good at human.*

Wilson waited.

Dogs do not hide, Thurman said. *Be human. Unhide.*

For a long moment there was silence, save the sound of buzzing insects, buzzing that grew louder and louder and louder...

Wilson closed his eyes and willed it all to stop, squeezed his eyes shut, tried to shut down his hearing and slow his breathing and become invisible. All those techniques used to work, but as he grew older, the old tricks had become less effective, to the point where he no longer knew what to do, how to escape, where to hide.

And that's when the tremors started, when the water began to feel alive, pulsing, wriggling, and the sunlight erupted into harsh shafts that blinded, confused, and dazed. He had to get up quickly, rushing to stand, pushing his palms into the wet grass that felt sticky, like honey, like blood, splashing out of the water, trembling, and his feet dripping, and his trousers wet at the cuffs, and his skin crawling, and he walked, no...he ran back into the house. He ran into the dimness, into the quiet, leaving his socks and shoes on the grass, and

Thurman, gently bobbing in the water in the afternoon sun, growling softly to himself.

—

Be human.

Thurman looked at the sliding door and saw his own reflection off the glass. He tilted his head.

Thurman realized he was looking at Thurman.

Good dog, he growled.

Then his lips moved, as if he were tasting a new word. Not all words came easy to dogs, and not to Thurman.

He growled softly, almost under his breath.

Then he tried it out, making the sounds for the first time, perhaps, and speaking it louder, so he could hear it as it left his throat.

Forgive, he whispered. Then he closed his eyes.

And he whispered again.

Forgiven.

Chapter Twenty

*H*AZEL RODE a cable car in San Francisco. She took the tourist ferry to Alcatraz. She had dinner in a Chinese restaurant in Chinatown. She drove to Los Angeles. She went to Disneyland by herself. She drove out to see the Hollywood sign. She parked by the La Brea Tar Pits, and came away totally unimpressed, having built up the site in her mind.

I read about the tar pits when I was little, she thought as she stared at it. *I guess I expected to see real saber-toothed tigers running around. Maybe I should go into the actual museum.*

She did not.

She got lost on the Los Angeles freeway system four times.

She stopped at an Orange Julius. Her mother had talked about them, saying how delicious the drink was.

It was okay. But not something I would tell my kids about. Probably not, anyhow.

And now, only days into her quest, she was beginning to feel dislocated, edging on disorientation.

Being free is harder than I thought.

She drove past an all-suites hotel just off the freeway and it took her twenty minutes to figure out how to circle back and exit at the right time to get to the hotel. She missed the correct exit twice, driving back and around three times.

She wondered if she would show up on any of the closed-circuit cameras posted along the highway and if any of the people who monitored such things would consider her a potential threat, trying to "case" the hotel before striking. Hazel did not consider that a real possibility, but it amused her to think of someone picking her minivan out of a thousand other minivans and applying special scrutiny to her and her alone.

She was given a nice two-room suite on the third floor, the bedroom not facing the freeway, but west, toward the ocean.

She was too far inland to see the ocean, but she took some comfort in the fact that it lay outside her bedroom window. She sat at the small desk and opened up the green leatherette folder that listed all the guest services and restaurants and room service options and churches in the area. She flipped past all of those sections until she found "Guest Laundry."

Washers and dryers are available to all guests and are located on the third and sixth floors. The machines are coin operated and detergent and fabric softener are available for purchase. Guests using these facilities do so at their own risk, and the hotel assumes no liability for any damages to clothing or lost articles.

"Third floor? Great."

Hazel now had something to do, something practical, something concrete, even if it was as simple as washing clothes.

She unloaded her second suitcase, the one she used for dirty clothes, and separated them into lights and darks. She looked at both piles, wondering if she had any delicates.

She did not.

I don't think I own any delicate clothing. Maybe a sweater or two. But I didn't bring them. Or did I give them away?

Water splashing in the atrium fountain echoed throughout the hotel's open interior as Hazel padded down the hallway to the laundry room tucked away in a far corner, next to the ice machine and vending area. As she neared the door, out charged a toddler, arms waving in the air, wearing nothing but a pair of shorts, laughing as only a toddler can laugh, with complete and utter abandonment. A split second later, a woman burst out of the room, giving chase, obviously the child's mother, laughing as well, but the laughter was a bit tired, and a bit concerned. She scooped up the toddler in her arms and spun about, carrying the wiggling child under her right arm, like a football player might carry a very active football.

Hazel hesitated a moment, but then continued.

I do have laundry to do, after all. And maybe they're almost done.

She stepped inside the very well-lit room, which contained a table and three washers and three dryers and a wall-mounted, coin-operated detergent dispenser. One slot offered a "special" laundry bag that Hazel knew was no more than a plastic bag with the word LAUNDRY printed on it.

The woman carrying the child waved at Hazel and pushed back an errant strand of hair from her face.

"I'm almost done. Clothes are in the dryer now. Washers are all yours."

"Thanks. I only need two of them."

The toddler, now being held by his mother in a standing position on the folding table, in between two mounds of freshly washed and dried clothes, let out a bloodcurdling scream. Hazel spun around, expecting to see broken bones or blood, but instead it was the toddler, bouncing, smiling, and readying to scream again.

His mother clamped a hand over his mouth.

"Inside voice," she hissed at him—not an angry hiss, but a firm one.

The toddler narrowed his eyes, and must have agreed, for when the hand came off his mouth he remained quiet, relatively speaking.

"Sorry. He gets rambunctious in the afternoon. Plays havoc on naptime, let me tell you. My naptime, that is. Not his."

Hazel had never been around babies or small children, so she was at a loss to know how to answer.

"No problem," she said, thinking that it was indefinite enough of an answer as not to offend a sensitive parent.

She doesn't seem like a sensitive parent—but you never know.

"So where you headed? By the way, I'm Jennifer. Which means you can accurately tell my age because everyone born in 1980 was named Jennifer. And this here is Axel. Don't ask. My husband picked it out. I got to name the first two. This one was his choice."

Hazel waved and introduced herself.

I like her.

"So where are you headed?"

"Well," Hazel replied, still unsure of how to describe her current journey. "Phoenix. But I don't have to be there until next week."

Actually, we didn't set a date. I said I would call when I'm in the area.

Jennifer listened, then sighed.

"We're actually on our way home tomorrow morning. Fargo."

Hazel nodded, wondering if she should make some comment on Fargo, another city she had never visited.

"We did Disneyland, SeaWorld, Magic Mountain, Legoland, Universal Studios, and Knott's Berry Farm."

"Wow," Hazel replied, obviously impressed.

"We love amusement parks," Jennifer continued. "And in Fargo you don't have many choices. Just the 'fun centers' with batting cages and go-kart tracks. No Magic Mountain in Fargo."

"Your itinerary is impressive."

Jennifer picked up Axel and set him on her hip, a practiced move, no doubt.

"But as much fun as all this has been . . . going home is the best part of any trip. Going back to our little house. I love California and the parks and all . . . but I love my home more than anything."

Jennifer moved Axel to face her and held him with both hands.

"Isn't that right, little Ax man? Do you want to go home?"

That question persuaded Axel to let loose his practiced, blood-chilling scream again.

And the scream, much to Hazel's surprise, elicited a wistful feeling in her, a wistful feeling for someplace called home.

⟶

Gretna waved as soon as she saw the figure at the end of the block.

"Emily," she shouted. "I'm already here."

For a moment, Gretna wondered if it had been proper to shout like that, for an old woman, that is.

Older. Not old.

And then she decided that she did not really care.

I'm already old. I can do pretty much what I like.

She smiled and waved again. Emily waved back.

Except get out of bed in the morning without groaning. Other than that, I'm good.

Thurman sat beside Gretna, grinning, patiently waiting. Gretna had told him that she was coming along.

"I thought you would like that, Thurman. And I get a little nervous, walking alone, with a dog."

Thurman had appeared wounded by that remark.

"In case I fall, Thurman—who would take you home?"

Thurman considered that and then nodded in agreement.

Good, he growled. *Good think.*

As Emily made her way up the front walk, Thurman began to do his retriever cha-cha-cha in anticipation, as Gretna explained it all once again.

"Thurman needed an afternoon walk. Wilson has some sort of professor meeting and he wasn't going to be home until later and he was worried about poor Thurman and I suggested that I could come and walk him and Wilson thought it was a good idea, but he suggested that I take a cab both ways but it is too nice a day for that, don't you think, Emily?"

"I do," she said and bent down to give Thurman a hug. He responded by offering a lyrical, happy growl. Gretna was not sure if he was trying to say anything, but he did sound happy.

"And I am glad you called," Emily said. "We can take our walk, then I can walk you back home. I have to visit my mother-in-law. It's been a few days."

"I know. She just sits in the lobby, you know."

Gretna saw the flash of pain on Emily's face.

"I didn't mean it like that. Even when you come, she still just sits in the lobby. You know what I mean. You could be there all the time and she wouldn't change."

Emily appeared a bit relieved.

"Well, let's walk," she said.

And the three of them set off down the block, heading east, in the direction of Wilkinsburg.

"So, you two had a nice time at that play?"

"We did. It's been years since I've been to a play. None of my children seem to appreciate that sort of theater. Unless there are robots and explosions, they want nothing to do with it."

Gretna nodded.

"Kids."

Gretna desperately wanted to ask more about the evening and probe down to a more personal level, but she had promised Wilson that she would not do that—under penalty of never seeing Thurman again.

Reluctantly, she had agreed.

And Gretna was mostly certain that Emily would have answered her questions—about the evening and about Wilson—but she was also certain that such information would not be volunteered on her own accord.

As they walked, they talked about the weather and how pleasant it had been, the prospects for a good season for

the Pittsburgh Pirates baseball team, which they both had
guarded opinions of, and how nice Thurman was to walk—
as dogs go, that is.

When Thurman heard his name, he looked back over his
shoulder and nearly stumbled off the curb, grinning at the
idea of being the topic of conversation.

The blocks passed quickly, and soon Gretna stood at the
front door, fumbling with Wilson's house key.

"I'll make sure he has water," she said as Thurman
bounded inside.

His bowl was nearly empty, so she let the water run for a
long time until it turned cool. Taking small steps, she placed
it near his food bowl, trying not to spill any.

When she stood upright, Thurman looked at her and
spoke.

You pray, he said, his growl gentle, almost kind.

"I am. I mean, I will."

Thurman nodded.

Prepare, he said.

"Prepare? For what?" she asked, absolutely certain that he
was speaking to her, none of this you're-just-a-fiction-of-my-
wounded-personality business.

Surprises.

"Surprises?"

And secrets.

"What?"

Thurman looked up at her with his expression indicating
that she had heard correctly. He then walked over to his bowl
and began to drink, making loud, slurpy noises with audible
gulps in between.

—

"Axel, do you want to go home? No more Disneyland?" Jennifer asked her son, who was now sitting on the folding table, kicking his legs, giggling about something.

In an instant, his face shifted to angry, his little eyes becoming slits.

"No!" he shouted and crossed his arms and pushed his chin into his chest.

Jennifer laughed.

"Even though he couldn't go on ninety percent of the rides, he still loves amusement parks. I'm guessing he'll grow up to design roller coasters or be a ticket taker at Great America. Either one is possible."

Hazel finished loading her clothes from the two washers into two dryers. She had only emptied half of a dainty-sized box of Tide detergent into each one.

No need to use too much soap. A half a box was plenty. And I wasn't digging ditches, and they smell clean.

"Do your other children like parks as much as Axel?"

"I think so. The oldest doesn't want to be seen with his family—ever—so we let him wander off on his own. He's happy. We're happy. The middle one, well...he's got leukemia and this trip was on his bucket list. So, yeah, he likes amusement parks."

Hazel was caught off guard by the casual and sudden turn of things.

"I'm so sorry...I mean...I didn't..."

"Relax. Of course you couldn't have known. And we've lived with this for two years now. We're doing everything we can to enjoy life as best we can. The doctors say it's a fifty-fifty proposition. You live with those odds for a while and you get used to it. I guess we think everyone should just be normal about it."

Hazel had no idea of what to say. It was obvious that Jennifer was used to the awkward silences and pained looks. She smiled, as if trying to comfort Hazel's apparent anxiety.

"Maybe the Lord will heal him," she continued. "Maybe he won't. But we are his, you know. We were never promised a rose garden—as the old song said. But we will do our best to enjoy the time he allows us to enjoy."

Hazel simply nodded in reply.

Jennifer picked up Axel, who had now gone quiet and appeared a bit droopy.

"So tell me, Hazel, do you know Jesus?"

Hazel assured Jennifer and Axel that she did know Jesus, and shortly after that assurance the dryer bell rang and Hazel offered to watch Axel while Jennifer carried a very large load of clean clothes back to their room.

"Normally I wouldn't bother doing laundry so close to the end of a trip," Jennifer said, "but none of us had anything clean to wear. Seriously. And five people in a minivan the whole way across North Dakota in dirty clothes is no picnic."

Axel stared at Hazel with wide toddler eyes the entire duration of his mother's absence, unsure of what to do and who this woman was.

They were both absolutely relieved when Jennifer returned.

After Jennifer and Axel departed with a "God bless you" wish, Hazel slumped in one of the two plastic chairs in the room and closed her eyes for a long moment. The laundry room remained empty, save for Hazel, for both her spin and dry cycles. For that, she was grateful. She did not think that she was up to interacting with anyone else that afternoon.

I have never faced adversity, have I?

She looked up when the dryer buzzed and began to slow, marking the end of its cycle.

I have never really been in any sort of trial. Sure, my mother died, and that was hard, but every parent, or most every parent, will die before their child does. But to see a child suffer. That has to be terrible.

She carried the dry clothes and dumped them en masse onto the table, and began to fold them.

I would hang some of them if I were home . . .

She realized what she had said, or rather thought.

There is no "home" anymore.

She paused, the shirt in her hands, feeling the lingering warmth.

But . . . sure, I haven't faced really tough times . . . she thought as she resumed folding, *but neither have I faced a triumph. Where is the big victory in my life?*

She wondered if any of this, any of this being free and unfettered, would get easier as the days and the miles passed.

I don't think it will.

That's what I'm afraid of.

It will never get any better than it is right now.

Or easier.

She took a deep breath and held it for a moment.

Maybe I should just go back to Portland and forget about

the wedding picture and my mother's husband and all the rest.
All of this can't lead to anything but ... but more uncertainty.

She tilted her head, as if in deep thought.

Then slowly, slowly, bit by bit, her mouth turned into a sort of gentle smile, a knowing smile, without truly knowing.

Or not.

She shook her head.

As they say, be careful what you wish for—because you just might get it.

She felt a cynical minor scowl take over her face.

Did I ever ask to be rich?

She sighed.

I am pretty sure I never did.

Chapter Twenty-One

H ELLO, DR. KILLEEN," Wilson called out.

Dr. Killeen was sitting on the small front porch of his home, not in the driveway, this afternoon. There was only room for the wheelchair and a large cement pot that held a breath of flowers and ferns and assorted greenery. The flowers were colorful but did not match—yellow and orange and blue and white and red and green and leafy— as if some color-blind planter had bought the leftovers of a plant sale. Martha Stewart would be aghast, Wilson thought.

Thurman, as was his wont, grew excited and eager to greet someone he knew, and he bounced and pranced the entire length of the front walk in a sort of canine dance revue.

"Hello, Wilson. And hello, Thurman. How are you both?"

Thurman responded by barking loudly and tossing his head backward.

Wilson had noticed him doing that on previous occasions, and had actually looked up the behavior on the Internet, but found no consensus of opinion on what it might mean, this head tossing. He likened it to the vague, subtle head nods that hipsters give each other as they pass, too cool for a wave, just a shade of movement of the head.

Cool.

But Thurman was no hipster, and definitely was not cool, but perhaps it was some manner of instinctual behavior.

Maybe the wolf packs way back when were made up of wolf hipsters who all practiced the very same canine head toss.

"We're fine, Dr. Killeen. And how are you?" Wilson asked, stopping a few feet from the front stoop.

"My name wasn't in the obituary columns this morning. So that makes it a very good day."

Thurman moved in closer and reared up, gently placing both front paws on Dr. Killeen's right thigh. The old man reached over and patted the dog's head; he cupped his hand under Thurman's chin and stared into his eyes.

"Good dog, Thurman. You've got deep eyes, you know that? The deep eyes of a prophet."

Thurman growled out, *I do,* but Wilson knew that Dr. Killeen would not understand his reply.

"Your dog thinks deep thoughts," Dr. Killeen said, now looking up at Wilson and squinting even more. "He's got old eyes, Wilson."

Wilson shrugged.

"I know. I didn't pick him, remember? He was thrust upon me."

Thurman turned his head and growled at Wilson, a growl that hinted at hurt feelings and scorn—but not really. A good-natured growling scowl.

"You mother stopped by a few days ago. She brought Thurman with her and was walking with some other woman whom I didn't recognize. And Gretna happily filled me in on all the happenings at her retirement...Village? Association? Condo?"

"Sorry about that. And they call it a village, although it's just one big building."

Dr. Killeen waved off his remark.

"I do enjoy talking to her. Well, I enjoy talking to anyone. Once all your friends die off, you get fewer visitors, you know?"

Thurman seemed to be comfortable half-standing there, his head and shoulders in the old man's lap, the sun on both their faces, the deep lines shadowed on the old man's face, the tremble in his hands more evident in the bright sunshine, the watery eyes held to slits.

"She told me, or rather she whispered to me, that she was going to become a grandmother."

Wilson nodded.

"It's an ongoing delusion. Ever since Thurman showed up. She's been telling others the same story."

Dr. Killeen stroked Thurman's head, and if Thurman could purr, he would have, his eyes shut in contentment.

"Is she feeling all right? I know she's old and sometimes an idea, no matter how ludicrous, can get stuck. But other than that, she was very lucid. Cranky, but lucid."

Wilson opened his palms skyward.

"The doctor says she's fine. Passes all his little memory tests. It appears that this becoming-a-grandmother idea is her only affectation. Well, one of her more noticeable affectations. Harmless, I suppose, but definitely on the odd side."

Dr. Killeen stopped petting Thurman and the dog looked up, then butted his head into the old man's hand.

"She said that Thurman told her."

"She mentioned that to me," Wilson replied.

"I said the knowledge must give her comfort—the fact that he promised her grandchildren."

Wilson had no reply for this.

Dr. Killeen cleared his throat, began petting Thurman again, and then said, "What gives you comfort, Wilson?"

"What?"

"Comfort. Where do you find comfort, Wilson? Or contentment? Your mother seems to have found it. To a degree, anyhow. Have you? Have you found it?"

From inside the house came a voice, calling out for Dr. Killeen. Except whoever was calling did not use his formal title.

"Clarence, do you want coffee?"

The voice was heavily accented. Wilson surmised Spanish, most likely South American Spanish. He had a knack for guessing the general origin of most accents.

Dr. Killeen winced, almost as if he had been stricken by some intense interior pain, and he looked up at Wilson, an imploring expression on his face.

"The secret is out. I went by C. Killeen—not Clarence—for so long...almost all my life. And now, betrayed by a very cordial caregiver."

He tilted to his left, trying to get a little closer to Wilson.

"You will keep my secret, won't you?"

Wilson grinned.

"Of course. I guess we all have secrets."

Dr. Killeen paused, then looked at Thurman.

"You're right. I hadn't thought of it that way," he said softly. "Secrets. Goodness. Well, would you like some coffee?

Margat is from Peru, and they seem to know how to make coffee that has some intestinal fortitude to it."

"I wouldn't want to bother you any more than I have already," Wilson replied. Apparently Thurman had not received the we-wouldn't-think-of-imposing memo, because he had already squirmed past the wheelchair and was nosing at the front door, happily growling in anticipation of seeing the inside of a new and different house.

"It's not like I have to do anything to make it. Please, stay." And he half-turned in his chair and called back, "*Dos cafes, por favor, Margat.*"

The front door opened inward and a small woman stepped out. She had long black hair, a round peasant face, and a beaming smile.

"Come in. I get coffee. *Dos.*"

With a practiced hand, the woman, Margat, grabbed the wheelchair and pulled it inside with a strength that belied her small stature. Wilson and Thurman followed them into the kitchen, the house holding faint odors of Vicks VapoRub, mothballs, and liniment.

Or is that witch hazel? I haven't smelled that in years and years.

Dr. Killeen was wheeled to the kitchen table and Wilson took a chair opposite him. The table was similar to Wilson's, with a shiny metal edge, flared metal legs, and a top with an amorphous squiggly pattern on it. Clarence's kitchen was much more out-of-date than Wilson's; the appliances and countertop all appeared to be at least several decades old.

Hospital clean and tidy and spartan, but old. Vintage, perhaps, would be a kind descriptive, Wilson thought.

In a few moments, after hearing sinister hisses from some sort of coffee machine, Margat brought out two mugs of coffee, both thick with cream, and a thin scrum of foam covering the top.

"I hope you don't mind a little *crema* with your coffee. It's the only way she knows how to make it, right, Margat?"

Margat nodded and slid a plate of cookies onto the table. Thurman's ears perked up and his nose went into third gear as he stared at the plate while obediently sitting a few paces away. His nostrils opened as wide as they could, inhaling as much cookie goodness as he could without being rude.

The two men sipped and nibbled at the cookies, which were some sort of vanilla sugar cookie, with enough variations of shape to indicate they had to have been produced at home.

Wilson noted Thurman's desperate look of hunger and longing. He broke one cookie in half and extended the smaller of the two pieces to Thurman, who almost leaped at the offer of sweet sustenance. He chewed the morsel carefully and slowly, smiling as he did so.

"You have a gourmet dog there, Wilson."

"He thinks so as well."

Again the kitchen was quiet, save for drinking and chewing. Thurman had another half-cookie.

"You came to talk, didn't you, Wilson? Your mother said she had been pushing you to talk. Not to me, necessarily, but to someone."

Wilson offered a weary smile.

"She has been pushing for the last forty years."

"A long time to be silent. A long time for secrets."

Wilson appeared to agree.

"You're a religious man, aren't you, Dr. Killeen?"

"I should hope so. It was in my job description. Being a pastor and all."

"Touché. But what I meant was, how do you deal with real life? At Pitt, we have professors who teach church history— or the history of religion—in the history department. I spent a painful evening between a pair of them at a faculty dinner. They may have known history, but not much else. I think they were both agnostics . . . at best."

Dr. Killeen cradled his half-full coffee cup in both hands, as if drawing additional warmth from it.

"I know the type," the old man said. "There are many pastors suffering from the same twelve inch problem."

"Twelve inch problem?"

"They have it in their head and not in their hearts. A distance of twelve inches . . . give or take an inch or two. To be honest, I think I was that way for years. Until I decided that knowing about God is not the same as living for God, that having knowledge is not the same as having wisdom. It takes a person willing to admit that they are flawed and human and that they only have a simple understanding of life to really get it—to get what life means—and to be fully aware of our place in the universe, and aware of God's place in relationship to us."

Dr. Killeen took a deep breath, the passionate explanation taking a toll on his breathing.

Wilson offered Thurman another half-cookie, as if he wasn't really thinking of what he was doing.

"Let me ask you a religious question, then," he said, his voice low, quiet, as if he was about to make a confession, about to open up to some sin in his life. "How long is God's statute of limitations?"

Dr. Killeen did not reply for a long moment. When he spoke, his voice was as raspy as leaves scabbering along on the street, dancing in an early winter wind.

"This is about the war. This is about what you did. Isn't it, Wilson?"

Thurman growled something, a long, low, guttural growl, as if he was adding an addendum to the question, a clarifying statement of sorts.

Wilson did not want to answer the question, and wanted to answer the question—both simultaneously, both in equal amounts.

"Maybe." He had spent most of his adult life not answering, not thinking about, not reliving, trying to be unaware of all that happened...back then.

But Dr. Killeen was a patient veteran of waiting, often waiting for hours or days until an answer became manifest, or years, or decades, until he could see God's hand in a life— God's direction, God's plan.

And so he simply sat, still, quiet, waiting.

Then he spoke, his words as even as words could be uttered, as neutral as words could be spoken.

"You saw things, didn't you?"

Wilson looked at his hands. He slowly clenched his fists, as if enduring a painful injection into muscle, into bone.

"You did things, didn't you?"

Wilson wanted to answer it but could not—not yet.

"Maybe."

"And you're not sure that God will forgive?"

Wilson shrugged.

"I teach writing for a living . . . and I don't know the words. For this. What I feel."

Thurman whispered his new word, louder this time, then growled it again.

Forgive.

Forgiven.

Wilson was certain that he alone heard it. And he was just as certain that the word, those words, were absolutely not from some deep place inside himself, not from a place that had been hidden for decades, not from a place where the guilt lived and refused to enter into the light of day.

The word came from Thurman. And Wilson did not, or would not, speculate on where Thurman had received that word.

Forgiven.

He closed his eyes and tried to imagine it.

How sweet the sound, Wilson thought. *And how impossible.*

━

Gretna stabbed at the TV remote, muting the sound, and slipped it back into the pocket of her favorite housedress, the one with the paisley pattern. She shuffled into the kitchen, her right arm out, fingers just grazing the wall—for security, she said.

"No one wants to fall down."

She scowled at the fruit bowl and picked up an orange. She examined it for a moment, then put it back down. She picked up a banana and put that back down as well.

"Too green."

She thought about making a cup of coffee.

"Too late in the day. I'll be up all night."

She padded back into the living room and stared at the TV.

"Stupid show," she said. "No one is that stupid. Real court-room drama, my foot. They're all unemployed actors."

She shuffled back into the kitchen and opened the refrigerator. She did not expect to find anything that she wanted, really, and did not.

She shut the door and stood in the middle of the room and folded her arms across her chest.

She thought about taking the almost crumpled pack of cigarettes from where she had hidden it—in the pocket of her winter coat—and sneaking outside and hiding around the block, away from the dozens of prying eyes that occupied the front lobby.

If passersby only knew some of the comments the seniors bestowed on the unsuspecting.

But that's too far to walk right now. And it's too hot. Cig-arettes don't taste good when it's hot.

Gretna stood and stared out to her living room window, without really seeing. Then she stopped and shook her head slowly, as if admitting defeat.

"So you really want to hear me pray about this again?"

She looked up at the ceiling. She imagined that God would want to make eye contact with people who bothered him like this.

"I talked to you before. You didn't answer. Remember? I could have saved myself a lot of time if you had just let me know early on that you were too busy doing something else."

She scowled upward, just a little.

"Maybe I'm being a little...harsh. Or judgmental, right? That's your job, I guess."

Then she looked down, a bit nervous.

"Sorry."

She kept her head low, her eyes averted.

"It's just that...Thurman...you know Thurman, right? Thurman told me things. That I would be a grandmother. And since Wilson is all I have...well, that means Wilson. And he's still...broken. Or wounded. I know he doesn't want to be like that. And I can't help him. I tried, but I can't. It hurts when a mother sees her child in pain and can't do anything about it. You know how that is, don't you? I see it in his eyes, every time we talk. Like he's hiding from something. Or trying to hide something. That he's hiding. That hurts. I know he's not at peace. He hasn't been at peace since he came home. And I can't die in peace, knowing he's broken."

Her voice wavered, and she did not like showing any form of weakness like this, when it left her with a wavery, quivery voice.

"And the pastor said I should pray again. So I'm giving this praying rigamarole one more shot. For Wilson. And for Thurman."

She swallowed and closed her eyes.

"And maybe for me as well."

She drew in a breath, steeling herself for her request of God.

"Please, please...give him peace."

She waited in silence for a long time.

"I can't think of anything else. I suspect you know all about this. I suspect you know what to do—and how to do it."

She opened her eyes and offered a smile to the ceiling.

"The way I figure it, if you didn't want to be bothered, why would you have sent Thurman to me? Right? Am I right? Or what?"

She waited another moment.

"So . . . amen."

She looked up.

"Okay?"

Hazel had an early breakfast and shuffled out of the hotel, dragging her two suitcases, one containing all newly washed clothes, to the car as the sun broke the horizon. She made a point of leaving early so she would not run into Jennifer or any of her family.

What would I say to them? And if I talk to the son that's sick, I'll probably start crying.

She tapped at the screen and entered the city of Phoenix on the Quest's GPS unit.

Once I'm close, I'll stop for the night.

The trip, according to the electronic map, would take her six hours and three minutes.

Longer if I get lost again.

She spent several minutes looking at the route so she would not be surprised or confused.

I'm sure I'll be confused regardless.

She said the routes out loud, thinking it would help.

"Take the 105 east to 605 north to 60 east to 10 east—and follow that the rest of the way to Phoenix."

Should be easy.

Traffic was either really thick or really normal, Hazel thought as she merged onto the freeway.

Hard to say if this is horrible traffic or not, she thought. *This is California, after all.*

She had previously decided to stay in the right lane, regardless of how slow it was, regardless if she was behind a semi truck or not, regardless if she was following a ten-car parade of ninety-year-old drivers with their blinkers on, so as not to be put in jeopardy again by being five lanes to the left as she whizzed past her intended exit on the right.

Steady and slow and certain.

She kept a check on both her mirror and GPS unit.

That saying should be embroidered on a pillow.

An empty school bus raced by her.

If I knew how to embroider, that is.

She had filled her old thermos, the one she had used while working, with coffee. This way she could have warm coffee the entire trip—and she could stop at a Starbucks to augment her coffee supply.

The one thing that Hazel had realized on this trip, the one thing that struck her more solidly than any other truth—and this was only after a week or so of traveling—was how much she missed dialogue, that simple, day-to-day, humdrum conversation with other people.

Conversations with the waitstaff at the roadside

McDonald's did not count; that was simply an order and an acknowledgment. It was not genuine, even if most of Hazel's previous daily conversation consisted of vapid comments on the weather, about the Seahawks' most recent game, or about the rising or falling price of gas.

She even began to miss some of her old coworkers, just a little.

There was always something to talk about with them: the latest problematic client, the latest ridiculous edict from human resources, the most recent wardrobe nightmare worn by Suzanne, the odd agent on the third floor. Had Hazel known that she would miss commenting on a purple blouse with a tangerine skirt, she would have thought the idea ludicrous.

"I do miss it," she said to herself.

She did not berate herself for talking aloud to herself. Her mother had been a self-talker as well, walking about her house chattering on, carrying on very complex conversations with herself, which often contained two or three contentious points of view.

"And here's what I've decided," Hazel said aloud as she finished the first cup of coffee and managed a double move, bringing the full cup to the nearest cup holder while shifting the empty to the vacated holder. "I've decided to let this trip to Phoenix determine my fate, as it were. Maybe that's a stronger term than I need, but I know what I mean."

Her intended exit was only two miles away, so Hazel readied herself for the exit and re-merge process.

"If the Army vet knows who that soldier is in the picture . . . well, that means I will go and try and find him. If he's still alive, that is. If he can't identify him . . . well, I think

I will travel a bit more and then head back to Portland. I'll get a small place in the woods. I'll live on the interest of the money. I'll volunteer at church—maybe offer to work in those apartments they have for the homeless. I guess I'm developing a soft spot for being homeless."

The large green-and-white exit sign slipped past and Hazel used her blinker for the announced distance of a half-mile until the exit, and smoothly transitioned to Interstate 10. That would be the last change in routes for the entire trip. She would have no other choices until she got to Phoenix.

By the time I get to Phoenix . . .

She heard that old song bubble up in her thoughts, and she tried to remember what the next line was, but it eluded her at the moment.

"I'll let it steep for a while. It'll come. Eventually. It is Glen Campbell, right?"

A FedEx truck whizzed past her, making the Quest vibrate and shimmy.

"And that's why I could never appear on *Jeopardy!*"

↩

Dr. Killeen adjusted himself in the wheelchair. He pushed himself up as straight as he could, despite the fact that his disease was slowly causing him to crumple in on himself, cell by cell, muscle by muscle, as it were. His arms quivered with the effort.

Wilson looked up.

He must have been an imposing figure in the pulpit . . . back in the day.

"Listen, Wilson, I told your mother that I served in Vietnam. Did she tell you that?"

Surprise was evident on Wilson's face.

"No."

No one spoke until Thurman warbled a growl.

"Where? When?" Wilson asked, his voice almost a whisper.

Pastor Killeen's face now had a serious, somber edge to it.

"I was commissioned into the First Armored. But once I was there, I went all over. Became a sort of traveling chaplain. And I was there the same time you were. We overlapped for two years."

Wilson, without thinking, drew himself tighter, folding his hands together, as if trying to avoid something, to make himself smaller, to make himself hidden.

"Wilson, whatever it was that happened over there . . . well, I saw it too. Chaplains participate in a lot of unburdening, you know. What soldiers did. Or what they didn't do. What they watched others do and did nothing to stop it."

Wilson just nodded, now mute, now powerless.

"I don't need to know what you did or saw or didn't do, Wilson. And I'm not sure I want to—unless you need to give it voice."

The air in the kitchen seemed to have disappeared. Even Thurman stood up and growled, a mumbling growl, as if asking for clarification, as if not understanding what was being discussed.

"But I do know that Jesus says, in many ways, that if we ask for forgiveness, forgiveness will be given. The act of asking precedes the act of absolution."

Wilson managed a strangled "No."

"Even for horrible things, Wilson. Even for those. Jesus offers forgiveness."

Wilson pulled himself back upright, almost upright. He started to speak, several times. Thurman growled a soft encouragement. Wilson tried again.

"I was a helicopter gunner, most of the time, in a Huey medevac. A machine gunner kills people. Sometimes they weren't much farther away from me than you are."

He inhaled a gulp of air. His voice grew more reedy and thin with each word.

"But to be forgiven, one needs to believe, right, Pastor?"

Pastor Killeen nodded and replied, "Wilson, I have been asked this before. I have held the hands of soldiers who were about to be dead. They often posed the very same question. I did not lie to them then. And I will not lie to you now. The answer is yes. Believe. Ask. Repent. Be forgiven. It is that simple. It is all you need."

Wilson shut his eyes and Thurman's growl had an otherworldly tone to it, as if he was trying to summon courage from a hidden canine source, or some understanding that Wilson could not find on his own.

The words were no louder than the petal of a flower, falling on dew-covered grass.

"I don't believe," Wilson whispered. "And I don't know if I can repent."

Chapter Twenty-Two

MARGAT TRIED to enter the kitchen silently, but she did not. There was a rattle of pills.

Wilson saw her out of the corner of his eye and flinched, his eyes wide with surprise and confusion.

"Clarence," she said softly. "It is time for pills."

Pastor Killeen made a face.

"They design them for horses, Wilson. Do I look like a horse?"

Wilson let his face soften. The air returned into the room. He could breathe again.

"No."

"All right, Margat. Pills it is."

Wilson stood and Thurman rose in response.

"We need to go. Thanks for the coffee."

Pastor Killeen waved it off.

"I will not push you, Wilson. Whether it's a conversion forced at the end of a gun or information a prisoner provides while being held, untethered, in the open bay of a helicopter at two thousand feet—neither of them are worth the paper they're printed on."

Wilson nodded as if he knew exactly what Pastor Killeen meant.

"Thanks."

"Go home with Thurman. And think about this. Think

about feeling at peace...at long last. You may not have another opportunity."

"I know."

Thurman growled out emphatically, *I say same.*

"So think about it. And come back. We'll have coffee again. And Margat will make chocolate chip cookies. No Peruvian delicacy, but I like them."

Thurman barked.

"He says we'll be back," Wilson said.

"Good."

And as Thurman and Wilson walked out of the kitchen, Wilson watched as Pastor Killeen grew smaller, almost deflating, as he meekly took the two large pills proffered by his caregiver, and reached out for a glass of water at the same time, his eyes losing the fire that had lit them with passion, with ferocity, only moments before.

Thurman barked at the front door and Pastor Killeen called out a final farewell.

Neither Thurman nor Wilson spoke as they started on their way home. Wilson did not know what to say, did not have anything to say, and Thurman must have thought that he needed time to think through things.

They walked three blocks in silence, but in step with each other.

Thurman growled softly, as if speaking to himself.

Think. Take time.

Wilson heard his muttering.

"I don't want to, Thurman."

Thurman looked up, veering slightly off the sidewalk and onto the grassy parkway.

Don't care. Not want. Need.

Wilson glared at him, scowled, and looked straight ahead as they walked toward the afternoon sun. The day was warm and Wilson felt a bead of sweat at his temples. He did not like to feel sweat on his face. That glistening had always been a trigger of memory, a trigger since... back then, when the heat of the jungle enveloped like a hot blanket, like multiple arms grabbing and constricting, the sweat coming from the heat and the terror and the fact that Wilson held the power of life and death in his hands.

"I've been fine until now, Thurman."

Not fine.

"I have been. I managed. I survived. No need to think of those things. They are in the past and forgotten. So why now?"

They stopped at the corner and waited for the light to change. It was obvious that Thurman did not know why traffic stopped on occasion, but it did, and he remained patient and still, and followed Wilson's lead in all matters of cars and trucks and waiting.

Wilson looked both ways, and over his left shoulder, and stepped off the curb.

Thurman followed, never more than an arm's length away from him when walking on the hot concrete.

Once on the other side, Thurman growled.

Now.

Wilson did not appear happy or understanding. He looked angry.

"I don't buy it, Thurman. Not now. Not ever."

Have to.

"I do not have to. I'm fine. Everything is fine. The way it was and the way it is is fine. I have gotten by for forty-some years this way."

They were within a block of home. Thurman sniffed, recognizing more familiar scents. He stopped and sat down and growled and stared up at Wilson. Wilson was forced to turn around to face the dog.

Accept. Peace.

Wilson put his hands on his hips, like a petulant child being told that he has to go inside.

"I can't accept that, Thurman. You don't know what I did. No one knows what I did. And no one will know what I did. Not now. Not ever."

Thurman's ears folded back and he growled, his growl more emphatic than ever.

God knows.

Wilson waited, as if waiting for some cogent thought, some logical rebuttal to Thurman's posit. But nothing came. He was left silent.

Accept. Live as human. What God wants. Peace.

"I am a human, Thurman," Wilson replied, looking around, making sure no one was near, that no one was observing him talking to a dog that growled, that no one was making a judgment on his sanity and his grip on reality. "And I am pretty sure that God was not in Vietnam . . . and I am not so sure he is here now either."

The street was empty of pedestrians.

Thurman remained adamant and re-growled.

Accept. Find peace.

"That is not a sequitur. Peace follows faith? It doesn't add up, Thurman. It doesn't."

You accept. Or . . .

Wilson had never heard Thurman use the word "or" before.

"Or what, Thurman? Or what?"

Thurman's eyes clouded, just for a heartbeat, a veil of sadness covering them. He spoke, plaintive and sad and barely above a whispered growl.

I leave.

Wilson stared at the dog, who stared back.

"You'll leave?"

Thurman did not speak, but looked over his shoulder and stood up.

At that second, Wilson knew that if Thurman were to begin to run, he would never catch him and Thurman would be gone forever. A dog as smart as Thurman would have no trouble finding a place to stay and people to take care of him, and Wilson would be alone again.

"Don't leave, Thurman," Wilson said, his raspy voice on the verge of tears, actual tears. "Please don't leave me."

Wilson realized, in that pellucid moment, that he did not want to be alone. He did not want to ever again enter a dark, silent house, filled with memories and ghosts and wisps of life and death, hovering, just beyond his grasp, the ephemeral remains of the lives that he had been responsible for taking. He could not face that terror now. Not alone. Thurman could not leave him. Thurman could not abandon him to the demons that followed him, in the dark, at the corner of his vision, at the edge of his thoughts.

"Please, Thurman. You can't."

Wilson was pleading. He had never felt risk like this before, heartstopping risk, not even when bullets shattered the doorframe around his gun position in the helicopter, not even when the copilot exploded along with a grenade, drenching everyone inside with his remains, not even when the darkness of a thousand nights fell.

"Please, Thurman. Please."

Thurman's hard face lasted for a single moment, then softened. While a dog does not cry, nor understand the permutations of sadness, Thurman's eyes welled up and he blinked several times to clear them.

He growled.

Think.

"Okay, Thurman. I promise. I will think about it. I will. I promise."

God hears, Thurman growled, his growl both hard and sympathetic, both hard and caring.

"I know. I know."

And with that, Thurman offered an affirmative growl and started to walk, with Wilson a half-step behind, walking to their house, walking, thinking that perhaps peace lay just beyond where they were, just beyond their grasp, not yet in sight, still elusive and hidden.

⌒

The words came to her two hundred miles from Phoenix.

By the time I get to Phoenix, she'll be rising.

That line came to her after not thinking about it for several hours. The rest of the song, however, remained opaque. Hazel knew she could find the lyrics on the Internet, but also knew the song was about a man leaving a woman and did not mirror her situation in the least.

"If I look up the words, it will stay stuck in my head for days. Better this way—to not know and not be bothered. Not knowing isn't a bad thing, really."

She had stopped for lunch at the Flying J Travel Plaza in Ehrenberg, Arizona, and had a small Wendy's hamburger and a small Frosty. She wasn't really hungry, but the offerings on Interstate 10 had not been exactly plentiful, nor did they show much promise until one got to the outskirts of Phoenix.

"Preventative eating, that's what it is," she'd said to herself as she pulled into the vast travel stop. "Just in case I were to get hungry later . . . and now I won't."

Being on a four-lane road, with trucks and very fast cars zooming past, unnerved her. She had never considered herself an intuitive, natural driver, generally driving with shoulders hunched and hands protectively clutching the wheel.

A thought came to mind midway through the hamburger.

Then why did I think driving around for the rest of my life was a good idea?

She managed to push the thought away by telling herself that she wouldn't drive forever, that she would find a place she liked, that she would locate a perfect spot to live, and then never have to drive again.

"And all I have to do now is get to Phoenix. I've never been to Phoenix."

She had her contact's address . . .

He's old and no one told him that giving out your phone

number as well as your actual address to strangers is dangerous.

... and he lived in a trailer park north of Phoenix.

As she had promised, she planned on calling him once reaching Phoenix. She spotted a suites hotel off the freeway after passing a sign indicating that Phoenix was only fifteen miles distant.

"I'll spend the night there. I'll call him, have dinner, and visit him in the morning. A good plan, if I say so myself."

The hotel was nearly an exact copy of the one she had left in California earlier that day.

She found the sameness both comforting and frightening.

"It's exactly the same," she said to herself as she wheeled her one bag toward the elevator. "I think that the artwork on the walls is even the same."

This time she was on the fifth floor and the bedroom window looked out over a parking lot and what appeared to be a flat desert beyond, lying to the south. It was only spring, and she could already see waves of heat undulating off the asphalt lot.

She sat on the end of the bed and picked up the TV remote, then put it back down.

"Too much chatter."

She walked into the living room and sat on the couch, and found herself holding the remote in that room as well.

She sighed, resigned to her fate, and switched the TV on, pressing buttons repeatedly. The hotel welcome screen came on and she scrolled through the channels until she came upon the cable weather channel. She waited until the local forecast came up, all the while stretching her legs and her back.

I should figure out how to use the cruise control on the Quest. But doesn't that seem odd—having a cruise control on one's quest? Seems anti-literary, if you ask me. If that's a word.

The local forecast came on and Hazel took note that the high temperature predicted for the following afternoon would be ninety-nine degrees.

There were no excessive heat warnings posted, as there would have been in Portland if it ever got to ninety-nine degrees.

If it hit ninety-nine degrees the governor would have called out the National Guard, probably. Each of them would be armed with a giant fan.

She smiled at the thought.

"Well, I guess I can scratch Phoenix off my list of places I could settle down in. If it's ninety-nine degrees now, what happens in August?"

She leaned back in the couch, and within minutes she fell asleep, watching the silent weather, holding the remote in her right hand.

After only a few months of residency at the retirement complex, Gretna had realized an important truth: If you really want someone to talk to, find a person in a wheelchair.

"They can't get away," she explained once. "They have to listen to you."

That afternoon, after a lunch of a tuna salad sandwich and tomato soup, Gretna spotted Lucille in the main lobby, staring out one of the front windows, brightly silhouetted in the brilliant spring sunshine.

"Maybe she's having a good day," Gretna said to herself as she made her way over to her. She scrabbled an upholstered chair closer to the window and the wheelchair. When she sat down with a loud huff, only then did Lucille take notice.

"Hello," Lucille said, smiling, and then her smile waned and she appeared just a squosh uncomfortable.

"Gretna," Gretna said, a little louder than she normally spoke. "Gretna. I know your daughter-in-law."

Lucille brightened and nodded with enthusiasm.

"With the dog. With... used to have a dog. Furby. No, that's not it. Thurby? No. Thurman. Right? Used to have Thurman."

"That's right. I did have Thurman the dog. He lives with my son, Wilson, now."

Lucille nodded again and put her fingers to her chin.

"He is a good boy, isn't he?"

"He is," Gretna replied, not knowing to whom Lucille was referring—but regardless, they were both good boys.

"And how is Emily?" Lucille asked.

Gretna was pretty sure than she did not know that her daughter-in-law had gone on a date with Wilson.

"She's good, Lucille. I saw her here with you yesterday."

At that, Lucille brightened.

"Oh, yes. She was. Such a lovely person."

Lucille folded her hands in her lap. In one hand, she held a handkerchief, the corner poking out like a rabbit's nose from an earthen hole. Gretna could see that the edges were done in a delicate lace.

I must have a whole drawer full of the same handkerchief.
I should use them. I know Wilson will just throw them away
after I'm gone.

Gretna blinked hard, several times, as if to clear those thoughts from her mind, and to bring her back to the subject that originally brought her to Lucille's side that afternoon.

Gretna adjusted her chair, tugging at the arm, trying to lift it over a rift in the carpet, saying mean things to it when it balked—all so she could face Lucille while she talked. She sat down with another huff, this one louder than the first.

I guess I could have moved the wheelchair instead. That
would have been simpler.

"Lucille," she began, her question plotted out even before lunch, "have you ever been surprised by God?"

Lucille tilted her head, like a dog hearing a high-pitched whistle, then smiled broadly. "I'm seventy-eight. I'm surprised every day I wake up and am not dead."

Obviously, Gretna wanted a more serious answer.

"No, that's not what I mean. I know what you mean, but not like that. Not like that surprise."

Lucille appeared deep in thought.

"Then like how?"

"Well, you know Thurman, right?"

Lucille smiled.

"He's a good boy."

"Well, Thurman told me that I was supposed to be ready for a surprise."

"Thurman?"

"Yes. Thurman."

Slowly, Lucille made an odd face of acceptance.

"Okay."

"And I told God that I was okay with that," Gretna continued. "But I don't know what sort of surprise I'm supposed to be ready for, or looking for."

Lucille offered a thinking frown, then replied, "Maybe you'll win the lottery."

"That would be a surprise all right, since I don't buy lottery tickets. Every time the jackpot gets to a gazillion dollars I tell myself I should buy one, but I don't think I know what store sells them."

Lucille appeared most assured. "Giant Eagle sells them."

"They do?"

"I think they do. I think I have seen signs for them."

"Do you buy them?" Gretna asked.

Lucille shook her head dramatically. "No, my granddaughter said I wasn't allowed to. She said they have terrible odds and prey on poor people who don't have any hope."

Gretna accepted that and then asked, "Lucille, do you like having a granddaughter?"

Lucille squinched her face tightly. "I guess I do. She seems to have a lot of rules, though. I thought young people were all supposed to be hippies or beatniks or something and not wear bras or shoes and grow beards."

"I guess they aren't," Gretna replied.

"No, they are not," Lucille replied.

Both women fell silent and stared out the window at two older women walking outside, in the real world, on the sidewalk, probably heading to lunch or tea or shopping at the Giant Eagle, perhaps.

Lucille spoke without turning. "You know you're supposed

to be surprised by surprises, Gretna. Otherwise they wouldn't be them. A surprise, I mean. I think you should just let surprises happen and not try to worry them into your life. Because then, well maybe then they won't come and surprise you."

Gretna looked over at Emily's mother-in-law and wondered if she was having a good day or a bad day.

So far, she couldn't tell.

—

Wilson sat at the kitchen table facing a small stack of ten-page descriptive essays from one of the three undergraduate courses he was teaching that semester. He preferred graduate courses, but when feeling charitable, he often felt that if he could make corrections early enough in a student's academic career, he might be able to prevent them from pursuing a writing degree if they were untalented, or nudge them to a more productive focus if they had glimmers of talent.

This class had a few promising students, a few not quite so talented but earnest students, more who were simply earnest, and a depressing few just occupying classroom space.

He clicked his red pen several times, and reluctantly pulled the first one off the stack and placed it in front of him.

Before he began to read, he tilted his head and listened.

It was Thurman. He was dancing, sort of, doing his version of a canine dance.

Wilson listened, leaning toward the family room, straining to hear.

Thurman's nails were clicking on the wood floor in the

den, and he was mutter-growling something over and over to himself.

Wilson soon translated Thurman's mutterings.

Think. Think. Think.

Thurman was repeating that word over and over as he danced about. Wilson could imagine the dog's back hips swaying, his back paws moving fast, trying to overtake his front paws, going to the left, first, then sliding back and trying the right side.

Think. Think. Think.

Wilson knew Thurman was probably expecting, or thinking, that for sure he would be listening. He smiled, a weary, forgiving, amused smile.

"Thurman?" he called out, his voice not much louder than normal conversation.

The clackering stopped, the noise that nails made when skittering on wood stopped, then slowly started again, more sedately, and Thurman entered the kitchen, his face a mask of uncertainty.

Think? he growled, posing the word as a question.

"I am, Thurman. Yes, I am thinking."

Thurman looked up, smiled, and waited, as if making sure that Wilson was telling the truth.

"I am thinking, Thurman. I also have work to do. So..."

Thurman nodded. Then he appeared to want to change the subject.

Swim? he growled.

Wilson offered a weary smile in return.

"Maybe later."

Thurman frowned, then nodded, more to himself than to

Wilson, and turned back to the family room. Once he was out of sight, the quick-paced clackering of the dog's nails started up again.

Think. Think. Think.

After a moment, he altered the words of his mantra.

Swim. Swim. Swim.

Chapter Twenty-Three

T HE DESERT SKIES MOBILE HOME PARK lay well outside of Phoenix, well beyond the standard residential areas and the standard strip malls and the standard four-corners-filled-with-four-fast-food-restaurants.

"This is like almost in the middle of the desert," Hazel said as she approached the main entrance. "The website said, 'Palm trees and views of the mountains.'"

As she slowed to make the turn, she glanced about.

"Mountains? Maybe if you stand on your roof."

She drove slowly, trying to make sense of the numbering system of the flat parcels of land, each small lot with a mobile home unit perched upon it.

"But it is very clean and tidy."

She rounded a corner.

"And it does have palm trees."

As she faced a long, narrow stretch of black asphalt, the heat was already shimmering at ten in the morning.

"And it is hot. Really hot."

She slowed even more, not because she needed to watch the lot numbers, but because a golf cart piloted by an older lady—a much older lady—wearing a thick sweater and a diaphanous pastel-colored scarf wrapped over her carefully coiffed hair and tied under her chin was in front of her Quest, puttering along at a very sedate nine miles an hour.

Or nine miles an hour according to the Quest.

Well up ahead, she spotted the number 12 on a small driveway, and it seemed to take another nine minutes to get there, Hazel unwilling to honk her horn, not knowing if honking was permitted, or if passing a golf cart was allowed at the Desert Skies. The extra time allowed her to take several deep breaths and to attempt to settle her nerves, which had been in a complicated jangle ever since she pulled off the main road.

"This will probably be a dead end," she said, steeling herself. "And that will be okay. I didn't know anything about him before, and my life was fine. If I don't know anything more, my life will still be fine."

She pulled off to the side of the narrow street, making sure there was more than enough room for golf carts to pass—two abreast, if the morning commute grew hectic.

She glanced at her reflection in the rearview mirror of the Quest. Her face, she thought, had grown more relaxed on this short journey. Even though she had many, many doubts and questions and uncertainties, she still felt more at ease, more at peace, and less stressed than she had ever felt in her prior life.

"Funny how having nothing to do, really, and no schedules, can make things more comfortable. Sort of. Kind of. Maybe."

She got out of the Quest and gulped, the hot air hitting her like a lead fist covered by an oven mitt, and she gasped again, trying to find a breath that did not feel like it was beginning the process of cooking her lungs.

As she walked around the car, the screen door of the

mobile home banged open. A scrawny older man stepped
out, his legs appearing to swim in his khakis, and his Hawai-
ian shirt probably two sizes too large. But his gray hair, what
was left of it, was neatly trimmed. He wore oversized glasses,
as if unwilling or unable to tolerate any uncorrected eyesight
at the sides of his field of vision.

"You Hazel?"

"I am. We talked yesterday evening. You're Woody, right?
Mr. Atherton, I mean."

He nodded.

"It's just Woody. You got your picture?"

"I do."

"Then come on in. It's already hot enough out here to
roast a lizard—and I mean that in the literal sense."

Hazel followed him inside and felt as if she were stepping
back into 1970. The wallpaper was a paisley riot of green and
white with shiny metallic accents. The sofa was off-white. The
kitchen, right next to the living room, was filled with white
Formica counters and blond wood cabinets. Most of the lighting was provided by round translucent globes hanging from
the ceiling.

But it was neat. Very neat. Nothing out of place, though it
did smell slightly of fish and coffee.

"You can sit there," he said, pointing at the sofa. "I got the
pictures in the other bedroom. Didn't want to leave them out
and clutter up the place."

On the walls were a few framed military decorations: a
folded American flag in a triangular wooden box, a porcelain
eagle captured as if in flight on a shelf above an old-style television set.

Woody returned carrying a battered cardboard box with PHOTOS/VIETNAM written on it in black marker.

"I went through all my pictures after I saw your post on Facebook," Woody said. "I had to use the computer in the rec center here since my computer went on the fritz. I studied the picture. Still have a good memory for faces. Not much else, I guess, but faces I know."

Hazel might have asked why he hadn't gotten his computer fixed, or printed a copy of the Facebook post, or asked for a copy to be mailed to him—but she didn't.

He must have his reasons. And I'm here now, so what difference would it make?

He opened up the box and pulled out two black-and-white snapshots, each tinged with a sepia tone at the edges, indicating their age.

"Used to take pictures all the time back then," Woody said with a hint of wistfulness in his words. "The guys in our photo unit would develop them for me for free, so I kept snapping away. I guess I shoulda taken more."

The first picture showed two soldiers standing side by side in a tropical setting, palm trees in the background. Both young men, boys, most likely, made the "V" sign with their free hands. In their other hands they each held a rifle, the butt end against their thighs. One soldier wore a helmet, cocked at a rakish angle. The other wore a cloth cap with a wide brim.

Hazel held the photo close to her face. Then she brought up her photo of her mother and the unknown soldier and alternated looking at one and then the other.

"I sort of see a resemblance, but not all that much," she said, a little regret in her voice.

"Yeah," Woody agreed. "That one was a little of a stretch. But sometimes the mind plays tricks on you, telling you that things are there when they're not, telling you that the wind moving the bush in front of you is just the wind and not the VC. So, you know, better to have a second opinion than to trust a first impression. You know what I mean?"

Hazel did not truly know what he meant. Well, she sort of did, but not really. She had no knowledge of thinking that a moving palm frond was a person with a weapon wanting to kill you first. But she did understand being confused and wanting clarification.

So she nodded.

"I do. I do indeed."

The second picture was of another young man, this one looking more gaunt and serious than the previous soldiers, standing in the open doorframe of some sort of helicopter, his hand resting on a machine gun, or some sort of large lethal-looking weapon, with a long barrel. The soldier's face was half-hidden in shadow.

The soldier was not smiling, but simply staring straight ahead, an absence of emotion showing, a blankness about his features, as he appeared to gaze at an object a thousand yards distant.

She had seen faces like that before, in books about war and battle, as if the men had vision, but had lost the ability to focus.

"This could be him," she said after comparing the two photographs. "It really looks like him."

"I thought so too," Woody said. "I looked at a couple hundred other photos, but that one was the closest match."

Hazel's heart began to race just a little, as if she was about to open the door on some new chapter in her life.

"Did you know him?" she asked, still staring at the man behind the gun.

"Not really. I mean kinda. Sort of," Woody said. "I remember him always wearing a shirt with a panther on it. The T-shirts were from the University of Pittsburgh. I guess they're called the Panthers. I remember him saying he was going to school there, then to teach and write books, after all the killing was over."

Killing? Killing?

Hazel did not say a word for a moment, and then another. She knew that wars could be brutal events, with death and all that, but never really considered, never fully embraced the possibility that the young man with her mother could have pulled the trigger of some gun and taken another person's life.

Woody's eyes wavered. He nodded, as if he knew exactly what she was thinking.

"No one wants to think somebody they know killed some other person. It ain't natural. I know. I know. I was lucky. Spent all my time on base. Was a corpsman. I saw plenty of death and busted-up buddies—but I never pulled a trigger."

Hazel stared at both photos and let silence fill the trailer.

"I still have nightmares. About what I saw. Somebody dying right next to you ain't nothing you ever forget. When it happens over and over, well, then you get the night shakes. Never leaves you, you know? Never."

Woody looked away, looked out the small window at the patch of very blue, very hot sky beyond, then wiped at his face with his hand. It made a small raspy noise of old skin scraping against stubble.

"Never gets easier, you know. Never."

Hazel wiped away the tear on her cheek as well.

"I'm sorry, Mr. Atherton. I am."

"Woody. Just Woody."

She nodded.

"And it ain't that bad. I mean, I don't have it that bad. Some bad memories. But I came back with everything I went over there with. Not like some guys who came back busted up and crippled. I ain't complaining. Could be worse. Could be a lot worse."

Hazel had simply not imagined this turn of events as she thought about the "what-ifs." Instead, she imagined finding a name and an address and then blissfully going on a quest to solve a small mystery in her life. But now, she realized, that might not be a reality that could actually, eventually turn out to be real.

After what seemed like a very, very long time, she managed to eke out a question in a small nut-brown mouse voice.

"Do you remember his name?"

Woody turned to her.

"I ain't sure exactly. Pretty sure. Steel, I think. Last name, of course. Might be with an extra 'e' on the end. Don't think I ever knew his first name."

"Steele?"

Woody shrugged.

"Yeah. But he never signed up for reunion news of the 25th. Ain't on any register that I have. A lot of vets, well, they don't want to remember, so they ain't signing up for reunions and newsletters and all that. Some guys who saw combat do. But not many, I think."

Hazel stared at the picture.

"Steele."

Woody nodded.

"If I was you, I would check with that university. Maybe they have a record or something. Or make up some story for the Vet Department in Washington that you're related or something—but that bunch of crooks in Washington probably don't give a rat's...you know, about anything 'cept their jobs."

"University of Pittsburgh," Hazel repeated, as if committing it to memory, although it was not a fact that would be easy to forget, like a phone number or a zip code.

"Yeah, start there. They probably have a department for vets or something. That's where I would go first."

Hazel found herself nodding.

"Woody, can I ask a huge favor?" she said, holding the old photo at face level. "Can I take this to get xeroxed or something? I would like to show it to him...if I find him."

Woody's face grew dark, then brightened.

"The computer in the rec center here. I think they got some sort of scanner thing. Could you do that? I...just don't want to let this get away, you know. I mean, this was one of the guys who went home, as far as I know. I want to keep that close, okay?" His voice wavered as he finished.

"Sure. I can do that. Will you ride with me to the center? Show me where it's at? And maybe I can take you to lunch?"

Woody took a deep breath and offered a weary, resigned smile, a half-smile.

"I can do that. Let me get my shoes. They got a real good deal at Denny's down the street. And I get a senior's discount, so I'll be a cheap date," he said, now smiling broadly, as if greatly relieved.

"That would be great. I like Denny's too."

—

Thurman must have heard the word "Emily," because he began to do his dance in the hallway by the front door, the hallway where Wilson made many of his phone calls—always standing up, always pacing after the first few words were spoken.

"Hi. This is Wilson."

Thurman danced about Wilson's legs, circling him twice.

"Yes. I enjoyed the play as well. Although I'm still not sold on the viability of the playwright. I still think he might be a flash in the pan."

Thurman danced with even more abandon as he heard Emily laugh, her voice coming through that thing that Wilson held close to his ear.

"I was just wondering... if you would like to go out this evening and get a cup of coffee or something. I guess it would be a date, but a minor date, if there is such a nomenclature for levels of dating."

Thurman stopped and listened, never having been told that eavesdropping was considered a rude activity.

"Good. That's good."

When Thurman heard that, he began to dance again, this time bouncing into both Wilson's legs and the wall on both sides of the hallway.

"I still have a two-inch stack of papers to grade. So could we make it at eight?"

Wilson and Thurman stood still and listened.

"Good. I'll pick you up."

And Thurman resumed his dance of a thousand canine joys, bouncing and bounding in the narrow hallway, the architect never having assumed to make the hallway wider to accommodate a joyous black Lab.

Thurman followed Wilson back into the kitchen, still dancing, and now grumble-growling *Emily, Emily, Emily.*

⟶

"This was unexpected, Wilson."

Wilson, for a short moment, appeared dismayed.

"Not bad unexpected," Emily quickly added. "Just unexpected. All the dating sites, you know, tell a man to wait a week, if not longer, to make a follow-up call."

"They do? I should have checked."

Emily touched his forearm with her hand, a delicate, yet intimate gesture of connection.

"Well, at least one site said that. Or an article. Or something. But it was most likely in reference to dating as a twenty-something. Not a two-or-three-times twenty-something."

Wilson turned to her at the stoplight and offered her a smile, a smile he hoped would appear honest and transparent and comforting.

Wilson did not truly know how to smile without considering it first, and thus was always concerned that the person he smiled at would read something untoward in his facial gesture.

But Emily smiled back. It appeared to Wilson that her face presented an honest reflection of how she felt.

"Is the Coffee Tree Roasters okay with you? Not quite as corporate as the other places. But the coffee is good."

"Sure. Any place would be fine, actually."

Coffee Tree Roasters in Squirrel Hill, often overtaken by hipsters, both Jewish and Gentile, was only semi-occupied this evening. Wilson and Emily ordered: a medium latte for Wilson and an iced green tea for Emily, with mint. They found two leather chairs in the front window overlooking the street.

"Well, this is nice," Emily said.

"Are your kids okay with you being gone? You know, short notice and all?"

Emily's pleasant expression spun toward a scowl, or a grimace, or sadness, none of which Wilson felt comfortable in guessing accurately, then quickly returned to a more neutral expression.

"They're at the age when me leaving is a good thing. For both me and them, I guess. I never thought there could be that many battles with two teenagers in the house. But there are. Clothes. Dating. Food. TV shows. Music. Texting. Phones. Homework. You name it, and they have a diametrically opposed view of it."

Wilson listened and tried not appear judgmental. Obviously, he had no valid opinion or experience in child-rearing.

"But I don't want to vent about them. I suppose that, all things considered, what I have is still better than the majority of the people in the world. And God never promises us a life free from problems."

"Apparently," Wilson replied. "And that is something everyone can agree on."

They sat back against their chairs, the leather groaning as leather does as it received the weight of their bodies. They both took sips from their drinks. Wilson closed his eyes for a moment. The lights of a taxi spun across the window, illuminating them both in a harsh, focused light for a second.

Wilson cleared his throat and opened his eyes.

"Emily..."

Emily leaned forward an inch or two. She looked as if she was steeling herself for something, something that she was not sure of, but something unexpected, and perhaps unwanted. Such is the way of interaction between men and women who were almost strangers.

"Yes?"

Wilson's eyes narrowed, as if dealing with a large and complex problem.

"Emily... I don't know... I mean... I don't know how to say it... but I simply don't know what to feel."

Emily's smile was sympathetic, comforting, and unexpected.

"And you think I do?" she asked.

Wilson wanted to nod, but realized that he should not.

Emily continued, not really expecting an answer to her question. "I have a little one... well, not little anymore... but I have a person in my house who has a dead man's face. Every time I see my son, when he first walks into the kitchen in the morning, I catch my breath. It's my husband, I think, just for a fraction of a second. He's home, I think. And then it all comes back, all the truth of the last few years, and all the pain."

Wilson did not speak.

"No, I do not have all the answers, Wilson. Maybe I don't have any answers," she said, looking down at her clear plastic cup. "Maybe no one does."

The two looked directly at each other.

"I don't know how to feel either. Or what to feel," she said, her eyes locked on Wilson. "And you have ghosts as well. I can see it in your eyes."

Wilson waited a moment, as if considering what to say or how to say it or if he should say anything at all.

"My mother must have told you some things." His words were softly spoken.

Emily's face gave no indication of having been told or not told any of the past.

"She usually does. About the war," Wilson added.

The lights in the Coffee Tree Roasters cast a softening glow on Emily's face, as if light were emanating from within her somehow.

"She did. A little."

Wilson looked down at his hands. He had seldom, if ever, really discussed his past, this part of his past, this painful set of memories that stood guard in his mind, keeping out strangers and confidants alike, making sure that no one came close enough to see what had happened . . . back then.

"Vietnam," he stated.

Emily offered the barest hint of an encouraging smile—not of acceptance exactly, but a smile of empathy. Wilson thought

he could tell her gesture was not forced, but a genuine response.

After all, she knows something about the results of war.

"I did two tours of duty in Vietnam with the 25th Division.
I joined the Army right out of high school and stayed on for
several tours—for almost six years. Then I came back and
went to Pitt...and I never left."

Emily's gaze did not waver, as a person uncomfortable or
silently willing the conversation to change direction might do.
She did not shrink and cower. Wilson had half-expected that
kind of pulling back. He had seen it happen many times. Perhaps that was one reason that the memories stayed hidden.

Emily broke the short silence.

"My husband did three tours. Two in Afghanistan. One in
Iraq. He was in for a career."

Her words were not spoken in an effort to one-up Wilson,
or to silence him, but in order that he understood that she
understood, or understood in some way, in some fashion.

No one really understands.

"I stood behind a .50-caliber machine gun in a medevac
helicopter. I provided security," Wilson explained.

Emily waited, then added, "My husband was a first
lieutenant...and a captain at the very end. He said that there
was no safe place over there."

A pained look came into Wilson's eyes, as if he was forcing a jagged memory away.

"Emily...I don't know if I have anything to give. To anyone."

Emily nodded at this, then put her drink down on the
small table and reached out and took Wilson's free hand.

"I don't know who Wilson Steele is, really," he said softly. "I don't think I have ever known."

She squeezed his hand.

"I don't know who I am anymore either," Emily replied. "Maybe no one does, Wilson, but I think the wounded find themselves in a very different place than normal people. People who have not experienced what you or my husband experienced or me or my family. They simply don't understand."

Wilson took a deep breath.

"Dr. Killeen said I have to believe. Without that, I'm trapped."

Emily nodded again, like a mother nods to a tearful child, offering a way out, a matter of solace, of refuge, of coming home.

"He is right, Wilson."

Wilson appeared lost and scared and confused.

"What if I can't? What if I can't believe?"

Emily squeezed his hand again.

"Wilson, you need to walk slowly on that path. Let's see what happens. If you can't see the bridge over the flooded river, you can't assume that it has been washed away. You have to make the journey. One step at a time. Then we'll see."

Wilson closed his eyes.

"Are you sure?"

Emily waited, then she laughed, a wary laugh, as if laughing in the face of danger, a lilting, small laugh that carried over them like a songbird singing loudly in a storm.

"No. But I'm more sure of this than I am of anything else. I am, Wilson. I'm sure of God."

It did not matter, truly, what Denny's location one visited in whatever state, they all appeared to be cut from the same cloth, the same cloying pancake smell mixed with coffee and bacon, and a portion of their clientele, regardless of the hour, apparently only minutes removed from a deep slumber.

Hazel found that ambiance to be terribly comforting, like a harbor that is known to all and always remains the same, unchangeable and immutable and ever-inviting.

Perhaps that is ascribing more to a restaurant chain than should be ascribed, she thought.

Woody waved to a waitress as they sat down. An elderly waitress, or perhaps her skin prematurely wrinkled by the desert sun, got up from her perch at the counter. Hazel wasn't sure which to blame—sun or age or both—as she approached the table.

"The usual, Woody?"

Her voice was sandpaper against sandpaper, either the result of a life of yelling or two packs a day for decades. The voice fit the face exactly.

Woody nodded. "You bet, Wilma. Don't like change."

Wilma scribbled on her pad.

"And what's for you, hon?"

"I guess two scrambled eggs and white toast, and coffee."

"Regular?"

"Yes, please."

"You got it."

They sat and looked out at the roadway and watched cars

speed past, the hot sun glistering off the metal, like natural strobe lights.

"Have you lived in Phoenix a long time, Woody?"

"Nah. I spent thirty-eight years in Austin, Minnesota, working at the Hormel plant. Hated the winters. So when I retired, boom! I headed for the desert. Been here ten years now. Feel like an old-timer, though. No one here seems to be from here. They all moved from somewhere else a year ago, it seems. Not that I'm complaining. I got nothing to gripe about, really."

"You have family back in Austin?"

"Some. My wife passed on over fifteen years ago. I got a kid, he's in the Navy and lives all over. He comes when he can. One or two aunts and uncles and cousins back there, I guess, but not all that much to speak of. Not a close-knit group."

Wilma served their food. Woody had a hamburger and fries and a Coke. Hazel ate without really tasting.

"Woody," she asked after putting a glob of strawberry-flavored jelly on her last quarter of toast, "do gunners on those medical helicopters...do they see much...combat? Or was the gun more for show? Since the helicopter had a big red cross on it and all."

Woody snorted, let out an expletive.

"Sorry, I don't mean to...I'm not around people all that much anymore. My language slips sometimes."

"It's okay, Woody. I've heard the word before."

"The red crosses just gave the VC something better to aim at, if you ask me. The birds came back pretty shot up sometimes. And the Army told the press that the gunner was just for security, but half the time they had to blast away as they were getting the wounded loaded on board. That's what they told me, anyhow. I never flew. Never in a million years would I go up there and hover in midair, just in range, so people could shoot at me. Nope. A death trap, if you ask me. But the gunners—yeah, they saw a lot of action. When everybody is shooting at you, you don't ask questions or tell them that it ain't kosher to shoot at the wounded."

Hazel listened and her heart lurched a little.

Did that soldier in mom's picture kill people like that?

"I mean, they didn't go out and strafe enemy positions or anything. But if they took fire, the gunners fired back. Toward the end, I heard that the VC would sneak in next to where the wounded were and give 'em everything they had. Knocking out a helicopter, no matter what kind, I guess, was a big deal for the VC."

Hazel tried to swallow the last bite of toast, which seemed to go dry and stale in her throat.

"Any gunner on any helicopter was fair game, and a great target. You could see where the tracers were coming from and every VC in the area would open up on it. Them gunners didn't have a real long life expectancy."

"Oh. I didn't . . . I didn't realize."

"That's okay. No one does. Or did."

Woody's eyes took on a faraway look, like he was staring backward forty years and seeing things he did not really want to see again.

"That's why I didn't want to give up that picture. He was one of them that went home. I saw him leave. He made it. Too many others didn't, you know. Kind of a success story. If there are any success stories that came out of that stupid war."

Hazel sat still and willed herself not to tear up, not to tear up over Woody's pain after forty years, at the futility of conflict, at the sacrifice so many young men made in courageous service to their country, not to tear up over this one unnamed gunner and his role in Hazel's life.

If he has one, that is.

Woody wiped at his face. If he was wiping away a tear, it was a practiced move so it would not look like he was doing so.

"But every G.I. says that about every war, I bet. You do your duty, and that's a good thing. Honorable. Noble, even. But after all the killing, after so many years have gone by, you sort of have to think and wonder if it was all worth it, you know?"

Hazel replied, "I do."

"I guess it was. I tell myself it was. I did what I was called on to do. And that's all I could do."

⟵

Thurman seldom climbed the steps to the second floor of Wilson's house. Occasionally he took the stairs, one at a time, with small, careful, gingerly placed steps, just to see if Wilson was okay and comfortable. Once he felt assured that all was well, he would make his way back downstairs, like a mountain climber descending a sheet of ice or the face of a glacier.

Wilson imagined that Thurman felt that it was his duty, as the dog of the house, to provide the first line of defense, in case of attack, or burglary, or intrusions by mailmen. Being close to the door and the window—midway, equidistant to both—was of prime importance to Thurman, so his preferred choice in sleeping locations was still his first pick the first day he arrived: situated on a thickness of folded blanket in the family room, adjacent to the couch.

Wilson had offered Thurman a fancy bed he purchased at the fancy pet store in Shadyside—tartan plaid on one side, imitation lamb's wool on the other. Thurman had tried it, both sides, decided to have none of it, and then somehow managed to nudge the door open and drag his blanket back out of the hall closet where Wilson had stored it "temporarily."

But tonight Thurman gave up on his task of protecting the house.

Instead, he followed Wilson up the stairs and sat beside his bed.

Wilson sat at the edge of the bed, wearing a University of Pittsburgh T-shirt with a snarling panther on the front.

Thurman came up silently and stared at Wilson.

"What?" Wilson asked.

Company.

"For you or for me?" Wilson asked.

Thurman growled his reply.

You.

"And you think I need company tonight? Why tonight?"

Thurman grew serious, as serious as a black Lab can make his expression, narrowing his eyes.

Emily. Sad.

Wilson took a deep breath and exhaled loudly.

"Maybe. But not sad."

Thurman did not buy it.

Sad, he growled. *Confuse.*

"You mean 'confused.' And maybe that's it, Thurman."

Sad.

Wilson reached out and put his hand on Thurman's head, and Thurman pressed back against it.

"Thurman, I know my mother prays. She has prayed. She continues to pray."

Thurman looked up, his eyes peeking through Wilson's wrist.

Pray.

Wilson did not speak. It appeared that he wanted to speak, but the words were trapped in his throat, trapped by a thickness there, a darkness that occurred when the pain rose up and squeezed at his heart.

"But after what I've done, Thurman, there is no redemption."

Thurman sort of shook the hand off his head and growled.

Redemp?

"Redemption. It means forgiveness, Thurman. When you do something bad. For me, there is no redemption."

Thurman was having none of this.

He backed up and half-jumped, so his front paws landed on Wilson's thighs, so his eyes were almost at Wilson's eye level. The dog stared as hard as a dog is capable of staring.

Bunkum.

Wilson just shook his head as if rejecting that evaluation.

Grace. Gift, he growled, his mumble-growls more emphatic than Wilson had ever heard up until this moment.

Grace. Gift.

Thurman's back legs did a little back-and-forth dance, as

he often did when he was trying to make a point, when he was serious about some aspect of life.

Grace. Grace. Grace.

"Yeah, Thurman, maybe for you. But you haven't done what I did. No grace."

Bunkum. Bunkum.

Wilson gently took Thurman's paws off his thigh and replaced them on the floor. Then he lay back on the bed and pulled the covers up and appeared to be trying to hide.

Thurman did something that he had never done before.

He jumped up on to the bed, his legs stepping with great care, not certain of the surface of a bed and how it would react to four paws. After a moment, he must have decided that it was safe to walk, and he took puppy steps toward Wilson and lay down, folding his legs under him, as gentle as a fawn, then laid his head on the second pillow and stared at Wilson, his dark eyes wide and open and welcoming.

"Thurman, what are you doing?"

Sleep. Not sad. Grace. Faith. God. Friend.

Thurman rattled off the words almost as fast as he could, words that he obviously hoped would provide rest and balm for Wilson's wounds, years and decades old, some open and festering, others hidden and covered by a thick patina of years.

Sleep. Protect. Not sad.

Chapter Twenty-Four

O N THE WAY back to her hotel from the Desert Skies Mobile Home Park, Hazel had stopped at a drugstore and had purchased a large road atlas. She could have used the map app on her tablet, but the small screen made it hard to really get the big picture. Plus it would be too tempting to start searching the Internet for more information. If she did that, she might lose her nerve to go at all. And so she had left the tablet buried in her other suitcase in the back of the Quest, where it would remain until she got to Pennsylvania. When she had returned to her room, she'd opened the book up to the two-page spread of the map of the entire United States.

She knew where Pittsburgh was, almost for sure, out east, but not as far as New York City, yet the land between her and that city remained a big unknown.

Geography was never my best subject in school.

It had taken a minute to locate Phoenix on the map.

I wonder if they still teach geography these days. Since everybody has a map on their smartphones, maybe not, she'd thought.

Between one finger placed on Phoenix and another placed on Pittsburgh, there was a very large swath of the country that Hazel had never once visited or seen or had even been curious about, for that matter.

I guess I was pretty provincial in my outlook. Maybe every-one from Portland is that way. You know, hipsters. It's in the water. There is no other part of the country that is as cool as Portland, so why bother with them?

There were all sorts of blue lines snaking across the mid-dle of America. Hazel had to flip a page to find out what the blue lines were and what the red lines were. Blue lines were interstates with limited access, and red lines were regu-lar roads, with easy access to Waffle Houses.

She'd brought the map with her to the huge, multistory atrium lobby of the hotel, had gotten a large complimentary coffee, which was served all day, and had sat, tracing one route and then another. She assumed that the GPS system in the Quest would pick the shortest and the fastest route, but now that she had a destination in sight, she felt a hesita-tion, as if the possibility of finding out the truth was a scarier proposition than she had first imagined.

I can get there soon enough. But I don't want to travel faster than . . .

She'd looked at the fountain in the lobby, the one that filled the atrium with a liquid sort of echo.

. . . faster than I don't know what.

She had a notepad with her and had jotted down the route:

Phoenix to Albuquerque. From Albuquerque to Oklahoma City. Then on to Wichita to Kansas City to Des Moines.

That's a long trip already. But I always wanted to see Wichita and Des Moines. My mother talked about both those cities.

Then from Des Moines to Chicago and then past Detroit and then to Cleveland.

From Cleveland, it did not seem like a long trip to Pittsburgh.

She used a torn piece of paper that matched the distance key to measure each section of roadway. It was a rough guess—some twenty-five hundred miles, give or take.

At fifty miles an hour, that will take...uhh...fifty hours. I could go faster, but I like to stop a lot.

She had finished her coffee and had debated getting a second cup, which would actually be her eighth cup of the day.

If I don't push the driving, and maybe stop once in a while to look at things, that could take me a week. Maybe ten days.

She decided on one more cup, pouring it from the urn that seemed to have a limitless supply.

That's not bad. A week or so until I find out.

She sipped at her eighth cup.

Or not find out.

⤙

Sharif Moses Yusry waited in his cab, listening to a baseball game, thinking that listening to native English speakers would help improve his English, although he understood little of what happened on a baseball pitch.

He did know that the team here in Pittsburgh were called the baseball Pirates.

Sharif and his cab were outside the Heritage Square Senior Apartments and Retirement Village, parked in the shade of a maple tree, waiting. He was the second of three cabs. Today was the fifteenth of the month, the day many of the residents received a government check—and also the day many of them needed a ride to the bank or the grocery store or sometimes the liquor store.

Sharif hoped it would not be the last place.

"Old people should not spend the money on such things," he said to himself after taking an old woman, tottering even when sober, to one such business.

But cabdrivers could not be selective in fares or their destinations. He would go where they asked to go.

Sharif watched two people make their way out of the front doors. They both headed to the cabstand. Gretna Steele was one of them. She allowed the other person to take the first cab and walked to the second cab. Sharif was out and opening the back door as she approached.

"Morning, Mizz Steele," he said. "Delightful, is it not? Outside."

Gretna eyed the driver with suspicion, scowled, and garrumped a short "Hello," and slid into the backseat.

"Where to go?" Sharif asked as he climbed behind the wheel and started the engine.

"Giant Eagle," Gretna replied. "I'm out of coffee."

"Most assured," Sharif replied.

"And someplace where they sell cigarettes," Gretna said, her voice low, almost a whisper. "You know of a place that sells cigarettes?"

Sharif shrugged.

"I do not use them. But the Eleven-Seven shows signs for them in their windows."

Gretna grumped, "Good. On the way back. Okay?"

"For certain," Sharif said as he pulled onto Negley Avenue and headed to the store.

Traffic slowed and Sharif looked in the rearview mirror.

"Mizz Steele, I see your son last night."

"What? Who? Where?"

"Your son, Mizz Steele. I know his looks. At the store . . . at de coffee shop. Some sort of Coffee Tree store."

"My son? Wilson?" Gretna leaned forward, which was difficult because of the slant of the rear seat. "When?"

"It was last night. Not late. With a woman. I think the woman goes to Heritage some."

Gretna leaned forward more and grabbed at the back of the front seat, as if wanting to hear every word.

"Black hair? The woman, I mean. Did she have black hair? Pretty?"

"Indeed. Pretty, indeed. I only drive past fastly. It was, as I have heard, a flash in de pan? Is that right?"

Gretna seemed much lighter all of a sudden, and much less prickly, much less caffeine-deprived.

"Almost right. But I know what you mean."

She leaned back against the seat with a smile.

Sharif turned the corner to the Giant Eagle.

"You wait here. I will be back in a minute," Gretna ordered.

"Will do that, Mizz Steele."

⟶

Hazel had decided to spend the night in Slippery Rock, Pennsylvania, well before the signs indicated that the city, and the college, lay only a few miles ahead.

With a name like Slippery Rock, it has to be cool.

Then she berated herself for using the word "cool."

At my age, I have no right to decide on what is cool or not.

She switched on her turn signal.

But it is still an interesting name.

She found an all-suites motel, having resisted staying at a single-room motel during her entire cross-country expedition. She wasn't sure why exactly, but having two rooms, and a bathroom, made it feel less transitory, and more like she was living in a series of very compact, very tidy apartments.

She had not expected to feel the negative effects of rootlessness, and of travel, as intently as she had.

Tour the country for months on end? What was I thinking? I can't do this much longer.

She wondered if Pittsburgh might be a good place to call it quits, to call an end to her very brief nomadic experience.

Pittsburgh sounds nice on the Internet. It looks pretty. I could live there. They have rivers I could live near.

She slooped her suitcase toward the elevator and the fourth floor. One wheel had already broken off, so the suitcase rolled sort of off-kilter, making a canvas hissing noise as Hazel dragged it across lobbies and down hallways.

The all-suites motel boasted free high-speed Internet access, so Hazel got a cup of coffee from the lobby...

They all have coffee in the lobby. Isn't that nice?

...and returned to her room to do a little research on her tablet.

She had resisted doing so until she got close to her intended destination.

If I found some tantalizing information, well, that would

just make me hurry to get there. Which might not have been so bad.

During her trip and its less than frantic pace, she did stop and see the sights in Chicago, and had spent an entire extra day walking along the city's lakefront. She had taken extra time in Cleveland too, where she'd also walked along the lakefront for much of a day.

Different lakes, though. I really think I should live by the water.

Now ensconced in the Slippery Rock Comfort Suites, Hazel accessed the University of Pittsburgh website. There was a page that described the overall academic standing and stature of the faculty, but did not offer a complete alphabetical listing.

Hmmmm.

However, there was a place that offered a "People Search," so she typed in the name Steele. But she waited to push enter on the tablet—waited because she was afraid that she might find him, and just as afraid that she would not.

Before doing anything, she stood up and walked around her two-room suite, not wanting to know as much as wanting to know. The closer she came to the truth, or the possibility of the truth, the more anxious and worried and concerned and nervous she became.

She took several deep breaths.

Then she sat down, picked up the tablet, and hit enter.

The little ball on the screen whirled for ten seconds, and then a name popped up: Wilson Steele, PhD.

And then a faculty profile picture and a very brief biography.

She almost dropped the tablet back onto the table. She stared at the picture for a long time. She had all but memorized the picture of her mother and the soldier, so she did not really need to refer back to it.

She stared.

"It could be him. It really could."

The biography was sparse in detail.

His PhD was from the University of Pittsburgh, as well as his MA and BA.

That must be unusual. Woody did say he intended on going to Pitt when he returned.

His area of specialization was writing and rhetoric and American literature. The information explained that he focused on teaching creative writing, mainly at the graduate level, but he also taught contemporary American literature at the undergraduate level. The web page included a long list of titles of papers he had written, mostly for academic-sounding journals that Hazel had never heard of, and three books—two on writing and one on rhetoric.

There were no other personal details mentioned.

She stared at the picture.

It really could be him. The eyes are similar. Very similar.

She looked up at the closed door of her two-room suite and did not think of anything for a long time. Then she went back to the tablet, went to Google, and typed in his name and added "University of Pittsburgh" in the search.

Instantaneously, several million links were discovered. The second item on the list, however, caught her attention.

The citation referenced an article in the *Pittsburgh Post-Gazette* newspaper, highlighting a Gretna Steele, who was the wife of the late Dr. August Steele, focused on her decision to return to the Pittsburgh area after having initially retired to Florida.

That could be his mother.

She tapped at the screen and the article came into view. Hazel read it carefully. It must have been from a local edition of the paper; the heading was "Squirrel Hill Comings and Goings."

The article was a breezy recap of the doings of the people in Squirrel Hill. Hazel looked it up and discovered that the neighborhood was not far from the University of Pittsburgh, and was formerly very ethnic, mainly Jewish. The article read:

> Gretna Steele, widow of Dr. August Steele, the well-known otolaryngologist (that's a sinus doctor for those of us who don't know Latin, now better known as ENTs), has recently moved back to the area. (She was born and raised in Squirrel Hill.) She is now residing at the Heritage Square Senior Apartments and Retirement Village (in our lovely village). Her reasons for returning to our cold winters and short summers? She didn't like the bugs or the heat in Florida and missed her son, Wilson. (Wilson is a professor at the University of Pittsburgh.)

Whoever wrote this really likes parentheses—if that's the correct plural version of the word. Spelling wasn't my best subject either.

Hazel stopped reading and simply scanned the rest of the piece, not noticing any more pertinent details about the

Steeles. The writer prattled on, detailing other former retirees who had moved to Florida and since returned to the Pittsburgh area in recent months.

Hazel went back to Google and typed in "Heritage Square Senior Apartments and Retirement Village," and immediately was connected to their website, with photos, phone numbers, and address.

She found her small notebook and wrote the information down.

Can it be that easy?

She hardly noticed that her heart was beating faster, almost as fast as if she had sprinted up four flights of steps.

Aren't I supposed to suffer more? Encounter more setbacks and obstacles?

She finished the last of her now lukewarm coffee.

This will not make a very good Lifetime movie, that's for sure.

Chapter Twenty-Five

*H*AZEL DID NOT LEAVE for Pittsburgh the next day as planned.

She encountered a bad case of nerves that morning, feeling jangled and wired and anxious, and knew that driving into a strange city would be more traumatic and perhaps even terrifying in her altered state.

Know, not know... sounds like a quote from Yoda, yet both results are equally terrifying.

Instead of traveling, she ate a very leisurely breakfast, which came free with her room, read the local papers, then drove to the campus of Slippery Rock University and walked around the bucolic and peaceful quad, spending over an hour in the bookstore, where she bought a Slippery Rock sweatshirt. She had lunch at Quaker Steak and Lube in the university's student center and got her fill of medium-spicy chicken wings.

After that, she began to feel normal again—unstressed, unvexed.

She went back to her two-room suite, took a nap, and watched a baseball game on TV—who was playing did not matter—while having a cheese-and-sausage pizza that Weege's Pizza had delivered right to her room.

The following morning she spent an entire shower

steeling herself—*No pun intended*, she thought as the words "steeling myself" popped into her mind—and, following a much lighter breakfast, headed south, toward Pittsburgh.

Her Quest's navigation system determined that the trip should take no more than an hour. Hazel always added 25 percent to the time estimates of the Quest. If the suggested route went through a major metropolitan area, she added up to 40 percent more time.

The map gizmo really doesn't know how I drive, which is slower than most—especially in congested areas.

The way was much less confusing than Hazel had initially feared, the suggested route veering left and right and around as it navigated the neighborhoods east of Pittsburgh proper. The GPS ticked the miles down, and soon enough announced, "Destination is ahead, on the right."

She saw the tall residential tower from a block away and tightened her grip on the steering wheel.

She pulled to the curb half a block away and once again attempted to calm herself down.

"What's the worst that can happen? The lady there says it is not her son. If that happens, then I'll try something else."

She checked the traffic twice, then pulled into the street and slowly drove into the small parking lot of the Heritage Square complex.

Is it a complex if it only contains one building?

She switched off the engine and took several more deep breaths. It did not really calm her down or settle her nerves, but it did buy a few seconds of time.

She took the photograph from the glove compartment.

She had sealed it in a clear plastic sleeve. And if anything happened to the Quest or her purse or its contents, well, she had scanned both sides of the photo and stored them digitally in the cloud.

She looked at her face in the rearview mirror.

A little panicked, I guess. But not crazed panicked. Just a normal panic.

She brushed a hand through her hair, straightened the collar on her blouse, and stepped outside.

She stopped.

Dear Lord, if this is meant to be . . . you know what to do, I guess.

She walked toward the front doors, attempting to think calm thoughts.

This looks like a pleasant sort of place. Clean. Well maintained.

She stepped inside and knew immediately that it was a place for seniors by the smell of mothballs mixed with Vicks mixed with the aroma of oatmeal and prunes. To her left was a long counter. She could see only the heads of two women sitting behind it.

"I would like to see a resident who lives here," Hazel announced, "but I don't know what room or apartment, or whatever, she lives in. Do I have to call first, or what?"

The closer woman looked up from a computer screen.

"Are you family or a friend?"

Hazel had not anticipated that question.

"A friend. I guess."

The woman shrugged.

"It doesn't matter. You just have to sign in."

Hazel signed her name in her small, neat cursive hand-writing.

"And who are you visiting?"

"Her name is Gretna Steele."

The woman behind the counter brightened.

"You're in luck. She's right over there. By the piano. In the green sweater."

Hazel heard a joint in her neck pop and crack as she quickly turned to look where the woman was pointing. In the middle of a pool of afternoon sun an old woman sat in an upholstered chair, looking out to the courtyard beyond.

"She's Gretna Steele?"

"She is," the woman confirmed. Then she called loudly, half-standing, "Hey, Gretna, you have a visitor."

Hazel blanched visibly. She had not anticipated that sort of introduction, but now that it had happened, there was no alternative but to smile, wave, and make her way toward the piano and the old woman in the green sweater.

The eyes are the same. They are.

⟶

Thurman paced back and forth, from the front door to the back door, not even stopping in the kitchen to see if his food bowl had been magically refilled during his half-minute absence.

Every time he walked by, he snorted, a little under his breath, almost as if in disbelief, or rather dismay.

This was Wilson's early afternoon; he had no classes scheduled, and for the first time in many weeks he did not have any papers or tests to grade. Instead of focusing on professorial tasks, he sat in the leather recliner in the family room and read a biography of Winston Churchill.

Thurman made his circuit again and again and again.

The soft, muted clacking of a dog's nails on the hardwood floors eventually got to Wilson.

"Thurman, what are you doing?"

Thurman stopped just outside the family room, on the far side of the arch that separated it from the hallway.

The dog looked over to Wilson and growled.

"You're nervous?"

Thurman appeared to nod his head.

"And what, pray tell, does a dog have to be nervous about?"

Thurman managed a grimace, then he smiled.

Food, he whisper-growled.

"Thurman, we have played this game too often for me to believe you. That's not it, I'm sure. What is it?"

How far I have descended into this canine madness, Wilson thought. *I am actually convinced that Thurman understands me. And worse, that I understand him.*

Thurman sat down and appeared pensive.

Nervous, he growled. *Worried*.

Wilson shook his head, at himself.

"About what, Thurman?"

Thurman wanted to shrug and tried to shrug, but never could quite accomplish it. He must have thought the gesture was excellent shorthand for all sorts of emotions and responses.

Instead of doing the shrug with precision, he growled instead, *Not know.*

Wilson stared at the dog for another moment, until Thurman got back up, shook himself energetically, and continued his pacing.

"Well, Thurman, if you don't know, I can't help you," Wilson said, and returned to his reading.

And Thurman continued to walk and make small worried growling noises, with no words attached to them, every time he passed the arch and caught sight of Wilson, who apparently did not care enough to investigate more thoroughly.

⌒

"Do I know you?" Gretna asked, her eyes narrowing as Hazel came closer. "You look familiar somehow."

"You are Gretna Steele, aren't you?"

Gretna was sometimes slow to become suspicious, not often, but sometimes.

"And who wants to know?" she asked, then smiled, almost. "Sorry. They have these seminars here that tell the rest of these old fogeys to be careful with strangers and never give out your Social Security number. You don't want my Social Security number, do you?"

Hazel looked a bit relieved. "No. No, I don't."

"Good. Because if you're after my millions, well, you're too late. You know, you could have a couple of million dollars saved up, but if you last long enough, it won't be enough. No sense in worrying about it. At my age, what do I need? Right?"

Hazel nodded in agreement. "You are right about that."

"So who are you? A daughter of somebody here,

checking up to see if this place is taking good care of them? Scoping out the place to see if you should send your parents here?"

"No, no, nothing like that," Hazel replied, already taking a liking to the cantankerous old woman. "I wanted to know . . . well, it's sort of a long story."

Gretna snorted. "It can't be too long. I don't have that much time left." She remained serious for a second, then laughed. "Sit down. If it's a long story, that is. I'll get a crick in my neck if I have to look up at you while you tell it."

Hazel pulled up a chair.

Gretna leaned close and whispered, "You don't have any cigarettes, do you? The cabdriver was supposed to stop at the 7-Eleven, but he forgot. Well, I forgot too. And it's too far to walk. And they don't sell them here. No one is supposed to smoke. A smoke-free facility, the signs say. But I know a couple of those old codgers up on the fifth floor that smoke, leaning out their windows. I'd ask them, but they can't hear and I'd have to shout and then everyone would know and they'd probably try and toss me out of this place for subversion or something."

"Sorry," Hazel replied. "I don't smoke."

"Rats."

"But . . . I guess if you wanted me to, I could go to the store and get you some."

"Well, that would be swell," Gretna replied. "Now that we've settled that, tell me your story. The long story. I got all afternoon."

Hazel had practiced what she was going to say a hundred times on her trip across the country, but now that she was called to remember what it was that she planned on saying, and how to phrase it, and how not to sound like a lunatic, all of that rehearsal simply slipped out of her mind.

"I'm Hazel Jamison," she started, her words hesitant. "I'm from Portland."

"Maine?"

"No, the other one. Oregon."

"Hippies and liberals, right?"

Hazel nodded. "Sort of. There does seem to be a lot of them out there."

"Why is that? The rain, maybe?" Gretna asked.

For an old woman, she is really sharp.

"I don't know. Maybe the old saying, 'birds of a feather,' you know."

"Makes sense. Go on," Gretna said.

"Well, it is a long story . . . but I guess I can get right to the point."

She reached into her purse and extracted the decades-old photo, now tucked into its protective plastic sleeve. She held it out toward the old woman.

"Do you know this person?" she asked. "The soldier, I mean?"

Gretna's eyes widened, not just from surprise, but also in order to stare at the picture. She looked up from the photo and stared hard at Hazel.

"Is that woman your mother?"

"She is. She passed away a while ago."

"Sorry to hear that. She must have been young."

"Sixty-three."

"That's young. You look just like her."

Gretna turned back to the picture. Neither of them said anything for a long moment.

"Do you know him?" Hazel finally asked, softly, almost under her breath, as if fearing what the answer might be.

"Yes. I know him."

Hazel began to take breaths again. She had been holding her breath for a while.

"He's my son. Wilson Steele. He was in Vietnam, you know."

"I do. Well, I don't, I didn't, but I assumed that. From his uniform. I had some hints, some help along the way to here."

"Was this taken in Portland?"

Hazel nodded. "I'm pretty sure it was. I don't think my mother ever left the area. Not even on vacation."

"She is very pretty."

"Thank you."

Gretna put her arm out and extended her hand. Hazel handed her the photograph and Gretna pulled it closer to her face, closer to her eyes, and stared at the black-and-white image.

"I don't think I have a picture of him in his uniform. I don't think he has any pictures of himself in uniform. At least none that I have ever seen. He was very young. Do you know what year this was taken?"

"I don't."

Gretna closed her eyes, as if she was considering some monumental choice, some hard-to-fathom decision.

"You should show this to Wilson. I think maybe he would want to see it. Now. Maybe now. Enough time has passed, I would say. He doesn't talk about this time in his life very much."

If there was a word for what Hazel was feeling, she did not know what it would be. She was nervous and excited and scared and more scared and hopeful and scared.

"Does he live nearby?"

"A few blocks away, actually. Maybe more than a few, but within five minutes."

Reluctantly, Gretna handed the picture back to Hazel.

"You should show it to him. He's home. Maybe he needs to see this."

"Now?"

Gretna's expression softened.

"Sure. How much time do any of us have left? Now is better than later."

↩

Hazel made good on her offer to buy cigarettes for Gretna.

She's obviously old. How much damage could they do now?

"Lucky Strikes. The kind without filters. I like to live dangerously," she whispered. "Here's five dollars. I don't know what they cost these days."

Hazel refused the money.

"No, this will be my treat. You helped me answer some questions."

When Hazel returned, Gretna palmed the cigarettes into the pocket of her housecoat, all the while looking about furtively to see if any of the staff had noticed the transaction. They had not.

"This is his address. It was the family home. He grew up there. You remember the directions?"

"I do," Hazel said, but she knew that the Quest's GPS would validate the rights and lefts and straight-ahead-at-the-light directions.

She put the Quest in gear, pulled out of the parking lot, and drove slowly, following the GPS—just in case.

In just a few minutes, she was on the opposite side of the street from a tidy brick home with neatly trimmed bushes and lawn, framed by a wreath of trees and foliage in the side yards.

"This looks like an old family home."

She got her purse, made sure the photo was inside, took a deep breath...

I should study deep-breathing techniques for stress reduction.

...and stepped out of the car, looked both ways, and walked across the street. In the larger window—the picture window—was the head of a large black dog, staring at her as she walked.

⌒

If anyone had asked Thurman why he was so rattled, so excited, so anxious, he would not have been able to tell them why—not exactly. Had Wilson been closely observant that day, he would have said that it simply appeared that Thurman had some manner of premonition, some foreboding, foreshadowing, of some upcoming event of some great import.

Thurman acted as if today was his birthday and he was totally expecting a surprise party, with people jumping out from behind the sofa, crying out, "Happy birthday!" but he did not know when exactly, so he kept imagining shadows lurking behind furniture and balloons to be delivered, out of the blue, as it were.

Once he saw the woman park her car, once he saw her exit the car and watched her begin walking toward the house, he could scarcely contain himself. He started his canine dance right there on the big soft thing in front of the window, dancing and whining and barking out repeated *Hellos*.

Then he jumped down, danced into the family room, yipping and crying and moaning and barking and muttering and whispering, and then danced back toward the front door, waiting, whining in great anticipation.

Wilson took out the bookmark, placed it on his current page, sighed, then firmly closed the book and placed it on the side table. He pushed the recliner to the upright position.

Must be the mailman. Or the UPS driver. Maybe Thurman thinks it's the pizza delivery boy.

When the doorbell sounded, Thurman launched himself into the air, as if trying to see through the small window located at eye level in the top center of the door.

Wilson swung the door open.

A woman stood there, clutching her purse with both hands in front of her, looking like a picture one would see in a 1950s *Life* magazine. A timid woman. In modest dress, holding a sensible purse, waiting for something, something unknown. Meek and unassuming and looking just a little frightened.

Wilson looked at the woman on his front step for longer than he would look at anyone else. In the past, he never truly saw the mailman or the UPS driver or the pizza delivery boy. They appeared and then they left, almost as if they were invisible. But not this woman. He looked at her face, seeing something that he did not yet comprehend. He thought it might be too obvious, his staring, that is, so he attempted to avert his eyes, just a bit.

Thurman continued his gentle caterwauling and dancing just behind Wilson, careful not to lunge or threaten or bark as if in responding to a threat or acting out because of stranger danger. He simply was lost in celebrating this new arrival, the new omen of something unexpected.

After what seemed to be a very long silence, Wilson nodded, just a bit, almost hidden, and said, "Can I help you?"

It was obvious that Hazel had lost the power of speech for that same moment; she seemed relieved that they both stared and did not speak. But now a question had been asked, and she was required to answer.

"I'm Hazel Jamison," she said. Then paused a long moment. "I saw...I met...your mother. She suggested...she said you would be home. I don't...want to be intruding...I mean, I don't want to intrude—that's it. I can come back later."

She actually took a half-step in retreat.

At that, Thurman doubled and redoubled his efforts to gain her attention and to prevent her from leaving.

Wilson was forced to turn around and glare at the dog.

"Thurman? Do you mind? We're trying to talk here and you're making this woman very nervous."

Thurman almost fell to the floor upon hearing that he might be the cause of her leaving.

Not go. Not go. Not go.

He growled and whispered other things, but in a tangle of syntax that even Wilson could not follow.

Wilson turned back to the woman who stood on his front step.

"I'm sorry. Thurman sometimes gets overexuberant. Sorry that he frightened you."

Hazel held up one hand as if she were wiping a blackboard clean of chalk.

"No. No. I like dogs. I'm not frightened. Not at all."

Thurman stood a little taller and growled out his hello.

"Mr. Steele, I'm Hazel Jamison. I saw your mother a few minutes ago. It's a long story, but I have a picture of my mother and . . . well, you're in the picture as well. Your mother said it was you. I found her through a Google search. The photo, it must have been before I was born. And I was wondering if you could shed some light on it for me."

Wilson was slow to respond.

"You're from where?"

"Portland. Portland, Oregon. Not the one in Maine."

Wilson's vision unfocused for a moment, then he spoke, softly, so quietly that Hazel had to lean closer to hear him.

"Portland. I was . . . I spent some time there—years and years ago."

"Oh."

"There was a VA hospital. Is it still there?"

Hazel shrugged.

"I don't know. It might be."

Silence again, except for Thurman, who continued his clattering dance in the foyer, but without the growling and barks.

"Could I see the picture?" Wilson asked.

Hazel seemed to snap out of a very short-lived fugue state, and opened her purse, with both hands, and pulled the picture and plastic protective sheet out into the sunlight.

Wilson took the photo, Thurman standing behind him leaning to one side so he could see it as well. They both remained quiet and still.

"It was the year I got out of the Army," Wilson finally said.

"It was?" Hazel asked.

"I would be out of the Army . . . in the fall. This was during the summer of that year."

Wilson felt a coil of sweat form on his back between his shoulder blades. His stomach lurched and his heart rate began to increase. He blinked several times, and then blinked again.

It was obvious that Hazel had a hundred questions to ask, but she settled on just one—perhaps the one most pivotal to why she had made this cross-country journey in the first place.

"Were you married to her? She wrote on the back of the picture, 'Our Wedding.'"

Wilson flipped the picture over. He tried his best to maintain his composure, but if one looked closely, one would see a slight tremor in his right hand, and a twitch in the muscles around his eyes—nothing writ large or obvious, but present nonetheless.

He shook his head slowly. His jaw tightened and then loosened.

"I don't know why she would have written that," he replied.

Thurman growled, his mumbling bark louder, and apparently a little agitated.

"I was there," Wilson replied, his tone flat, unemotional, almost practiced. "I don't know why she would have written that. I was a guest."

Thurman appeared to grow more restless, pacing back and forth in the narrow entryway, growling, his nails clicking a staccato rhythm.

Hazel drew in a large breath, as if attempting to maintain her composure as well.

"Then do you know who it was that she married? She never told me a name. In fact, I never knew that she had been married. She never told me about it. I just thought she was a single parent. I'm not looking for anything . . . you know . . . to get anything out of this. It's been so long. I just wanted a name."

Wilson swallowed several times, blinking, still looking at the photograph.

"I'm . . . I'm sorry. It was just another soldier I met at the hospital. I don't . . . I mean, it has been a long time. I don't think I remember his name. I wasn't . . . friends with him. Just an acquaintance. From the hospital. He asked if I wanted to go to his wedding. I said yes. I went. That's all there was to it. I simply spent an afternoon at a wedding of two people I did not know. I was happy to go because it got me out of the hospital for a while."

Wilson's words seemed fast and unfocused and off target, somehow. Thurman bounced up and down, bringing his front legs into the air and then dropping down again, barking and mumbling and growling.

Wilson turned again.

"Thurman, stop it!" he shouted. "I mean it. Or else you get put out back."

Thurman appeared stunned, and he slowly backed up three steps, yet still growling and mumbling and regarding Wilson defiantly.

Wilson turned back to Hazel.

"I'm sorry. It is me. In the photo. But that's all I can tell you about that picture."

Hazel nodded, the question still written on her face.

But then...why did she write that? Why would she have kept a picture of a guest she hardly knew? Why would she have saved just one random picture of a random guest?

She clearly wanted to say all those things, ask all those questions, but she did not. She looked at Wilson's face and into his eyes and must have seen something dark and cold and cautionary. She formed a question in her mouth...but did not ask it.

"Okay."

Wilson stood silent, even as Thurman was whispering and growling.

"Well, okay," Hazel added, her voice like cotton.

She slipped the picture back into her purse.

"You've been helpful," she replied, not meaning a word of it, and then feeling guilty at her reaction.

She took one step backward.

"Listen," she said softly, almost as if she was pleading, but she wasn't—or tried not to sound like she was. "I'm staying in

Pittsburgh for a couple of days, at least. I'm over at the Wyndham University Center. I think it's on Lytton Avenue."

"It is," Wilson said. "That's almost on campus. I work there. At the university."

"Oh. Okay."

Hazel almost forgot to ask what she wanted to ask.

"Well, I know that I'm an unexpected visitor. And the picture was unexpected. But maybe if you remember the groom's name . . . you could call me. Or leave a message."

Thurman almost howled, in a singsong, howly way, as if he was insisting that Hazel not leave.

Wilson let out a long breath, as if he had been holding it in for a long period.

"Sure. I will think about it. That day. And if I remember anything else, I will call. At the Wyndham University Center."

Hazel managed a nod and stepped down from the stoop.

"Thank you, Dr. Steele. I appreciate it."

"You're welcome," Wilson replied and pulled the door shut, silencing—almost silencing—Thurman, who was still grumbling, still whining in the background.

⤙

Hazel pulled onto the street and looked back at the house one last time. She saw the dog, Thurman, barking silently through the window, his front paws on the back of the sofa, barking directly at her. She saw the dog turn his head to look behind him for a brief moment, then turn back again to continue barking as she drove off.

He won't call. Maybe he was just a guest. Maybe she lost

all the other pictures marked "Our Wedding" and this was the only one she saved. Maybe there was a fire or a flood or a burglary.

At the stoplight, the GPS instructed Hazel to turn left.

She did, and as she did so, she began to cry—not a lot, but some, crying over a lost moment of her past, a past that she knew little about and that was now more permanently lost and gone and buried.

That was what she cried for.

And cried during the entire trip to the Wyndham University Center.

Chapter Twenty-Six

WILSON PACED around the house, not looking at anything, not paying attention to the machinations of Thurman, not hearing, not seeing.

He looked at his watch.

Emily had called earlier that day—well before the strange woman appeared with the strange photograph from his long-buried past—had called and asked Wilson if he might like to take a walk that afternoon. The weather was bound to get warmer soon, probably hot and most likely humid, and this specific day promised to be perfect: mild and sunny and well suited for a stroll around the neighborhood with Thurman in tow.

Wilson had not thought of a reason to decline, or thought of it in time, so he had agreed.

The doorbell sounded again and Thurman launched himself toward the front door, obviously hoping it was that woman who had come earlier.

When Wilson opened the door and Thurman saw Emily standing there, he managed a canine double take, but quickly went from confused to delighted.

One of Thurman's most endearing traits—a trait of all dogs, most likely—was the ability to go from grumpy to ecstatic in a heartbeat, with no angry residue polluting the present. Dogs did not, probably could not, hold grudges or seek revenge. Such emotions were not in their DNA; certainly it was not in Thurman's DNA.

Seeing Emily brought him joy, and he would choose no other course of action than to show it, and to welcome her with open arms—or paws, as it were.

"Hello, Thurman," she called out and knelt down to greet him. "Are you ready for your walk?"

Thurman obviously knew the word "walk," and he was even more delighted after hearing it, showing his delight by repeating his retriever dance, rear legs swinging back and forth like a semi truck fishtailing as it barreled down a snow-covered mountain road.

She grabbed Thurman and hugged him to her. This delighted him even more and he mumbled and whispered and growled happily in reply.

"I know, Thurman, I know," Emily said, repeating the words many pet owners tell their pets, as if expecting the animal to understand. But Thurman understood and looked at Emily with a quizzical look, as if to ask what it was that she said she was understanding.

He growled a whispered response and Emily tilted her head as if trying to understand him.

Wilson returned to the front door after finding and putting on his shoes.

"Ready?" Emily asked.

"I am," Wilson replied.

"I didn't want to pressure you on this walk thing," Emily explained as they made their way down the front pathway of the house. "But I feel awkward sometimes if I walk by myself.

I feel like people are either watching me or judging me some-how. Or think that I'm lost. Or a stalker."

Wilson looked surprised.

"I feel the same way," he said. "But now with Thurman, that fear is gone. I think that's why so many insecure people have dogs."

Thurman growled a reply, and it sounded like he was dis-agreeing with Wilson.

No. Like dogs. People like.

Emily's face reflected her puzzlement.

"Does it ever sound to you like Thurman is actually trying to form words?"

Yes. Words. Thurman.

Wilson pondered the question, not trying to figure out if Thurman was trying to talk—that he knew was true—but pondered on how to tell Emily that the dog wasn't talking and that it simply sounded like words.

"Maybe. Sometimes," he replied. "But I think we're just projecting."

"Really? That's too bad."

They turned the corner onto Negley Avenue.

"I actually asked one of the psychology professors at school about it. His office is a few doors down from mine. He said that lots of people with dogs think that. That their dogs talk. Or understand English. He said they don't, but it was normal for people to think that way. Well, not normal, but not unexpected."

"Hmmm."

They walked in silence, Thurman happy to tack from one side of the sidewalk to the other, a furry sailboat in the wind, sniffing passionately, looking up into every tree for elusive squirrels. There was a squirrel, or many squirrels—Wilson could not tell them apart—that appeared to live in his backyard, and whose sole purpose in life was to torment Thurman by scampering away from him, circling tree trunks, making the dog think they had disappeared, and chattering at him, scolding him with great agitation from a high branch, chattering from safety, well out of Thurman's leaping range.

Wilson wondered why Thurman did not come back into the house with a crick in his neck from spending so much time staring up into the leafy upper reaches of trees, trying to force one of the squirrels to fall off the limb solely through the strength of his canine will.

Thurman did not appear to want to do violence to the squirrels—at least that's what Wilson understood him to say. He just wanted to play with them.

Play. Squirrel play. No.

As they walked, Wilson wondered if he should take Emily's hand. They had been out together three times, and for Wilson, that number of "dates" stood as a record achievement. But they had only talked, never expressed anything in the physical realm, and he could not be sure if she wanted anything more out of their relationship than simple friendship and adult conversation.

And as they walked, Wilson kept pushing the image of that photograph from his mind.

She'll never return, he told himself. *In a few days, she'll be back on her way to Portland. And I will never have to think of . . . of that time of my life, ever again. Never.*

"What are you thinking about, Wilson?" Emily asked after

they had gone four blocks without exchanging a single word. "You seem a bit preoccupied. Schoolwork? A paper you're writing?"

He could have answered using either of those explanations, but neither felt right, and neither reply was honest.

And that conflicting emotion surprised Wilson. He was not a person with particularly high moral standards, and had not held himself to high standards in the past. He had used ruses to deflect inquiries away from himself, to prevent people from drawing too close.

But today it did not appear that he would resort to those old, well-established, and deeply entrenched behaviors.

Instead, he simply replied, "I'm not sure what I'm thinking about. Just letting my thoughts wander, I guess."

That's less of a lie than I would normally tell.

"Okay. I get that way sometimes," Emily replied, and she reached over and, without appearing to give the action much thought, took Wilson's hand in hers.

Thurman recognized it immediately.

He began to jump, dance and whisper and growl, *Good. Good. Good.*

They walked that way for nearly a block, without speaking, save the whispery growl of Thurman repeating, *Good. Good. Good.*

The three of them stopped at a red light on Wilkins.

Thurman continued to mutter and growl.

"You sound like a Muppet," Emily said to Thurman.

Thurman stopped speaking and stared up at Emily, a confused look on his face. He tilted his head, as if hoping for an explanation.

She knelt down and placed her hands on the sides of his head.

"A Muppet, Thurman. They are sort of like puppets. It's a children's show on television. *The Muppet Show.* They are very cute little creatures. Funny and fuzzy and cute."

Thurman tried to sound out a word.

Emily looked at Thurman, then up at Wilson.

"Is he trying to say, 'Muppet'?"

As Wilson shrugged, Thurman danced about, trying to repeat the sound of "Muppet."

"I can see why your mother thought he was talking to her," Emily said.

Muppet. Muppet. Muppet. It was obvious that Thurman liked the sound of his new word.

"The light's changed," Wilson said. Emily stood and the three of them crossed the street while Thurman growled and whispered, *Muppet, Muppet, Muppet.*

The air felt good—not cool, not hot, as if the weather was invisible, wrapping itself around everyone in a comfortable embrace, everyone who was outside. Such perfect days were rare for Pittsburgh. Chilly, humid, hot, windy, cold, really hot, really cold, frigid, jungle humid, Arctic cold, frosty, sticky— those conditions were normal in the city, and when a perfect day arrived, it took many people by surprise and led them quickly to feeling a sense of total well-being, almost happiness.

Wilson was not immune to such nudges and realities. It did feel good to be outside, walking with another person, walking with Thurman, enjoying the scents and the sounds and the fact that he was still alive.

Yet despite this perfect day and all its unspoken expectations of contentedness, he felt something inside, a feeling that he had seldom if ever felt before, a feeling in his heart as if a thick wrapping was being removed, as if a box was being opened and the sun and the warmth and the freshness of the air was reaching the heart for the first time in years and years and years.

It was pain, but not really pain. It was new, but not really new. It was revelatory, but . . . it was not revelatory. Wilson had not let his heart move anywhere, or expand, or feel for so long that he had forgotten it was there.

Thurman's arrival had marked the beginning of the change in Wilson, by simply being there and participating in his daily existence. Thurman's acceptance of Wilson at face value had at first been unsettling and had sometimes brought Wilson to the edge of panic. But now he could not imagine life without Thurman, without those eyes of expectancy every morning, sitting by his empty food dish, without his unbridled and unexpected joy over just about everything he encountered, from a tennis ball in the backyard to a rawhide bone that he hid under his blanket in the family room.

Midway down the block, Thurman seemed to grow serious, growling and muttering to himself. Then he sat down. Both Emily and Wilson had to stop and they both turned around.

"Come on, Thurman. You're not tired. You're a big dog. You can make it," Emily said in the well-practiced voice of a mother offering encouragement to a recalcitrant toddler.

Thurman shook his head and growled.

Emily looked over at Wilson.

"Is he trying to say something?"

Thurman growled it again.

"He is, isn't he?"

Wilson closed his eyes, for just a moment, feeling the sun on his eyelids, seeing the gold behind them.

"He is," he replied.

Thurman growled it again.

"I'm pretty sure he's trying to say the word 'honest,'" Wilson said.

Emily looked at Wilson with a surprised smile.

"It does sound like that, doesn't it?"

Thurman said it again.

"It does sound like 'honest,'" Emily repeated. "That's amazing."

Wilson did not want to say what he was about to, but felt he had to.

"Thurman wants us to be honest with each other."

Emily's face showed an incredulous expression that quickly changed to that of belief.

"He does?"

Thurman said it again.

Honest.

"I'm sure," Wilson replied. "I think I'm sure."

Thurman growled out *Yes.*

"As sure as I can be of a talking dog," Wilson added.

He and Emily looked into each other's eyes.

"And now...who do you think is the most outlandish here? Me, you, my mother...or Thurman? Or are we all deluded?"

Emily did not reply—because she had no answer to the question.

⌐

Hazel found the Wyndham University Center all-suites hotel without any problems, though the steep streets and twisting roads of Pittsburgh were a new experience for her—and for her Quest.

Couldn't they have found a nice flat piece of land to build a city on?

She turned into the hotel's parking lot.

And land was cheap back then. Why couldn't they have built wider streets?

She got out her smaller, this-I-bring-into-the-hotel-with-me suitcase, plus the larger case, filled with clothing that needed to be washed again.

I'll be here for a couple of days. I'll have time.

Check-in went smoothly and Hazel was given a room on the third floor, with a bedroom that looked out over a very large skyscraper sort of building in the middle of a large block filled with lawns and trees and walkways and benches.

That must be something from the university. It looks old.

She stared up toward the top.

It looks like something out of Europe.

She walked back to the bed and started unpacking her laundry first.

Except I've never been to Europe either, so I'm making an educated guess.

She stacked the clothes into two piles—lights and darks.

And so far, I like Pittsburgh. Hardly a hipster in sight. It does not seem like a granola sort of place. More blue-collar, but not bad blue-collar. I'll make a list of the places I want to see here before I . . . leave? Stay?

She found two plastic bags in the closet and filled them with the two loads of laundry. Then she used the Lilliputian-sized coffeemaker and made a free cup of coffee, complete with artificial sugar and some manner of white powder that turned the coffee grayer than mocha.

She sat in the upholstered chair in the sitting area and sighed.

Lord, you never promised me an answer. I know that. But . . . could you sort of help me decide on what to do next? I'm not asking for a sign or a burning bush or anything cinematic like that. But maybe . . . maybe I could just put a settled feeling in my heart. That would work too. That would be swell.

She sipped at her gray coffee.

Oh . . . and thanks. Or Amen.

She tried to smile. She wasn't sure God was all that a smiley of a deity, but she hoped he was.

Or whatever. You know what I mean. Thanks. Really. I really mean that. And whatever you decide . . . I'll be okay with. So . . . Amen, again.

She took one last sip and decided that she would have to see if they had real coffee and real cream in the lobby.

I guess you have to say "Amen" to make it official, right? So . . . Amen.

~

The three of them ping-ponged looking at each other—Wilson to Emily to Thurman and back to Wilson to Thurman to Emily. The three-handed silent conversation went on for some moments.

Thurman growled again.

It sounded like *Go.*

She stopped and looked at Wilson. "I am terrified of all this. You, me, whatever this is. It scares me."

Wilson did not disagree.

"And . . . you don't know what I've done. My past, Emily. What happened back then."

Emily offered him a look of understanding. Thurman growled in support.

"You're not still doing it, are you?"

Wilson appeared surprised—more than surprised, appearing as if he had never once considered being asked that specific question.

"No. No. I'm not. Of course not."

Emily's face did not change. It did not grow worried or anxious or nervous. She maintained a comforting half-smile.

"Then it is over. Isn't the past the past? I mean, it won't come around again."

Wilson waited.

"No. I guess it won't," he said, then added softly, "I mean, I know it won't."

Emily's face did show a shadow of pain and regret, for a moment. "My husband, my late husband, he could not let it go. He could not let go of whatever happened over there . . . he could not let it go. It stayed with him. Or he kept it close on purpose. I don't know which."

Wilson tried to keep his expression neutral, but it was

obvious that he knew exactly what her husband had felt or did not feel.

Wilson's voice grew small. "Did he kill people?"

Emily did not appear surprised by his question. People who have endured the same sort of trauma are not surprised when that trauma is openly discussed. Other people may be kept out, but those who knew pain understood those in pain.

"No...well, I don't know for certain. He might have. He did not tell me much. The stress got to him, I think."

Emily's hand clenched into a fist. Wilson recognized the gesture as a way of coping.

"He saw too much," she said. "But he...before we married...he was sensitive, almost delicate. I don't why the military appealed to him so much. I think he had something to prove to himself...and maybe his father. They had a difficult relationship."

Wilson found himself nodding in agreement, in sympathy, in empathy.

"I don't think he was ever totally honest with himself," she said. "And maybe not with me either."

A part of Wilson wanted to step closer to Emily and to embrace her in a hug of comfort.

But he did not.

"You have to tell the truth to yourself," she added. "And you have to be honest with God—if you ever want to find peace. And without God, I could never survived, going through that pain. Not alone. You need God's grace to endure. I know I needed it."

⟵

That night, the evening spread out against the sky with only a few very bright stars making their presence known. Wilson stood out on the back steps, in the dark, watching, or actually listening to, a black dog circumnavigate the yard in an inky darkness. He could hear him rustle about, nudging against the bushes that outlined the backyard of his childhood home.

"The trees weren't as big when I was a child," Wilson said aloud, softly. "The sky looked bigger because of that."

Thurman bounded back to the house from the darkness, grinning.

He seemed always to grin as he ran toward the house.

Perhaps it was knowing that the inside of that house promised warmth, softness, and security.

Wilson wondered how long Thurman had been in the dog detention unit at the animal shelter. His mother never asked, and Wilson knew that if he went back there now, no one would remember one specific, isolated dog from the hundreds, or thousands, that had been processed since Thurman had been adopted. *Maybe they have some sort of paper trail,* he surmised. *But not knowing is okay as well. I can imagine his history, and it doesn't matter now.*

Thurman took the last two steps in a leap and slid into the family room, nails scrabbering on the wooden floors, headed, no doubt, to the kitchen to check to see if the kibble fairies had visited his food bowl while he was outside.

He grumbled the same way every night seeing an empty bowl.

Wilson locked the back door and double-checked the lock's hold, twice, as he always did every night. He knew that if a burglar or intruder really wanted to get in, a glass pane in the door would prove little to no deterrent.

Yet the locked door, and his checking, made him feel secure, although it was never a feeling of overwhelming security.

He switched off the lamp in the family room. The oven light provided enough illumination for Thurman, he was sure of that. He never once saw or heard Thurman run into anything in the dark.

Thurman kept up a soft, under-his-breath, whispery growl as Wilson made his rounds. Most evenings, Thurman stood, silent and observant, by his bunched-up blanket as Wilson got the house ready for the night. But tonight he stood by the stairs. When Wilson climbed the stairs, Thurman followed him, climbing slowly and carefully as he always did, as if he were unsure of how to make all four legs work in partnership as they found footing on uneven surfaces.

Wilson knew he was following.

Wilson got ready for bed and Thurman waited just outside the doorway, as if respecting Wilson's need for privacy—something that dogs, in nature, had no need of, nor understanding of. Yet there Thurman was, outside, waiting. When Wilson walked to the bed for the final time, Thurman entered the room. He did so slowly and with a sense of deliberateness.

The dog sat down on the small throw rug by the side of the bed and looked up at Wilson. Thurman could form a severely serious look on occasion, and this was one such occasion.

"What?" Wilson asked.

Thurman tried to pose a question, adding his version of a querying inflection to the tone of his whispered growls.

Be honest?

Wilson appeared to know exactly what Thurman was asking and why.

"It's about this afternoon, isn't it? About Emily? And us? Being honest? About telling the truth."

Thurman nodded.

Honest.

Wilson knew that Thurman had problems making a "th" sound, so the word "honest" covered for the word "truth."

"I know. I know."

Past is past.

"I know. But I don't know . . . you know what I mean?"

Thurman's look was hard, almost brittle.

No.

"I'm guilty, Thurman. I have done so many bad things . . . back then. Things no civilized person would do. I am tired of feeling guilty."

Forgive. He forgives.

Wilson looked back at Thurman, trying to read his eyes, his expression.

"You mean that, don't you?"

Yes.

Wilson closed his eyes.

"You know, I'm just projecting all this onto you. You don't really talk, you know. You growl in weird ways and make odd noises in your throat that I hear as words. But you don't do any of that, not really."

I do.

"You don't."

I do.

"Thurman...back then...in the war...the people that I...killed. Sometimes it was at close range. I could see their faces. And when that happened, I felt...something like joy. I felt happy, Thurman. I was happy over it. I won. I survived. I got to come home. Victorious. But that was then. Now, when I think of it, I realize that only a monster takes glee in killing people. And that's what I was, Thurman. I can't escape that. I can't forget that."

Thurman stood and head-butted Wilson's knee.

Past. Past. Gone. War past. Gone.

"That's what you say, Thurman. 'Gone' is easy to say. But it isn't that easy. I can't do it."

Past. Gone. Forgive. Gift.

Wilson sighed.

"But I can't believe it is just that simple. To ask for forgiveness. To ask for a new start. To be right with God. Ask him into your life, the preachers on TV say. And expect everything to be wiped clean."

Honest.

"I can't, Thurman. Too much water under the bridge. Too long ago."

No. Can. Do. Gift. God gift.

Wilson knew that if he stayed as he was, Emily would never stay with him. She didn't want another closed-off person like her husband. She wouldn't want another dishonest man. Unless something changed in his life, Wilson knew with a dreadful certainty, he absolutely knew for truth, that he would be alone. He would be alone now and for the rest of his life. His mother would die and then Thurman would die and he would be alone and die alone, and that scared him almost as much as anything else in the world. He had seen fellow soldiers die in Vietnam, but if someone was with them, if someone was there to hold their hand and say, "There, there, it will be okay. I'm with you," then regardless of the specter of death, the wounded soldier became quiet, as if...as if the peace of Heaven filled them. Wilson saw it happen dozens and dozens of times, when a chaplain would fly with them and offer comfort on the return flight to the sick and dying. When a chaplain, or another soldier, made a connection, a sometimes final connection, then the dying would not die alone. They would be facing death with a friend.

Wilson yearned to have that peace while he was still alive.

He did not want to die alone. He did not. He could not imagine reaching out, at the very end of days, and finding no human flesh to hold on to, to comfort, to...to love.

He had read much on the subject—about guilt and pain and forgiveness and alienation and stress and walling off feelings and not actually living a life, but merely being a spectator. He had read much. He knew much. That was his job, his profession. To read. To understand. He had read books. He had read portions of the Bible. Maybe all of it by now, in bits and pieces. He had listened to sermons, on TV, usually. He knew the way. He knew the path. He knew the words.

But knowing...and doing...were poles apart, worlds apart, lifetimes apart.

Wilson had thought, up until Thurman arrived, that being alone was his destiny.

Now he realized that maybe, just maybe, it was not.

The words were there, in his head, but on the way to his heart, they remained stuck in his throat.

He swallowed hard.

Thurman whispered.

Do. Say. Honest.

Wilson looked down at the dog. Thurman looked back. His eyes were filled with hope and expectation and unbridled honesty. He nodded, his canine head bobbing, as he tried to will Wilson into speaking the words.

"Okay, Thurman. Okay."

He swallowed again and closed his eyes.

"I'm sorry. I accept. I'm tired of fighting. Please forgive me. God, please forgive me. Please. I accept the gift. I am... yours."

A sense of relief started—first a trickle, then as a torrent of blessed, sweet freedom, blessed relief. Wilson felt his heart unbound and free, for the first time in many decades.

Perhaps this was the most singular, pellucid moment of existence that he had yet encountered.

And Thurman began his dance, hips to the left and hips to the right.

Forgive. Forgive. Forgive.

Dance. Dance. Dance.

Happy. Happy. Happy.

"Thank you, Thurman. Thank you."

Happy. Dance. Happy.

Wilson wiped at his face.

"Tears? Really?" He looked at his wet hand with some curiosity, as if he could have never imagined shedding them in the past.

He looked down at Thurman, whose face exhibited a marked degree of concern. He figured the dog had never seen him cry—or perhaps never seen anyone cry.

"It's okay, Thurman. Tears of relief, I guess. It's normal. Sort of. Relatively speaking."

Thurman's head bobbed again and he looked relieved.

Wilson sucked in a large breath of air, as if trying to cleanse the toxins of the past out of his body.

"It might take a while," he said.

Thurman grinned.

After another moment, Wilson spoke.

"I should call her," he said.

Emily, Thurman growled. *Good. Pretty. Good.*

"No, not Emily. The woman who was here this afternoon. With the picture."

Thurman's eyes opened a bit wider. It was not that he had forgotten her, but Wilson was sure he had no idea of how she figured into his life.

"I need to call her," Wilson said. "Is it too late?"

Thurman tried to shrug.

"It's only nine. That's not too late."

Wilson used his cell phone to find the number of the Wyndham. He pressed call.

"Hazel Jamison, please, she's a guest at your hotel."

Wilson heard an electronic hustle and whistle, then the sound of a cautious "Hello?"

Wilson reached over and put his hand on Thurman's head.

"Hazel? This is Wilson Steele. You were at my house today. I think I have some information about that picture."

The phone was silent. Then came a very tentative "Okay."

"But it's not the sort of information that's easy to pass along over a phone. Will you be in town tomorrow? Could we meet somewhere?"

Again, a long moment of silence ensued.

"I will be in town . . . for a while. Maybe longer. I was going to do some sightseeing. Are the cable cars—the incline, I think it's called—on Mount Washington worth a visit?"

Wilson smiled.

"Absolutely. The view of Pittsburgh from there is fantastic."

"Okay. I was going to do that in the morning. And then I was going to the Phipps Conservatory. I like plants. My mother was a great gardener—not at the end, but when I was growing up. She always had flowers. Is that Phipps thing worth a visit?"

"It is. Could I meet you there? Maybe at two?"

Again, a long moment of silent decision making.

"Sure. But . . . could you bring your dog?"

Wilson nodded to the phone.

"Sure. Thurman will be there as well."

⌐

Why did I ask him to bring his dog?

Hazel had been propped up in bed, watching the local news and wondering if she could ever feel comfortable with a new set of newscasters and weathermen. How long would it take her to decide which local news team she liked best?

And why couldn't he just tell me over the phone what he re-membered?

Maybe he found a picture or something.

She tapped at the TV remote control.

Well, tomorrow is another day.

She switched off the bedside lamp.

I've never been on an incline before.

She stared at the dark ceiling.

Or a cable car, for that matter. Or does the one in San Francisco count? Maybe.

Chapter Twenty-Seven

T HURMAN WASN'T SURE about getting into the car, wasn't
sure about where and how to sit in the car, and wasn't
sure about the ride in the car. He had been in cars before, of
course, but never felt at all settled riding in one. And instead
of hanging his head out the window as other dogs might have
done, he instead stared at Wilson's floor mats as Wilson navigated the relatively short drive from his home to the Phipps
Conservatory.

Wilson had called in to the university that day to cancel
his classes. He had claimed an illness and did not feel guilty,
since he so rarely canceled class—perhaps only once every
two or three years.

"My students will be thrilled," he told Thurman as he hung
up the phone. He assumed that some aide would post notices
on the doors of his three scheduled classes but wasn't all that
certain of the protocol involved.

He pulled out of his garage at one o'clock, knowing it
would only take five minutes, if that, to drive there. But he
wanted more than enough time to find a parking spot and
another long period to try and put his jangled nerves in
order.

In the past forty years, Wilson had done his best to avoid
any situation that might cause jangled nerves and anxiety
and nervousness. And he had for the most part succeeded.

He did not have any truly close friends. He had not been ro-
mantically involved in all those years. His professorial career
had not been without some bumps and turns, but nothing
had been unexpected and no circumstance ever rose to the
keeps-one-up-all-night sort of worry.

Wilson had walked through his life as a dispassionate observer: alive, present, but not connected.

This . . . this event, these recent events and decisions, had
changed his life. He did not yet know how to describe it, and
the change was disruptive and unsettling and scary, but not
in a bad way.

That didn't make sense to him, and he knew it, but he was
allowing it to happen. Giving up the fight had changed his
life, was transforming his life and his heart, and he had not
yet had the time to figure out just what it all meant.

That's why he left early. That's why he thought a half-hour
sitting on a park bench, in the sunshine, might be a path to
enlightenment—no, not enlightenment, for that had already
occurred—but a way to incorporate that enlightenment into
his mind and heart and body.

He felt at the verge of being overwhelmed, not in a panicked way, but like falling into a cold mountain lake on a
hot day—a shock, but a shock that would provide welcome,
soothing, cooling relief.

Good fortune was with Wilson that morning. A spot
opened up just as he entered the small parking lot. He attached the leash to Thurman's collar.

"I think all dogs have to be on a leash, Thurman," Wilson
explained. "I know you would behave, but not every dog is
as good as you."

Thurman thought for a moment, then nodded.

Okay.

They walked toward the ornate Victorian-era greenhouse, now with more modern additions. Wilson actually began to experience a sense of peace about what he was facing.

That sense of peace was new and different. Wilson had seldom felt at peace, even when alone and quiet and in the dark. It had become an elusive quality in his life and had been so for decade upon decade. He may have appeared at peace, but inside, in his heart, in his mind, he had never truly felt settled or complete or content.

This new peace felt odd, but good odd, he decided.

He spotted an unoccupied park bench, shielded by a copse of trees, on the pathway to the admissions pavilion.

"She will have to come this way, Thurman. We are sure to see her when she comes."

Thurman had been busy sniffing and snorking in the grass along the sidewalk, looking up into the trees, checking for squirrels, listening for birds, and staring at anyone, any human within hailing distance.

"And now, Thurman, we wait."

Thurman appeared to nod and sat down at Wilson's feet—watching, waiting, and whisper-growling, almost as if only to himself, *Happy. Happy. Happy.*

⟵

Thurman spotted her first. He stood and growled and whispered, *Lady.*

Wilson shook his head slightly to clear his thoughts. The

woman who had visited him yesterday was walking toward them, about a half-block distant.

Thurman began his welcoming dance.

"You need to behave, Thurman. Okay? No wild celebrations. I have enough to think about."

Thurman looked over his shoulder at Wilson, as if trying to ascertain if Wilson was just joking or being up-front and honest.

Okay.

Thurman must have decided that Wilson was telling the truth. So the dog dialed back his dance moves to a few degrees of wiggle in his back hips—an inch or two at most.

Wilson waved and the woman, Hazel, waved back.

"I'm so glad you stayed in town," Wilson said. "I couldn't remember if you said you had seen the sights or were going to see the sights. But I'm glad."

Thurman barked his affirmation.

They sat down, Thurman on the ground between them, so he could stare at each as they talked. He must have been a lip-reader, because his preferred mode of conversation was when he was making eye contact.

Hazel spoke next.

"So what information about the photo? You said you had remembered something?"

Wilson nodded and appeared to bite at his bottom lip, just for a heartbeat.

"Miss Jamison," he said.

"Hazel, please."

"Hazel, I lied to you yesterday. About the picture. I remember it."

Hazel's look went from unsure to expectant in a heartbeat.

"So you remembered who the groom was?"

"I do."

Wilson took a deep breath, perhaps stalling for time, perhaps building up courage.

Thurman growled, *Tell.*

Wilson was sure that Hazel did not know that Thurman had spoken.

"That's me in the picture. And that was... that was a picture of our wedding. Your mother and me. We were married."

A veritable wave of expressions seemed to emanate from Hazel, going from shock to acknowledgment to concern to confusion. It was obvious to Wilson that she struggled to look interested and not alarmed.

"The reason she wrote 'Our Wedding' is because it was our wedding."

Hazel appeared as if she wanted to speak, ask a question, shout, but could not decide on which question or which shout was most appropriate, most important, most critical to be answered first.

"How? Why?"

"All my life, I've been teaching students to be aware of context. And I don't want to be guilty of ignoring that fact now," Wilson said, although it was apparent that Hazel had not been worried at all about context. She simply wanted an explanation.

"I was in Vietnam. I was young... we were both young... the whole world was young back then. I had done two tours of duty in Vietnam. I think I was proving something to myself. Vietnam... the war... neither was a healthy place to be, not physically nor emotionally. But here's what changed from all the previous wars: In Vietnam, you could be in a firefight in the jungle or in a helicopter shooting at some unseen enemy, and within twenty-four hours you could be back in America eating a McDonald's hamburger and chocolate shake. I think every soldier who saw combat and returned home suffered a whiplash of emotions. Back then, we weren't exactly welcomed stateside with open arms, and our decompression was too rapid. Every soldier seemed to suffer from the bends, as it were. I know I did."

Hazel listened, trying to keep her expression blank, trying to keep tears or smiles or anger away, attempting to be simply neutral in all emotions—at least for the moment.

Thurman stared up at Wilson, his eyes showing a glint of sorrow.

"I was sent stateside near the end of my second tour. I had taken shrapnel in my shoulder and back—nothing too deadly or too serious, but I needed some physical rehab. I got that at the VA hospital in Portland."

Hazel nodded.

"And you met my mother there?"

"Not at the hospital. But in Portland. There was a big bookstore in downtown Portland—Powell's."

"It's still there."

Wilson smiled, a sad but satisfied smile.

"Good. That makes me happy. I went there during rehab. I met your mother there. Looking for books. And we started talking. And she had the most wonderful laugh. Musical. After so much killing and flying next to so many dead soldiers . . . it was like a drug, her laugh. It made me believe that the world was not a cesspool of evil—but that there was hope and that I could have a future."

"How long were you in Portland?" Hazel asked, not knowing if that was the most important question or not.

"I had four months left in my enlistment. We met, your mother and I, a month after I got back. And we got married within a month of our first meeting."

Hazel just stared at Wilson, as if trying to imagine him young, trying to imagine him as impetuous and willing to risk everything on a woman he hardly knew.

"I know. It sounds crazy. And it was. Getting married seemed like the right thing to do. I was lost. So many soldiers came back feeling lost and adrift and hopeless. Your mother...offered me hope. She offered me an anchor. Or what I thought would be an anchor. Something to rebuild what was broken and shattered inside me. She offered me laughter and hope and the chance of a future—all the things that I was certain I had lost in the war."

Hazel looked at him, then looked down at her hands.

"Did it work? How long...I mean, how long were you together?"

At that moment, Wilson experienced an overwhelming desire to get up and to run—run as far and as fast as he could until he could stop reliving the pain of his past. Perhaps yesterday, had this meeting happened yesterday, before he saw the light of God, he would have run. But now, still unknowing, still a novice in faith, he simply knew that he had to see this through. He had to see this to a conclusion, whatever personal pain he might endure. He had to set the past right again—not just for himself, but for this lost and confused woman sitting beside him on a park bench outside the Phipps Conservatory, a stone's throw south of the Cathedral of Learning, where Wilson had spent the last forty-some years in hiding.

"It lasted three months. I'm sorry. I was sorry then. As soon as it happened, I knew that I could not stay. I was broken. Badly broken. And she knew it as well. I think she knew it from the very beginning. I am sure she thought she could save me. She offered me a way to salvation, but I was too broken and too wounded—emotionally—to understand it then."

Hazel looked up.

"I'm so sorry," she said, as if she truly meant it.

Wilson waved her sorrow away.

"I was at fault, not your mother."

Thurman stood up and barked. Twice. And looked decisive.

"Hazel, I have to feed Thurman. That was his 'I'm hungry' bark. But there is a lot more I need to tell you. Would you ride with us back to my house? I'll bring you back afterward. Did you drive here?"

"No. I walked. The man at the hotel said it was like ten minutes. So . . . you can take me back to the hotel . . . whenever. Later. That would be fine."

Thurman started to dance, wiggle left, wiggle right, whispering and growling, *Food, food, food.*

Wilson felt a stirring in his chest as he stood, like a heart being unwrapped, like a candle being lit in the darkness.

He decided, as they walked toward the car, that it was a very good feeling.

⟿

Wilson had to push Thurman into the backseat, Thurman growling and grumping and complaining during the entire rump-shoving effort. Wilson's car was a two-door sedan, so human passengers would naturally be offered front-row privileges.

Thurman was forced into the car headfirst, and clumped onto the backseat headfirst, and that is how he stayed during the short ride home—staring straight out the rear window of the car. Hazel looked over her shoulder several times, and called out his name, thinking that it was only natural that a dog be facing forward. Thurman paid no attention to her, and remained statuelike during the seven-minute trip.

He bounded out of the car with great enthusiasm, however, as if feeling certain that his dinner would be forthcoming.

Wilson led the way into the house, allowing Hazel her choice of chairs in the kitchen while he got Thurman's kibble ready for serving.

Hazel chose the chair where Wilson always sat.

"Okay. He has his dinner," Wilson said. "Would you like some coffee? Tea? Water?"

"Coffee, if it's not too much trouble," she replied.

"I have this fancy pod coffeemaker. It'll take a minute to heat the water. I need to run upstairs to get something. Bathroom is down that hall, if you need it. Make yourself at home."

"Okay."

And Hazel was alone in the kitchen with Thurman, whose

head was engulfed in a bowl of kibble, making happy chewing, crunching noises as he ate, his tail wagging slowly.

The pod coffeemaker hissed and stopped making boiling noises. She looked around. There was a small metal carousel of pods on the counter. She selected one that sounded strong, but not overly bold. She opened a cabinet door where she would have stored coffee mugs. A gathering of disparate coffee mugs took up the first shelf. She selected one that showed a Pitt panther on the side. Then she pulled open a drawer where she would have put spoons and the like, and the drawer held exactly that, in neat little bins, the spoons all spooning each other in one stack. She was careful not to dislodge any other than the top one. The top shelf on the refrigerator door held a carton of half-and-half, which she took out and left on the counter, assuming that Wilson might have coffee himself.

Her coffee brewed quickly. She added cream and returned to her seat at the table.

Thurman had finished his meal and clattered up closer to her and sat down, licking his chin and whiskers with his rather long, thick tongue.

"This is very nice," she said softly.

Thurman appeared to nod.

Nice.

Hazel stared at him, thinking that she heard him repeat what she had just said, but she knew that dogs couldn't talk. Or least none of the dogs that she had met during her life could talk. She assumed Thurman was no different.

Wilson came back downstairs holding a metal box the size of a large shoebox, or a shoebox that would have held boots.

"Good. You found the coffee and all that."

"I did. I hope you don't mind."

"Not at all."

Wilson busied himself with his coffee, making small talk, holding off the important details until he could be face-to-face.

"So, Hazel, do you work in Portland?"

Hazel swiveled in her chair.

"I do. I mean, I did. I quit some weeks ago. Sort of picked up stakes in Portland, and I guess I'm looking for a place to settle down."

Wilson nodded as he poured cream in his coffee.

"Did you want sugar? I put the sugar bowl in the refrigerator. I read that it keeps ants away. I've never had an ant issue. Maybe the refrigerator thing works."

"No. No thanks. I'm okay. I use it sometimes. But not all the time."

He came and sat down opposite her at the table. Thurman remained where he had been, able to see them both very clearly.

Hazel appeared to want to explain.

"I would never have done this . . . quit a job and sell everything and just travel . . . but my mother sort of left me . . . I guess I would call it an inheritance. I never knew she had it and only discovered it while cleaning out her house."

"What sort of inheritance?" Wilson asked, hoping that the question did not appear intrusive.

If Hazel had taken offense, she did a wonderful job of masking it.

"It was some stock. She had it for years and years and it was fairly valuable."

A seriously bemused expression filled Wilson's face, as if he knew the answer and was equally puzzled and delighted.

"Was it Apple stock? The computer company?"

It seemed to be Hazel's turn to look bemused.

"It was. How did you know?"

"It was a lucky guess. Or an educated guess."

Wilson must have seen that this answer was not nearly as complete as it needed to be.

"I have something I need to show you," he said, and pulled the metal box toward himself and carefully lifted the lid.

The sheet metal box, gunmetal gray, looked like it had been handmade by a young boy forced to take an industrial arts class back in the time when such classes were required.

"This has been sitting on the top shelf of the second closet in my bedroom, under a stack of blankets, for the last forty-some years. I have never taken it out, but I know everything that's in here."

Hazel watched as he placed the lid on the table; it made a chilly metallic sound.

Hazel could see inside and on top was a tattered and stained T-shirt—or what looked to be a T-shirt—with a University of Pittsburgh logo and panther on the front.

Wilson appeared almost hesitant to reach in.

Thurman did not move, but his snout was in the air, and his nose flexed wide to capture the scent of whatever this box held. Obviously he did not think it was kibbles, or he would have been on all fours trying to investigate.

"I was wearing this under my uniform when I was wounded," Wilson said, his words coming out slowly and carefully, as if he was trying to keep any emotion at bay. "I kept it because... well, I am not sure why I kept it. Perhaps it signified survival."

He touched it with a delicate tracing of his fingers.

"There are a few other things in here: pictures of people I served with, some medals, some trinkets from Vietnam. Dog tags. I suppose I thought it was important to keep them."

He reached in, felt under the shirt, and pulled out an envelope. Hazel stared at the handwritten address, recognizing the flowery strokes as well as the hand that wrote it.

"That's from my mother, isn't it?" Hazel asked.

The kitchen became a solemn, somber place; the only noises were the tattering hum of the refrigerator and the heavy breathing of Thurman, almost a panting. And that was all. It was as if neither Wilson nor Hazel drew audible breath.

"It is. I think it is the only letter that she sent me."

"Can I read it?" Hazel asked in a nut-brown mouse voice.

Wilson handed it to her and Hazel slid the single sheet of paper out and unfolded it.

As she began reading aloud, Wilson moved his lips as well, as if he had memorized that letter.

Wilson,
I am with child. I thought you should know.
I don't need anything. Honestly.
I will be fine. I have many friends and my family will help.
I hope you are okay.
I know you are only doing what you must do. I know how hard it is for you.

I know you wish it could be otherwise.
I hate that war because of what it has done to you.
I hope—and pray—that your soul finds peace.

Love,

Florence

Hazel's voice had begun to quiver and quake midway through the short note, and at the end she could barely be heard. To Wilson, it was no matter. He knew what the note said.

"I could not have been a father then," Wilson said, staring at the letter that Hazel held in trembling hands. "Biological, yes. Emotional, no. I was in such deep and troubled waters and I wasn't sure that I would stay afloat. There were drugs and alcohol. I used anything to dull the pain. For years."

Thurman stood, stepped to Wilson, and jumped, his front paws on Wilson's thigh. Wilson put his hand on Thurman's face.

"I managed to graduate and do graduate school and work on my doctorate—but it was all done in a self-medicated fog."

"Was the war that bad?" Hazel asked.

"Death is bad. Violent death is terrible. Violent death that you begin to enjoy is the most corrosive acid your heart and soul will ever experience."

"Oh," Hazel replied, obviously not knowing what to say.

"I have only recently been able to think of the war without nightmares, without crushing guilt. I know it was wrong to leave her...your mother...but being there would have been worse. Had anyone been close to me, back then, they would have been damaged as well. I would have made sure of that. Lashing out. Being creatively cruel. I could not do that to her."

"Oh."

"I sent her money. Not right away, because I didn't have it then. But two years later, I received a book advance. I sent all of it to her. Twelve thousand dollars. I told her that she should use it to make her future easier. I told her that I had heard good things about Apple computers. I told her that maybe she should buy some stock in that."

Hazel's face gave way to a curious smile, a half-smile, a slender smile, but a smile.

"So you paid for me to come here," she said.

Wilson tried to smile in return. "In a way, I guess I did."

Thurman appeared to be confused. He bounced down from Wilson's thigh and turned his attention to Hazel. He butted his head into her knee, and she responded by patting his head.

The silence returned as they both remained still.

Hazel was the first to speak into that silence.

"So, you're my father?"

Her eyes were sad and hopeful and frightened and resolute.

Wilson nodded.

"Yes. I am sure that you are my daughter. You are."

Thurman turned back to Wilson.

Daughter?

Wilson sighed.

"I think Thurman is slowly figuring this out. The relationship. Our relationship."

Daughter?

Wilson pointed to Hazel, who was allowing a semi-baffled and delightfully confused smile to form.

"Yes, Thurman. She is my daughter."

And at this, at this startling confirmation, Thurman bounced down and began the happiest of his happy dances—back hips going left, front legs going right, all four paws dancing in some sort of madcap calypso, canine rhythm.

And Thurman began growling as he danced.

Wilson wondered if Hazel heard his words.

Happy, happy, happy.

⟶

An hour later, the three of them—Thurman, Wilson, and Hazel—stood in the lobby of the Heritage Square Senior Apartments and Retirement Village, in front of Gretna Steele.

"Yes, she is my daughter," Wilson reaffirmed.

"Seriously?" Gretna asked again.

Daughter. Daughter. Daughter.

Thurman's whispered growls were equally insistent and authoritative. Gretna wavered a bit, then sat back down, heavily, in the chair she had just risen from.

Her face was beatific, at peace, happy.

"Thank you, God," she said staring upward.

"Now I can die happy," she added. "But maybe not for a little while."

Epilogue

THE FALL SUNSHINE played long shadows over the backyard of Wilson Steele's home, warming and comforting, the air still, the leaves going to reds and gold.

An informal semicircle of chairs arced around the shallow end of the reflecting pool. Emily sat at one end, then Wilson, then Hazel, and Gretna at the other end. None of them had talked much—they simply sat, warm, full from lunch, enjoying an autumn environment that would soon turn to gray and cold.

But not today.

Today was near perfect.

Hazel had found an apartment in Shadyside, only minutes away. She began to talk to Wilson . . . talk to her father, about returning to school.

"You will get a family discount, you know," he told her. "After all these years, I can finally take advantage of that."

This afternoon, Thurman sat in the middle of this arc of humans—smiling, eyes shut, tongue lolling to one side, happy, deliciously happy.

Wilson spoke, quiet, firm.

"It will be a long journey. I know that much. The journey that all of us are on. Are now on."

Hazel nodded her agreement.

"But we have started," Emily said. "And that is what is important. We'll get there."

"And I think your friend, Dr. Killeen, has already helped so much," Hazel said. "Helped all of us."

There were nods from everyone, including Thurman, who stood up, stretched mightily, and began to growl and whisper.

God.

"And of course, faith," Emily added. "Thank you, Thurman, for reminding us of the obvious here. That without God, we would all still be lost."

Thurman smiled, nodded in acknowledgment, and began to dance, just a little.

Muppet. Muppet. Muppet.

It had become one of his most favorite words. He walked and danced around the pool—sniffing, looking, sniffing again.

"Go ahead," Wilson called out as Thurman got to the far end.

Thurman waited.

"I said it's okay," Wilson added. "Really."

At that, Thurman launched himself into the air and into the water, the splash well removed from his humans. He paddled about, snorting and smiling, the water rippling off his fur, making tiny kaleidoscopic jewels on his black fur. He swam for a bit, then made his way to the shallow end of the pool, the safe and warm end of the pool, the end of the pool where all his humans gathered.

He closed his eyes, then smiled to himself and then tilted his head upward and smiled to God above.

Happy Muppet. Happy Muppet.

The Dog That Whispered

Reading Group Guide

1. All of the main characters are dealing with the effects of either long-hidden secrets or long-term unexpressed guilt. Which one do you think is more detrimental to emotional well-being?

2. Wilson finds it important to keep everything in his house exactly the way it was when he was growing up. What do you think is his motivation behind this? Is he driven by a desire to live in a simpler, less-complicated time, perhaps?

3. Wilson is not noted for being jovial and welcoming or even friendly. Do you think that all of his social shortcomings could be blamed on his Vietnam War experience? Or do you think some of these traits can simply trace back to the way Wilson is wired emotionally?

4. Wilson has suffered a lifetime of inner turmoil for things he did while serving in the war in Vietnam. Do you think his guilt is justified—or should he be able to defend his actions as "just following orders and doing what a soldier has to do"? Do you think that Wilson's guilt got easier or more difficult to deal with as he grew older?

5. Thurman, the dog, somehow enables Wilson to give voice to the pain he has hidden for so many years. Why do you think Thurman is able to do that—to be the catalyst for Wilson's eventual truth-telling and coming to grips with his guilt? Why a dog rather than a pastor or a close friend?

6. Wilson sought out the help of a trained psychiatrist—who apparently is not a believer. Was that a wise choice on his part? Should he have only sought council from spiritual, theologically trained counselors?

7. If Thurman was helping Wilson see the error of keeping secrets and the inner corrosion that guilt causes his soul, and if Wilson was actually the one interpreting Thurman's growls as words and advice and admonition—why couldn't or why didn't Wilson achieve that awareness on his own?

8. God can use anything He chooses to bring an awareness of Himself to people. Do you think He would deliberately use a dog like Thurman to open a man's eyes? Do you think that Wilson could only have found faith through such an unconventional method?

9. Emily was a believer when she met Wilson, and she knew that he was not. Would you have encouraged Emily to agree to date Wilson—or would you have mentioned the Scriptural caution against being "unequally yoked"?

10. Do you think that Hazel's mother was responsible for Hazel's "small, uninspired" life and existence?

11. Do you think Hazel would have ever made her trip of discovery if it had not been for her mother's secret inheritance? Do you think that without the money, Hazel would have stayed where she was, remained at her job, never to find the truth about her past?

12. Wilson knew he had a child, yet did not want to admit it, even when Hazel appeared at his front door. Why do you think he was so reluctant to admit the truth?

13. Do you think that Hazel, after finding the truth out about her father and mother, will be able to move on to become spiritually healthy? Or will her past continue to haunt her?

14. Do you think that anyone who has faced combat and the horrors of modern-day warfare can remain unaffected? Was it reasonable for Wilson to have concealed the truth—especially since he returned to an America that was, at the time, largely unsympathetic to war veterans?

15. We sometimes tend to label people as antisocial or simply mean—when there may be pressures and tensions in their lives that we know nothing about. Has this book changed the way you view "prickly" people that you know?

ALSO LOOK FOR THIS HEARTWARMING, HUMOROUS NOVEL BY BESTSELLING AUTHOR JIM KRAUS

THE DOG THAT SAVED STEWART COOLIDGE

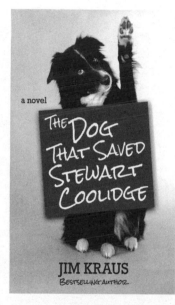

When a stray dog helps himself to a bone from a display in the supermarket, he has no idea that his actions will ignite a romance between two humans. Working at the store, Stewart Coolidge is instructed by his determined boss to catch the thieving animal immediately. Stewart's cute neighbor, Lisa, is an aspiring journalist who is delighted to write the story for the local paper. When the dog starts showing up on the doorstep of their building, Stewart and Lisa grow closer through harboring the furry fugitive. She mistakenly believes Stewart is a Christian, like her, and invites him to go to church. Smitten, Stewart decides to play along. Meanwhile, the wanted dog, who has a divine sense of how things should be, recognizes how much Stewart needs Lisa, and decides to do all he can to bring them together.

Available now in print and electronic formats from FaithWords wherever books are sold.